THE HAPPY EVER AFTERLIFE OF ROSIE POTTER (RIP)

When Rosie Potter wakes up one morning with what she assumes is the world's worst hangover, the last thing she expects to discover is that she's actually dead. With a frustrating case of amnesia, suspicious circumstances surrounding her untimely demise, and stuck wearing her ugliest flannel PJs, Rosie must figure out not only what happened last night, but why on earth she's still here. Slowly the mystery unravels, but there are many other secrets buried in the quiet Irish village of Ballycarragh, and nobody is as innocent as they first appear. Aided by the unlikeliest of allies in her investigation, Rosie discovers that life after death isn't all it's cracked up to be, particularly when you just might be falling in love . . .

THE HAPPY EVER AFTERLIFE OF ROSIE POTTER (RIP)

KATE WINTER

ISIS
LARGE
PRINT

First published in Great Britain 2014
by
Sphere
An imprint of Little, Brown Book Group

First Isis Edition
published 2015
by arrangement with
Sphere
An imprint of Little, Brown Book Group

A catalogue record for this book is available
from the British Library.

ISBN 978–1–78541–113–7 (hb)
ISBN 978–1–78541–119–9 (pb)

Published by
F. A. Thorpe (Publishing)
Anstey, Leicestershire

Set by Words & Graphics Ltd.
Anstey, Leicestershire
Printed and bound in Great Britain by
T. J. International Ltd., Padstow, Cornwall

This book is printed on acid-free paper

For my Mamma. Wise, Witty, Warm,
Wonderful Wendy.

Acknowledgements

I was reluctant to even do a thank you page, so terrified was I of leaving important people out. So just to start off, I want to say THANK YOU to everyone. Everyone who read my book, is going to read my book, ever mentioned my book to me, ever told me my hair was looking well, or even winked at me in the street. Unless it was in a sleazy way. In that case, stop it, you should be ashamed of yourself.

Right, so now everyone's thanked, I think I should name a few specials.

Mamma Wendy, who is the best editor-mother to ever refrain from making any editorial noises whatsoever, instead just being encouraging and awesome and my favourite person in the world. I love my mum.

Leonie and Armando and the whole Cornelius family, who are my extended family, not through blood but through choice. Your love and support are invaluable and you make me feel safe and inspired all the time.

Guy and Shannon and Niamh, thanks for all the brainiac advice (smartest people on the planet) and for being so flipping cute (that's you, Niamh. Although you're obviously very clever too).

The first readers of this book, outside of family: Clo and Siobhan. You stand out in my memory as being my first reviews, and your genuine, glowing praise made all the difference to me as a budding writer. THANK YOU.

Ajda Vucicevic, you are my champion. Thank you for believing in my words and for not forgetting about me. You made my fairytale come true . . . and I promise it's not over yet.

My agent Amanda Preston and all at LBA Books, I still get all goofy and proud when I mention "my agent" . . . which happens a lot.

My editor extraordinaire, who made my book a much better book, with the lightest touch and a core of steel — I admire you so much, Manpreet, thanks for your excellent help and your ability to kick my ass gently.

To my Facebook family, and the creative community in Sligo. You are all amazingly supportive and your pride in me and my work makes me want to do more, better, faster, all the time.

And to the real Charles Walker. You know who you are. Thanks for inspiring me to write this book.

CHAPTER
ONE

It's early. It must be very early. This, I can tell without even opening my eyes. To be honest, I really don't want to open them yet. I've got that very special feeling one only gets on particular mornings; the feeling that everything is fine and will remain so as long as one doesn't move a muscle, doesn't crack an eyelid, doesn't commit to being awake at all.

Despite following all these self-made rules in order to fool my brain into drifting back to the safety of dreamland, I become acutely aware that something is very different about this "special feeling" scenario. The weirdest sensation, like nothing I've ever felt before. I could only describe it as feeling tightly squeezed into my own skin. Like a sausage. A sausage under a too-hot grill, about to burst its pressurised constraints and split open with a great sizzling release.

Well, that's just lovely, Rosie.

The part of my brain that's still present and correct is unimpressed, and quite certain that I'm not a sausage. This must be some new, bizarre form of hangover. I mentally check my entire body for symptoms, taking care not to move as I do so, for fear they'll all manifest fast and furious if I do. No pounding head as yet. No sawdust mouth or churning stomach. No chills in fingers or toes, nor aching muscles. Interesting. Perhaps I discovered a new wonder drink last night, the only ill effect of which is a vague sausagefeeling. I could live with that, to be honest, compared to some of the cracking sambuca-induced hangovers I've endured.

Last night. That's another odd thing. Trying to cast my mind back is leading me to an absolute dead end. Somehow I'm failing to conjure up even the faintest memory of the events leading to the present situation.

I suppose I'm going to have to open my eyes. With the utmost care, I do so, first focusing on the cracked and cobwebby ceiling of my bedroom for a few moments, then lifting my head to peer around gingerly.

I'm wearing my very comfy, very ugly, blue-flannel PJs. I must therefore deduce that I can't have left the house last night. Seeing as most nights I return home and find the concept of undressing for bed far too much like hard work, it's practically impossible to consider the idea that I would have come home, disrobed and then carefully clad myself in these hideous pyjamas. Anyway, I usually sleep naked. Which means, Watson, that it must have been a cosy night in on the couch with Jenny, my best friend and housemate. Which is good news, as we definitely needed one of those. Things have been a bit strained of late.

But why can't I remember anything? And why do I still feel like a pork product?

"Jenny!" I bawl at the top of my voice.

Our cottage is pretty small, so she'd probably hear me through the draughty old walls if I just muttered her name half-heartedly, but we do like to yell at each other. It's just one of those housemate games. Like hiding obscene *Playgirl* pinups in the cereal box, or pretending the guy your friend fancies has just walked in when she's been squeezing her spots and rubbing olive oil into her hair for twenty minutes. I still owe her for that one, come to think of it.

She doesn't seem to be in. That, or she's ignoring me and trying to get some more sleep. Fat chance I'm going to let her.

I wear out my vocal chords appealing to her in every tone of voice and with every nickname I can muster up. Eventually when there's no response at all, not even a peep, I realise that I must accept defeat. Either she's got seventeen pillows piled over her ears, or she's gone out already. Isn't it a bit early for that though? I try to turn my head to look at the bedside clock with as little physical exertion as possible.

That's when I finally register the chaotic scene around me. My bedroom is absolutely *trashed*. Now, I'm not a neat freak or anything, but I'm not a messy, dirty teenager anymore either. And this room looks worse than it ever got in my teen years. Evidence suggests that a very small, very precise hurricane hit right here in the epicentre of my bedroom. My clothes, shoes, make-up and jewellery are strewn around willynilly. Nothing is where it belongs, and even from my not-so-vantage point I can see that a lot of stuff is broken. Only one painting remains on my wall, and even that one is hanging at a very precarious angle. The rest are scattered in ragged pieces amongst all the other debris. One particularly vicious-looking shard of mirrored glass is sticking up right in the centre of the room, like a modern art installation. I must warn Jenny before she barges in, which she inevitably will when she finally gets her act together.

What in God's name went on here last night?

I'm contemplating getting up and investigating further when I hear movement coming from the kitchen. Why, from the sounds of it, the little minx is home after all. This is all a bit too strange and I have a sudden premonition of doom. I hope she's not mad at me again. Maybe we had another fight over Jack last night? I'm about to call out to her in a more polite manner when there's a tentative knock on my door.

Right. We must have had a fight. Jenny never knocks.

"Enter!" I try to force a jovial tone into my voice, but it sounds strained even to my ears.

There's no response on the other side of the heavy wooden door, until after a good ten-second delay, "Rosie?" Jenny's voice whispers through as she pushes the door open just a crack.

"That is I," I speak a little louder, "Do come in to my delightfully tidy boudoir."

But she's speaking over me now, "ROSIE?" Quite unnecessarily loud, to my sensitive ears.

"YES!" I bellow back at the door, getting irritated at this point.

4

She finally pushes the door all the way open. I hear the sharp intake of breath as she takes in the carnage around me.

"I think I've been burgled!" I joke lamely, in a bid to ease the strange tension in the air.

Jenny's gaze shifts from the wreckage of my room to where I'm lying prone on the bed. Her already large brown eyes grow even bigger and rounder, and her little rosebud mouth falls open in an expression of abject horror.

"Jeez, I know I probably look rough, but aren't you over reacting a li —"

My wisecrack is cut short by an ear-splitting scream issuing forth from my housemate's now gaping mouth. She spins around and disappears from sight. From the huge slamming sound that reverberates in her wake, I'd say she's just exited at high speed through the front door.

I think it might be time for me to get up.

Once I do finally drag myself out of bed I no longer feel all that bad. As a matter of fact, I feel really good. Strong, fit and healthy. The sausage-feeling has abated entirely and I have the completely unnatural urge to go for a run. And believe me, I don't run. Ever.

I pick my way carefully through the rubble of my own little Ground Zero, into the kitchen. There are several empty wine bottles and a pair of well-pawed glasses loitering by the sink, which adds fuel to my theory of a girls' night in.

I can see Jenny pacing like a caged animal at the gate through the window, mobile phone pressed to her ear, gesticulating wildly towards the cottage. I wonder what's gotten into her. It's a miserable, grey, drizzly morning and she's bound to be getting soaked out there. She seems to be looking in my direction, so I give her a little wave, but there's no response forthcoming.

Definitely mad at me then. Maybe if I make her breakfast she'll defrost a little. I open the fridge and ponder the contents, chewing on my bottom lip. Not much inspiration to be found here unfortunately. Half a browning banana, a badly re-wrapped chunk of Cheddar that's sprouting some impressive mould patches, an almost-empty carton of milk, and a jar of relish that's been lurking there in the back ever since we moved in.

I swing the fridge door shut, harder than I meant to. I'm not even hungry, which in itself is a little unusual, being as I'm damn near *always* hungry. My appetite is pretty legendary around here. But then, I am a "whole lotta woman" as Jack likes to tell me. Not fat, as he hastened to clarify the first time he said it and my lip curled in a warning growl. Definitely not fat. Delightfully well proportioned, in fact, seeing as I stand five eleven in flats, and sport some rather impressive size eight-and-a-half feet (which, much to my eternal frustration, make shoe-shopping a night-mare).

I wander back towards my bedroom, planning on slipping on some warm clothes and going out to check on Jenny where she's now perched on the gatepost like a strange little gargoyle.

6

It's only when I reach the doorway and look from this new perspective into my own room that things start to get really messed up. Aside from the room looking like a bomb has hit it, there is a strange figure sprawled on my bed.

My first (ridiculous) thought is: *Hey, how did I not notice that someone was sleeping with me?*

My second (more appropriate) thought is: *Oh shit, look at all that blood!*

The prone body has a blueish tinge to its skin, and there's a large, dark pool of blood spreading right beside its head. From where I'm standing it looks like it's coming from a small, deep wound just above the poor woman's temple.

How did this happen? Who the hell is this very dead-looking stranger in my bed? But then, with a leaden drop in my gut, the realisation dawns that this is no stranger.

That mop of red hair looks disturbingly familiar. I recognise those worn-looking, blue-flannel PJs. Those are, without doubt, size eight-and-a-half feet.

"HOLY SHIT!"

I stagger backwards, groping for the kitchen counter to hold me up. No wonder Jenny freaked out. This has to be some kind of overboard Halloween joke. When I find out who's responsible for this, I'll be giving them a piece of my mind. This kind of fright could cause a heart attack.

I realise all in a rush that my grasping hand hasn't made contact with anything, despite the fact that I've stumbled, flailing, into the centre of the kitchen. Where the kitchen table should be.

Where the kitchen table still is.

Where I am standing, smack bang *in the middle of* the kitchen table, wearing it like some kind of haute couture wooden skirt.

It's my turn to scream.

CHAPTER
TWO

Jenny and I moved into Honeysuckle Cottage about eighteen months ago, shortly after she moved home from Dublin. She's been my best friend ever since she turned up in the school playground and berated Melissa McEvoy for stealing my packet of Frisps. Even then, she was the most exotic creature I had ever laid eyes on (but then, that's not saying much when you've been born and bred in a small Irish village like Ballycarragh).

She was about half the size of every other student in our class. We all thought there had to have been some kind of mistake, and kept expecting her to be moved back down a few classes to where she belonged. But she was insistent that she was seven years old and belonged with the rest of us seven and eight year olds. When it became apparent nobody in charge was going to prove her wrong, we had to accept it as fact.

She was the cutest-looking little thing. From the moment I laid eyes on her I was in a kind of jealous awe of her dainty features and delicate beauty. She looked like a little china doll. She still does, in fact. Big, brown eyes dominating a small, heart-shaped face, with rosebud lips and a tiny upturned nose. When she was

9

little she had a head full of tumbling black curls, but once she hit her teens she sheared it all off, favouring a tousled crop that basically just does its own thing and always looks astonishingly chic.

Men go la-la over Jenny. They see her as this delicate, innocent little flower that they can protect and admire, and feel all manly and strong around. Unfortunately for them, this perception is a million miles from the real Jenny. She's tough and ballsy, with a mouth like a whole den of sailors and a real *don't-mess-with-me* attitude. Of course, she's soft and loving, and tender and considerate too, but most men don't tend to stick around to discover that, once their idealistic fantasies have been shattered by just one tongue-lashing from her pretty mouth.

We made a real odd couple in school. I was already standing a good head above all the boys in my class, let alone the girls. By the time I was eleven I was showing signs of being pretty well endowed in the curves area too, while poor Jenny didn't even start to manifest boobs until she was almost fifteen. For most of our teen years we would bitch and moan and complain to each other for hours on end about how we each wished we could look more like the other:

Jenny wanted my long, thick, red hair.

I wanted her big brown "Bambi eyes".

She wanted a full, oversized smile like mine.

I wanted her cute little nose.

She wanted my considerable tits and ass.

I wanted to be feminine and dainty like her.

10

And then we got over it. Somewhere around sixteen we sort of realised that we were both pretty lucky — neither of us resembled a hunchbacked crack whore and we quite liked being ourselves actually.

It was around that time that Jenny met and fell instantly in love with Tom Devine. I'd be lying if I said I'd never felt a stab of envy about their relationship, but it was impossible to resent Tom. He was generous with his time and never made me feel like I was a third wheel. In fact, over the years he actually became like the bonus member of our cosy little friendship more than an intruding male. He loved Jenny to distraction, often boring me with incessant talk of how cute and sweet and funny she was when we were alone. But he gave me good advice regarding the string of short-lived affairs I went through, and was always understanding when Jenny and I needed some time alone. To be honest, he was the perfect boyfriend. No boy I ever met measured up, that's for sure.

Jenny and Tom moved to Dublin the year we all turned twenty-one. That was a real blow to me. I wasn't sure how I would cope in Ballycarragh without them. I made many complicated plans to move away myself, but never actually followed through on any of them. I'm not sure why. I always planned to do plenty of travel, but I tend to spend whatever money I manage to cobble together. And the summer job I took (that somehow managed to turn into my full-time job to this day) as a barmaid in McMorrow's pub didn't exactly fill my pockets. I did visit Jenny and Tom in Dublin quite a bit, and they came down home often enough too, so in the end it wasn't quite as traumatic as I'd thought it would be.

Jenny worked in a rather upmarket hotel in the city centre and Tom was a self-employed carpenter. They were tremendously happy and after a few years were already talking about getting a mortgage, making babies and the rest. They got engaged, which came as no surprise to anyone. What did come as a surprise, however, was that almost a year to the day after Tom proposed, Jenny walked out and moved back home. No explanation. She never told anyone what really happened, not even me, and she usually informed me of *everything*, even that extremely disturbing erotic dream she had about Bertie Ahern once. She was adamant there was no big mystery behind her decision, that it was just a fact that we all needed to accept and then move on, but I knew her too well to really believe that.

Tom was devastated, but I didn't really get to talk to him after the fact. I only saw him once, briefly, that Christmas, when he was in McMorrow's for a pint with his brothers. I felt slightly disloyal to Jenny, but I had to serve him his pint, didn't I? All he said to me when I made a subtle enquiry as to what had really gone down between them was, "I loved her so much, Rosie. But she just stopped loving me."

I put it to Jenny that night when I got home. I didn't tell her what Tom had said, but I did ask her straight out why she had stopped loving him. Her reply was heart-breaking. She said in a flat voice, "I'll never stop loving him. But I don't deserve his love."

After that, she refused to be drawn any further. I tried on many occasions (usually when we'd had a little too much wine) to get her to open up and fill me in on why she felt this way, but there's no-one as stubborn as Jenny when she's made her mind up about something, and she never spoke a peep about it ever again. Sometimes I would catch a look in her eye that suggested she was lost in a world of her own. Whenever I saw that faraway sadness come over her it maddened me that I couldn't help.

Tom Devine didn't move home. He rarely visits Ballycarragh nowadays as he lives in California with his wife and daughter. He was married barely nine months after he and Jenny split up, and a baby came along suspiciously soon after that. Rumours abounded in Ballycarragh that the new wife had been his bit on the side and that Jenny had left him because she found out. Or that "The Yank", as she is affectionately referred to around here, was just a rebound thing that had gone too far and that any day now he would snap out of it. Jenny has no comment at all on the whole thing. Personally, I hope he found love again and is very happy. And I hope even more that one of these days the same will happen for my gorgeous best friend.

Sometimes I wonder if her experience with Tom is what makes her so weird about my relationship with Jack. My gorgeous boyfriend, Jack Harper, can do no right in Jenny's eyes. She knew him before I did, of course. But the arrogant, self-important wanker she describes from those days is certainly not the same sweet, handsome, sexy man that I met and fell in love with around this time last year. I do try to be understanding of her feelings, but to be honest it's lately got to the point where we simply don't talk about him. Every time we have, we've ended up rowing. At the end of the day, I'm not going to let any man, no matter how wonderful he is, come between my best friend and me. That said, I'm not going to let my best friend come between my man and me either. So it hasn't been the easiest situation to manoeuvre all in all. And now it seems like things are about to get even more complicated, due to the small fact that I seem to be dead.

CHAPTER
THREE

I leap clear of the kitchen table like a scalded cat, regarding it suspiciously from a safe distance. This can't actually be happening, can it? I have to be having some kind of crazy realistic dream. But there's no way I'm getting back into that bed with my own gruesome-looking corpse to try to sleep it off. My body is tingling with adrenaline, and it feels like my heart's beating at a thousand times the normal rate. And yet, how can this be, if that bleeding, blue lump of flesh in there is my actual body? I look down warily to where my body usually resides. Yes, here I am, standing in the kitchen in my flannel PJs and bare feet. I pinch my arm, and though it doesn't hurt, I feel my own skin between my fingers.

This is seriously weird. I'm still breathing but, hang on . . .

Yup, as I suspected, I can stop just like that. It's like the sensations of my breath and my heartbeat are just memories, habitual repetitions of the real thing. If I concentrate, the heartbeat feeling goes away, and so does the breathing thing. But that just feels wrong, so I hurriedly bring back the familiar thump-thump, in-out-in-out.

Okay, Rosie, get yourself under control. What do we know for sure?

My dead body appears to be lying prone in the bedroom next door. Fact.

My best friend has discovered this and is currently (understandably) freaking out. Fact.

I'm a ghost. Fact?

This last one proves too much for me. I've got to get out of here. I can feel the blind panic rising in me on a tide of cold, dead blood. I rush to the front door, only to discover that I can't get a proper grip on the door handle. My damn hand (the ghost of my damn hand) just keeps swiping through the solid metal knob. A frustrated, anxious noise, somewhere between a cat wailing and the whine of a strained engine, escapes me as I grasp thin air again and again.

Why can't I do this? I could have sworn I opened the fridge earlier, didn't I? Maybe I just imagined it. Or worse, maybe I've completely lost my mind along with my corporeal form. What did I do differently with the fridge? Dammit, I didn't even think about it that time and I managed. Now here I am, trying to do the simplest thing in the world and it's like banging my head against a brick wall.

This thought stops me in my distressed tracks. I realise there's an alternative. After all, I've seen this kind of stuff in the movies loads of times. Surely it's the same in real life. Surely a silly little thing like a brick wall, or for that matter a wooden door, can't stop me. I take a deep (entirely unnecessary) breath and step purposefully through the slab of solid oak that is our front door.

I pop out the other side successfully, and stand spluttering in the damp morning air. What they absolutely don't mention in the movies is the grossness of that experience. It feels like being sucked in, chewed a few times, then spat out with the force of a champagne cork. But worst of all is the *taste* of it! I would never have thought a door could have a flavour, but I know better now. I feel like I just swallowed a mouthful of sawdust. Smokey, slightly damp-smelling, woody sawdust, with a lingering aftertaste of varnish. I will not be doing that again in a hurry.

Gurning and spitting like a cantankerous camel, I wander over to where Jenny is still engrossed in her phone conversation. Her voice is simultaneously shaky and exasperated.

"Yes, that is correct. A *dead* body . . . Yes, I'm quite sure it is . . . Yes, blue . . . As I said, Ballycarragh."

A small muscle in her jaw is starting to twitch. A sure sign that something's really starting to get on Jen's nerves. Sure enough, after a brief pause in which I clearly hear the person on the other end of the line saying in a disbelieving voice "So you think there's a dead person in your bedroom, is it?" Jenny explodes, shrieking, "I HAVE JUST FOUND MY BEST FRIEND'S DEAD BODY!"

She takes a deep breath before returning her voice to its usual volume. Now her tone is calm and ominously friendly, managing to suggest grievous bodily harm and cupcakes all at once. "And I need you to send the

17

police *right now* or . . ." The unspoken end of that sentence hangs in the air for a moment, throbbing with Tarantino-esque threats, before there's a muffled response on the other end of the line, and Jenny chirps brightly, "Thank you! Have a nice day!"

She hangs up with all the force one can muster when pressing the red button on a smartphone. I can't help chuckling. Even in a crisis she's sharp as a tack. She shoves the phone back into her pocket and tucks herself up inside the old over-sized coat she's wearing. Mine, I realise with a pang, finding it horribly touching how small and vulnerable she looks with her knees tucked up inside it and the sleeves covering her hands. It's just her tousled little head poking out the top; her face pale, her eyes red. I step in front of her, harbouring a wild hope that perhaps she'll be able to see me in my ghostly form and we could have a joyful reunion and then maybe spend a few days causing havoc around the village. She could pass on all my messages to my loved ones and I could still live in Honeysuckle Cottage, and there'd be no need for anyone to be sad . . .

Not a flicker. Not even when I wave my hand millimetres from her nose. So I'm destined to wander the earth undead and lonely. All of a sudden a thousand questions are clamouring for attention inside my head.

Why the hell am I here? Where's the bright light I'm supposed to be heading towards, or the friendly, rosy-cheeked relative come to greet me, dressed all in white and smiling beatifically?

18

I can't even begin to answer those questions. Not with the day I'm having and all the shock and horror I've had to deal with so far already. Instead, I try a little harder to communicate with Jen. I always was more interested in the life of the living than deep philosophical questions about the afterlife — it seems that even death can't shake me out of some habits.

"Jenny . . ." I croon, in a desperate and rather spooky sounding voice. "JENNY!" I bark, right in her ear.

No response. She just sits there, staring up the road, no doubt waiting for the police to arrive before she ventures back into the house. Well, I'll just wait with her, I suppose. There's no way I want to go back in there on my own. And I've got nowhere else to be. I suffer a sudden, ridiculous moment of panic as I realise I'm supposed to be opening up the pub this morning, swiftly followed by an equally ridiculous feeling of glee as it hits me that I never have to go back to work again.

I suppose Jack will realise I'm not turning up, and he'll open up for me. Then he'll start trying to call me and get no response, and then, eventually, he'll get worried and contact someone. Oh, my poor baby, then he'll hear the news and I can't even imagine how horrible that's going to be for him.

I can hear an engine in the distance. It doesn't look like Jenny has noticed it yet. It gets louder still. I'm pretty sure it must be on our road now. She's still not reacting. Just before the silver car rounds the corner, Jenny sits up straighter and cocks an ear. It's the Gardaí Síochána — the local Irish police force — which means

Sergeant Seán O'Flaherty and his mini-me son, Seán Óg O'Flaherty, the left arm of the law in Ballycarragh.

"Oh well, now." I can't help myself instinctively trying to have a bit of a moment with Jenny. "There's nothing to worry about with these two on the case!"

Of course, she doesn't crack a smile. She clambers down from the gatepost looking solemn and shaken. Even when I start humming the *Magnum, P.I.* theme tune as the two men exit the car, she resists joining in. This is something Jenny and I have done since we were kids every time we spot Sergeant O'Flaherty. He's had the same Tom Selleck moustache for as long as anyone in Ballycarragh can remember. Rumour has it he was born with it. Poor Seán Óg has been trying to grow his own for years now, but unfortunately all he can manage is a sparse scattering of fine hair which could only be described as bum fluff.

As soon as Seán Óg sees Jenny, he flushes bright red and starts looking down at the gravel with intense concentration. We all went to school together, you see, and Seán Óg always had the biggest crush on her. Usually Jenny is outrageously flirtatious with him, which only makes him go redder and redder and become completely unable to string a sentence together at all, much to our cruel delight.

Today however, to my continued disappointment, she greets the two men with a minimum of words, let alone coquettish fun.

"I thought she stayed at the pub last night," she explains, leading them into the house. "But then, this morning, I saw her coat and . . ." She stops well short

20

of my bedroom door, gesturing queasily. "She's in there."

With that, she drops into a chair at the kitchen table and puts her head in her hands, clearly worn out from the effort of trying to maintain her composure. I don't have the stomach to go in there and watch that pair poking and prodding at my defenceless body. It would just feel too undignified. So I crouch beside Jenny and try with all my might, one last time, to telepathically communicate with her.

The thing is, I'm pretty sure I've never really come across any instructions as to how to psychically contact the living from beyond the grave, so what I end up doing is mentally stamping my foot and ranting, *Why can't you hear me, dammit?*

Unsurprisingly, she doesn't answer. And I don't have long to practise my sophisticated technique, as the O'Flahertys are out of my room in under two minutes.

"Definitely dead, so she is," says Seán Senior, shaking his head solemnly. "I've not seen the like in Ballycarragh in over thirty years."

Seán Óg's usual pink flush has entirely left his cheeks, now he's even paler and more shaken looking than Jenny. He stands behind his father, breathing shallowly and gripping his hat with white knuckles.

Jenny just continues to stare straight ahead, not reacting at all to either of the Gardaí. Her gaze seems fixed on a point a long way off through the window of the cottage and quite possibly all the way into the next county.

"Well, what the hell happened to me then?" I demand impatiently, standing up and glaring at Seán Senior.

For a moment, it actually seems like he's answering me, but the quick flash of hope fades as I realise he's clearly addressing Jenny. "We'll have to wait for the fellas from the city before we touch anything in there. They will investigate the environment and subsequentially will remove the caddyver from the scene of the crime. It'll be sent off to Dublin for some ferronsic tests and the like, and an aupotsy." He pauses, obviously delighted with the opportunity to abuse such technical terms.

I'm clearly in good hands here.

"Nothing can be confirmed at this junk-tour, but my initial investigation would suggest that Miss Potter has what appears to be a bullet hole just above her left ear. Also, her surroundings are in an considerable disarray suggesting a struggle or attempted robbery. So we must consider foul play in our investigation. We could well be dealing with a homistide here."

What? Hang on a minute. Bullet hole? Foul Play? Homistide? Does this mean I was murdered, is that what ol' Garda O'Flaherty is saying? Oh bloody hell. I suddenly feel very light-headed. It appears that Seán Óg experiences pretty much the same feeling, as he makes a sudden dash for the front door, his hand over his mouth, eyes watering.

Try being the one who's been viciously executed for no good reason!

What have I ever done to deserve this? Who the hell would want to hurt me? KILL me?

"Jack Harper." Jenny says, under her breath.

"WHAT?" I spin around, my eyes bulging out of their sockets. "Oh, no, no, no, Jenny, don't you even dare . . ."

Jenny raises red eyes to Sergeant Seán O'Flaherty Senior. My heart sinks as I see the cold, hard hatred in those pretty brown eyes.

"Jack Harper did this," she says, loud and clear. Then once more for good measure. "Jack bloody Harper."

Shit.

Shit, shit, shit.

CHAPTER
FOUR

Jack Harper walked into McMorrow's bar one chilly evening last November as I was pondering just how bored I'd have to get to strike up yet another conversation with Seamie Doherty (one of our regular customers) about cars. Seamie only talks about cars, you see. The rest of the time he just sits staring into his pint, giving each new patron who walks into the bar a slight jerk of the head as his greeting.

Or perhaps I could encourage Auld Ross Moriarty (from a safe olfactory distance of course because, *phew*, that man is ripe) to break into song and serenade the small gaggle of lost-looking tourists gingerly sipping their long-flat pints of Guinness in the corner.

Imagine my delight, then, when as a third option I was blessed with this gorgeous ride of a man walking through the door. He was all wrapped up in a thick duffel coat, gloves, scarf and a beanie hat pulled down over his brows, but the little I could see of him was very promising. Let's face it, though, if it walks on two legs and has the Y chromosome in Ballycarragh it's pretty promising.

His (sexy, blue) eyes swept the room as he slowly pulled off his gloves, finger by finger. I watched him taking in the low-beamed ceiling, the big open fire, the crooked shelves running higgledy-piggledy around the walls, the long stretch of dark-wood bar and finally, me, standing behind it, polishing a wine glass to within an inch of its life. I realised I was holding my breath and tried to surreptitiously let it out while he held my gaze, a devastatingly sexy smile slowly lifting the corners of his mouth.

Ah, Jesus. I literally felt a sharp stab of desire in my lower belly. What a treat on a dismally quiet, rainy Sunday night. Just wait till I told Jenny about this!

The handsome stranger pulled off his hat to reveal a tousled head of blondy-brown hair as he walked over to where I was standing. He stuck out one (clean, tanned, neatly maintained) hand and greeted me with a twinkle.

"Hello, gorgeous redhead behind the bar," he drawled, in an accent somewhere between South Dublin and downtown New York.

I was grinning like the Cheshire Cat at this stage. I put down the very shiny wine glass to clumsily shake the hand he proffered. He lifted my (pale, freckly, slightly-sticky-with-Guinness-residue) hand to his lips and planted a firm, dry kiss.

"Jack Harper, at your service," he said, causing me to instantly start fantasising about the many exotic services I would require. "I'm the new entertainment manager here."

Ah, yes. I had heard something about this, the latest madcap plan of Roger Smith. My boss was a big-city business mogul, who had several years earlier moved to

Ballycarragh to start a family. He took over the local pub, and ever since then he had been introducing marketing scheme after promotion plan after grand expansion idea. The truth was, there wasn't another pub for miles around and McMorrow's would probably have run itself, left to its own devices. But Lydia Smith had yet to produce any new members of the family and Roger was obviously a man who liked to keep busy, so we all tolerated the fancy big business attempts to glamorise our local pub. We'd all been having a great laugh just the previous night at the very thought of some city slicker coming in here and trying to "inject a little glamour" into the place, as Roger had boasted the entertainment manager would do.

However, I was rapidly rethinking my exclamations of "Glamour, me arse!" and "I'll not entertain any new managers around here!" now that I was faced with the real deal.

"Rosie Potter," I squeaked, my voice somehow managing to come out sounding like a bad impression of a *Sesame Street* character. Clearing my throat hurriedly, I continued in my normal, low voice, "bar manager."

I was bursting with the news as I let myself into the cottage later that night. Jack and I had chatted for a good hour before he disappeared upstairs to move himself into the small, attic apartment above the pub. I was ecstatic that he was going to be living there; nowhere to hide! Now, I realise I may sound like I have a touch of the stalker about me, but I can't stress enough how rare it is to see a new face in Ballycarragh, let alone such a pretty one.

Besides, I was generously considering the possibility of handing this one over to Jenny. She still hadn't had so much as a sniff of another man since returning from Dublin after the whole Tom Devine debacle. Never mind that I kind of wanted him for myself, I thought magnanimously, her need was greater than mine. Then again, one must give a lad the opportunity to choose for himself. It's not like men don't have a mind of their own. Either way though, it would probably be best to lay the groundwork quickly; before every unattached female in a six-mile radius started to come sniffing around.

"Oi, Jammy!" I called, as the front door slammed behind me. I found her in the sitting room, curled up under several blankets looking pretty doleful. Glancing at the TV before her, I could see why. The kissing-in-the-rain scene from *The Notebook* filled the screen. I've lost count of how many times we've watched that film. I'm surprised she can't recite the entire script from heart.

I rolled my eyes at her exaggeratedly, but she just sniffed at me and returned her gaze to the movie.

"Cup of tea?" I chirped. "I have some news . . ."

"Hmmm?" She didn't seem all that interested.

I made my tea, generously making one for her too, even though I wasn't sure she deserved it, the grumpy wench. Then I flounced back into the dark little sitting room, which was lit only by the flickering fire and the

27

bluish glow of the TV. I flicked on the side lamp by my favourite armchair and flopped down with a loud sigh.

"Oh, what a day, what a day!" I muttered, ostensibly to myself.

She vaguely tilted her chin in my direction, not shifting her gaze from the screen at all. Stubborn mare! I was definitely rethinking my generous donation of Jack Harper. I decided I was just going to have to lob my news in like a grenade if I wanted to gain her attention at all.

"The new ents manager arrived today, and he's certainly not the vacant blonde PR princess we were expecting," I said, loudly. "In fact, he's a drop-dead hottie."

Calmly, Jenny lifted the remote control and snapped the TV off. She turned her whole body towards me, swinging her legs over the armrest of her chair and making herself comfortable as she fixed me with big, interested eyes.

"Do tell," she said, in a measured tone that belied only a hint of excitement.

"Ha!" I barked, delightedly. "I'm not sure you deserve my juicy news now, wench!"

We both chortled wholeheartedly for a few moments; the sort of shared giggles that have many years of friendship and experience behind them. And then I told her all about the gorgeous creature who had walked into our local pub that evening and who, joyously, seemed likely to be sticking around for quite a while. Jenny whooped and sighed and "oohed" in all the right places, right up until I said his name.

"Jack said he's going to try to do at least one themed night a month, and there'll be no admittance unless you're in fancy dress. Can you imagine some of our regulars all dressed up? Seamie Doherty in drag? Auld Ross as Spongebob Squarepants?" My laughter petered out as I noticed that Jenny wasn't sharing in the hilarity of it all.

"Jen?" I enquired, confused. What had brought on this sudden change of mood?

"What's his second name?" she asked bluntly, her voice clipped and strangely anxious-sounding.

"Er . . . Harper, I think," I replied, still somewhat bewildered by the turn this conversation was taking. "Middle name 'Sexy'!"

My weak attempt at lightening the atmosphere certainly didn't do the trick. Jenny just continued to stare through me, seemingly lost in her own thoughts, a stressed-looking frown creasing her brow.

"Why do you ask, Jenny?" I asked gently.

She didn't answer for a long moment. I almost thought she hadn't heard me, the silence stretched out for so long. Finally she spoke, standing up from the armchair by the fire abruptly.

"I knew a Jack Harper in Dublin. He did some work at the hotel. He was a complete *bastard*!" She spat the word out with such venom I was taken aback.

"I just hope to fuck it's not him. And if it is, you'd do well to stay the hell away from him."

With that, Jenny stalked stiffly into her bedroom, closing the door firmly behind her.

What the hell was that all about?

Taking myself off to bed that night, I resolved that it simply couldn't be the same Jack Harper. There was no way the cute, charming man I had met that day could be the same one who had inspired such hatred in my best friend. Jenny could be harsh, for sure, but she rarely took against someone unless they really deserved it. She'd meet this Jack and see that he was lovely and sweet and sexy, and we'd all have a great laugh at this mix-up someday in the future.

Wouldn't we?

Apparently not. When Jenny walked into McMorrow's the very next day, it became clear that my Jack and her Jack were one and the same. He was sitting up at the bar, innocently sipping on a coffee and generously providing me with some eye candy when Jenny came through the door. The instant she laid eyes on him, she turned a deathly shade of white and spun on her heel.

Too late, it seemed, as Jack had already spotted her. "Jenny!" he exclaimed, with what sounded like genuine warmth to my uncertain ear. At the sound of his voice, Jenny froze mid-step. She didn't turn around.

"What a pleasant surprise!" He was on his feet, moving towards her rigid back.

As I looked on in mounting discomfort, Jenny seemed to come off pause mode. She didn't reply or look around. She took two long steps towards the door and shoved it open with somewhat excessive force, before vanishing back into the wet day outside.

Jack turned back towards me looking a little confused and very embarrassed. His gaze stayed on the floor as he headed for the back stairs leading up to his flat. Then he seemed to change his mind and swerved back in my direction.

"That *was* Jenny McLoughlin, wasn't it?" he asked, his wounded eyes making my heart swell with sympathy.

I just nodded, not sure what to say. I certainly had no explanation for my best friend's weird behaviour.

He shook his head sadly and shuffled off up the stairs, not to be seen for the rest of the day, much to my disappointment.

This lack of "Yummy Jack" time led me to be in a fairly grumpy mood by the time I got home. Fine, if Jenny wanted to hate him, I could live with that. But she had some pretty serious explaining to do if she wanted me to stop fancying him. She'd never even mentioned the guy before now; he can't have played that much of a dramatic role in her life in Dublin. I had to get to the bottom of this.

"JENNY!" I roared, all set to have it out with her as I stormed through the front door of Honeysuckle Cottage. Unfortunately, she happened to be directly in front of me as I did so, so we ended up screaming in fright into each other's faces, which actually helped to lighten the mood, seeing as we couldn't help giggling hysterically as we recovered from the sudden rush of adrenaline.

We prepared a light supper together, not really talking much, both very aware that we had something to tackle. Finally, when we sat down to eat, I asked her

31

the question that was burning a hole in my mind. "Why do you hate him so much, Jenny?"

Her reply was not very informative. "He's a pig."

"Ah, I see. That explains it then."

I took another mouthful of salad and considered what to say next. "He seems like a really nice guy to me, I have to be honest."

"Well, he's not." She didn't seem to be willing to elaborate. "You'll just have to trust me on this one."

"Jenny!" I dropped my fork, exasperated. "Tell me what the hell this guy has ever done to you and maybe I'll understand. Otherwise, I'm going to have to just go on my own opinion of him."

She looked at me for a long moment, her eyes softening a little. "Rosie, you always see the best in people, it's one of the loveliest things about you." She took a long slug of water before she continued. "But he's a black-hearted swine and I swear to God, if you get involved with him, you'll end up very fucking sorry."

CHAPTER
FIVE

Honeysuckle Cottage isn't far from McMorrow's pub. That said, nothing in Ballycarragh is very far from anything else. It usually only takes me about fifteen minutes at a brisk walk to get to work. Today, I do it in two. I can hardly believe how fast I'm running. And I'm not out of breath in the least, either.

Then again, I'm not sure if I actually bothered to breathe.

It's only when I see the familiar stone façade of McMorrow's before me that I start to wonder exactly what use I'll be here. It's pure reflex that made me come running to Jack's side in his hour of need.

Well, that's love for you, isn't it? I tell myself self-importantly. Even if he doesn't know I'm here, I am. He's about to get possibly the worst news one can get in a lifetime. The love of his life is dead. Murdered in cold blood, according to the local lawmen. God, I hope they don't ask him to identify the body. I look terrible dead.

Auld Ross Moriarty stumbles out the front door and I take the opportunity to slip in past him, which saves me having to taste wood again. Whoa, he really does smell bad. It seems my senses have been somewhat primed by my undead state, making the local booze hound even more malodorous than usual. Despite what his nickname might suggest, Auld Ross isn't that old, he's actually somewhere in his early fifties. He just looks twice that, thanks to his fondness for drink and fags and the fact that he never found a wife. Instead, he lives with his mammy and apparently avoids soap and water at all costs.

My eyes adjust quickly to the dark interior of the pub. And there he is. My gorgeous boyfriend, balancing precariously atop a stool, taking down the last of the Halloween decorations. He's talking to Roger Smith, who sits in his usual position at the end of the bar, reams and reams of mysterious paperwork spread before him. His wife, the Botoxed and buxom Mrs Lydia Smith, stands beside him looking surprised. She always looks surprised, though, thanks to the monthly botulism top-ups, so I don't really give it a second thought. The two men are laughing at something Roger has just said.

Jack's white teeth flash as he laughs. Hell, he's a whole lot of *fine*. He climbs down and sits on the stool, carefully folding up a "Happy Halloween" banner. I move right up beside him, wishing he could sense me here, that I could prepare him somehow for what's coming. He looks so happy and relaxed. I bet he's made up some excuse for me already, probably by saying that I had asked him to cover me this morning and he forgot, or something like that. They certainly don't look too worried that I haven't shown up for my shift.

I reach out, in pure habit, to brush back the one lock of glossy blondy-brown hair that always falls forward over his left eye. My ghostly hand doesn't do what it's supposed to, of course. It passes straight through his head, feeling all warm and squishy and weird. Jack involuntarily shudders.

Hey! He felt that!

Yes, it caused him to shudder in apparent revulsion, but it's something. He gets up as Roger is leaving, and follows him outside. I'm left alone with Lydia, pondering how best to use the new shudder-inducing skill I've just discovered. I'm just about to start practising on her when the Sergeants O'Flaherty enter the bar.

"Oh hellooo, Gardas!" trills Lydia in her high-pitched, little girl voice. "To what do we owe this pleasure?"

No doubt she's worrying that they're here to administer a slap on the wrist for the illegal (but highly lucrative) late-night lock-ins her husband turns a blind eye to several nights a week.

"Howaya, Missus Smith," bawls Seán Senior, while his son struggles to remove his gaze from the impressively enhanced décolletage before him. From the pink in Seán Óg's cheeks, it seems Jenny isn't the only female in Ballycarragh he's got a bit of a thing for. His father maintains eye contact with Lydia admirably, despite the extravagant display of bosom.

"We're just here to have a quick word with young Harper. We won't keep him long."

"Of course, Sergeant," Lydia simpers, sycophantically. She beams her trout-lipped smile at the younger of the two men with a coquettish flutter of thickly mascara'd lashes. "He's just outside with my hubby — he'll be back in a flash.

"Would you like a little drop of something nice while you wait?" she asks, making even this innocent query sound like a dirty promise.

I snort, watching the two men as their brains start to melt southwards. Bloody ridiculous if you ask me. After an almost indecent pause, Seán Senior pulls himself together.

"Cuppa tea would be grand, Missus Smith. We'll just be waiting in the cubby."

With that, he drags his dazed-looking son into the snug at the front of the bar while Lydia busies herself brewing them some tea. I take the opportunity to get a closer look at this oversized Barbie doll. Lydia has always been a bit of an object of ridicule to the women in Ballycarragh (and clearly an object of desire to the men). Her porn-star looks have prompted all number of rumours to circulate about just how much work she's really had done. The Botox, the lips, the breasts; they're all pretty obvious. However, there has also been some fairly wild speculation about full-face transplants and removed ribs, sex-change operations and fat transfers, black-market placenta milkshakes and the like.

I have to admit, as I peer closely at her face, looking for tell-tale staple marks or other incriminating scars, that her skin is truly flawless. Underneath all that make-up, I actually think Lydia Smith might be quite a

36

pretty lady. I'm about an inch from her right ear when she suddenly jumps and squeals like a stuck pig.

I nearly jump out of my skin (oh, hang on, I've done that already haven't I?), staggering backwards with my ears ringing.

"Jack!" She giggles like a teenager, and I can see why now. Jack has snuck back in through the back entrance and taken her by surprise, poking her in the ribs from behind. He loves sneaking up on people and giving them a fright. He hid in the linen closet at the cottage for almost an hour once, just waiting for me to finally put away the laundry, so he could leap out like a crazy bird man and scare me out of my mind.

He's laughing now, his sexy blue eyes all crinkled up at the corners. It breaks my heart to see him so happy, when in just a few moments he's going to get some news that will shatter his world.

"The Gardaí are here to see you, Jack." Lydia twinkles obscenely at him. "Have you been a naughty boy?"

I feel like smacking her.

Leave him alone, you lecherous thing!

A flicker of something uneasy flashes in Jack's eyes, but his smile remains fixed. "Always!" He winks at Lydia, pours himself a pint of water and saunters towards the cubby.

I follow miserably, like a loyal dog with its tail between its legs. I feel so bad for being dead. Poor Jack. My poor, poor baby. I'll just have to will him to be strong. Not too strong, of course, that would just be

37

weird. Maybe a couple of restrained tears, a whispered declaration of undying love, that kind of thing.

"All right, lads, you've got me, I'll come without a struggle!" Jack jokes, as he enters the small room.

It always seems so much more cramped in here in the cold light of day. At night, with the little pot-bellied stove roaring in the corner and the two small tables overflowing with half-full drinks, you'd be astonished how many people can squeeze in. Right now, though, just the four of us are uncomfortably close. I end up standing awkwardly, with my arse in Seán Óg's face. I'm not willing to move though. This is the only way I can remain beside Jack. It may not be the most comfortable of situations, but feck it, what the young Garda doesn't know won't hurt him. Besides, if he could see me he'd probably be delighted with my positioning, the little perv.

Awkward "hellos" and some basic pleasantries are exchanged, before Seán Senior gets down to business.

"Now, Jack, I need you to tell me," he begins, his voice taking on a special tone that I suspect he thinks of as his "Interrogation Voice".

"Where were you on the night of October thirty-first?"

Jack looks like he's struggling for an answer.

"Oh, that's not good, sweetheart!" I mutter, willing him to pull his act together. "You look pretty suspicious right now!"

Then he asks, "Do you mean last night, Seán?"

"Yes, yes," Seán Senior blusters a bit, looking at his notes as if for help. "Last night, the thirty-first of October, what was your location please?"

Jack replies smoothly this time. "I was here," he says, calmly. "I was DJing at the Halloween Ball all night."

"And are there any witnesses to support this claim?"

"Er . . . Yeah, pretty much the entire population of Ballycarragh was here." Jack cracks a cute lopsided grin that has me almost clapping with glee. Yes, he's doing really well! There'll be no framing him if he keeps this up.

The Gardaí do not find his flippancy amusing. At least, Seán Senior doesn't, and Seán Óg swiftly wipes the smirk off his face when his father glares at him.

"Sorry." Jack's still smiling a little. He's so relaxed, so obviously unaware of what's happened. How could they suspect him of anything? He tips his glass in the younger investigator's direction. "If I recall, Seán, you were propping up the bar for most of the night with Katie O'Shea? You'd be a pretty reliable witness for me, wouldn't you say?"

Seán Óg is beet red as his father turns to him and asks through gritted teeth, "Is that the case, Seán Óg?"

"Well, yes." He talks very quietly, staring intently at his boots. Then he looks up, slightly apologetically, at Jack. "But I don't actually remember seeing you at all, if I'm telling the truth."

My stomach hitches. What? This isn't good. But Jack's shaking his head, still smiling, still unperturbed.

"It was Halloween, yes?" he says. The two Gardaí look at him blankly, so he continues, as if explaining something simple to a very small, very stupid child, "I was in costume."

Seán Óg's face lights up. "Ah, Jaysus, was that you in the mad hairy-wolf outfit? That was class. Me and Katie were wondering all night how you got the face to look so real, and them claws —"

Seán Senior cuts off his son's enthusiastic babble with a loud and extended throat-clearing fit. When everyone has quietened down, he continues with his line of questioning.

"All right, so," he says, shuffling his scrawled notes again. "Can you tell me the last time and place you saw Rosie Potter please, Jack."

Now the smile is gone. Instantly, Jack is sitting up a little straighter and his face is very serious.

God, he looks sexy.

"Yesterday. She helped me with the set-up before I started work. Why? What's this got to do with Rosie?"

Sergeant O'Flaherty doesn't answer the question. Instead, he asks, "And where was that?"

"Here," snaps Jack, shortly. "In my apartment and in the bar."

"And when was the last time you were in Miss Potter's house?"

"I don't really hang out there much." Jack's looking very uncomfortable now.

I whisper close by his ear, "Easy, now. Easy, boy." And then feel immensely glad that nobody can actually see or hear me talking to my boyfriend like he's some kind of frisky thoroughbred horse.

"Can you answer the question?" Seán Senior is suddenly resembling a real policeman and the atmosphere in the cubby is tense.

"Probably last week. Yeah, I walked her home last Wednesday from work. Can you tell me what the hell this is about? Is Rosie okay?"

"Just a couple more questions, son." At least Sergeant O'Flaherty doesn't look like he's relishing being the bearer of the news he has to impart. "Was Miss Potter present here at McMorrow's during the course of events last evening?"

"No. She was meant to be coming, but she texted me to say that she was staying in with her housemate, Jenny."

"Do you know of anyone who would want to harm Miss Potter?"

"No!" Jack is on his feet. I don't know exactly what he intends to do, but I have to resist the urge to try to hug him.

"What the hell is going on here?" He looks panicky. "Why won't you tell me? Please tell me, has something happened to my girlfriend?"

My poor baby. I can feel tears pricking at my own eyes as Seán Óg stands and gently guides Jack back into a sitting position.

"Jenny McLoughlin found Miss Potter's body at their home this morning," Sergeant O'Flaherty says, his flat voice betraying no emotion. "It appears that there was some form of struggle and the circumstances of her death are currently being considered suspicious."

Jack goes white as a sheet. He doesn't say a word. Nobody says anything for several drawn-out minutes. I'm almost starting to feel bored of all this blank staring when Jack speaks, his tone remarkably even. "And you think I have something to do with this?"

"We have to explore all avenues. You have been identified as being a potential suspect."

And then Jack's face crumples and two fat tears trace shiny tracks down his tanned cheeks and my heart is absolutely breaking watching him grieve.

At the sight of the tears, it's like someone has lit a fuse under the O'Flaherty men. They hurriedly gather their things and exit, muttering platitudes a-plenty and promising to bring the scoundrel responsible for this travesty to justice. I snort aloud at their sudden change of tune. Looks like Jack's in the clear then.

Jack doesn't even seem to notice them leave. I sit in silence with him, just watching. It's all I can do really. His expression is blank. He doesn't shed any more tears, though a shiny trail of salt glistens on his face. I feel completely helpless.

It really sucks being dead.

CHAPTER
SIX

I'd be lying if I said I took Jenny's dire warnings re: Black-Hearted Jack too seriously. She can be quite a dramatic creature after all. And she didn't exactly give me a lot of information to go on. But it did make me take a step back and resolve to really get to know him before leaping all over him and demanding some "quality time", which was a new experience for me, the Queen of Instant Gratification.

I kept a close eye on him for the next couple of weeks. I tried to squeeze more of a story out of Jenny too, but she got so stiff and uptight whenever his name was mentioned, I eventually just stopped trying. She had started avoiding McMorrow's completely, which, though awkward for my social life, was pretty good news overall. It meant I could relax and enjoy Jack's company at work without having to worry about her glowering over my shoulder and offering further predictions of doom.

And his company was *so* enjoyable. On quiet days in the bar we'd spend hours chatting about everything under the sun. His gorgeousness refused to diminish. In fact, he seemed intent on being the most sweet and attentive man I had ever come across. He made no secret of the fact that he had a huge crush on me, but he was never, ever sleazy or even mildly suggestive. Instead, his flirtations were subtle and imaginative. One morning he arrived downstairs with a slightly drooping bunch of wild flowers he'd picked up while out walking the Smiths' terrier the previous night. On another occasion, I got home to discover that my handbag had been sneakily filled with prettily wrapped chocolates while my back was turned at work.

He never made a big deal of it. In fact, when I thanked him effusively for such things, he merely smiled a soft smile and twinkled his blue eyes in my direction. He seemed to sense that I was a little unsure, so was treating me like some kind of skittish, old-fashioned lady of virtue. And I *loved* it. I wanted him more and more as the days went by and he retained a respectful distance, while still making eyes at me across the glasswasher. No matter how close an eye I kept on him (and I kept a very close eye on him, be sure of that) I never once caught a glimpse of the rat my best friend insisted lurked beneath his beautiful exterior. He paid little or no attention to other girls, even when they threw themselves drunkenly at his mercy at the end of a busy Saturday night. He was polite and well mannered to all the customers, though he did do devilish impressions of them behind their backs for my entertainment.

Round and round went my mind: I should definitely *not* go there, out of loyalty to Jenny. Why the hell *shouldn't* I go there if she refused to give me any good reason not to? I should trust Jenny's judgement and leave well alone. I should throw caution to the wind and offer myself to him on a platter, man-devil or no man-devil.

God, my head was wrecked. And it was Lydia Smith, bizarrely enough, who prompted me to take action in the end. She swept into the bar one wintery evening, all puffy blonde hair and bee-stung lips. She appeared rather cheerful, considering she usually seemed to think that smiling was a wrinkle-inducing threat to her youthful looks. It was a very quiet day in McMorrow's, and my only company was Auld Ross Moriarty, perched on his favourite stool at the bar counter. Jack had gone off to the town to pick up decorations for the upcoming Christmas period.

"Hellooo, Rose!" trilled Lydia, seemingly in the mood to chat. I think I can count on one hand the number of times Lydia Smith has actually addressed me by name. She generally tends to save her breath for the men-folk around here. Then again, on this occasion, her options were me or Auld Ross. I'd go for me too if I were her. She slid past me behind the bar and helped herself to a large glass of Chardonnay, winking at me conspiratorially and whispering, "Don't tell Daddy, he might punish me!"

It took a huge effort to suppress the shuddering revulsion that threatened to engulf me. Horrible images of strange S&M games taking place between Mr and Mrs Smith flashed through my mind unbidden as I tried desperately to grasp control of my subconscious mind.

Thankfully she switched topic fast, leaving me reeling. "So, how are you finding our new ents manager, Rose?" she asked, batting those ridiculous false eyelashes at me coyly. "Isn't he a sweetie?"

Much as I didn't particularly feel like having a girly chat with Lydia Smith, I was delighted with her choice of subject matter. "He's great!" I answered enthusiastically. "He's doing really well for this place. There's been a much younger crowd in on Sundays of late and his ideas for the Christmas are —"

"Oh, piddle!" Lydia stopped me with a dismissive wave of one bejewelled hand. "I don't want to talk *business* with you!"

I gaped at her, unsure whether I was infuriated or intrigued, or perhaps a little bit of both, as she continued in her breathless, little girl voice.

"Don't you think he's rather a dish?" she enquired, not waiting for a response at all. "I believe he's got every female within a ten-mile radius on heat!" She let out one of her ear-splitting peals of laughter at this, causing poor Auld Ross to slop Guinness all over his already fairly grubby sweater. She lowered her voice to a hoarse stage-whisper. "Haven't you noticed though?" She smiled, taking another long slug of wine. "He only has eyes for one girl around here!" She winked at me conspiratorially, which unfortunately lent her the appearance of a drunken sailor rather than the cheeky minx I'm sure she thought she looked like.

My own mouth felt rather dry all of a sudden. I could only manage to squeeze out a high-pitched "Hmmm?"

She just stood there grinning expectantly at me, waiting for a better response.

"Um, are you sure about this?" I asked finally, not quite sure what else to say.

"Oh, yes, dear." She patted my cheek like a particularly annoying aunt might do. "Trust me, the boy has it *baaad!* And really, who could blame him?"

And with that last, strange contribution, she drained her glass and disappeared as suddenly as she had arrived, leaving me staring after her in a complete daze. As I poured a fresh pint for Auld Ross, I started to feel a fluttering in my stomach.

Jack Harper was nuts about me. Everyone could see it. Even Lydia Smith had noticed. And here I was, giving off mixed messages, unable to make up my own mind about what to do, when really I was completely head over heels falling for him. He must have been driven demented by the way I kept blowing hot and cold. The poor guy probably didn't know which way to turn. Perhaps he had even confided in Lydia and asked for her help in finding out how I really felt? Right then and there I decided it was time to follow my own instincts. Jenny would come round eventually, I reasoned. My excitement mounted as my mind filled with cheesy, Hallmark-esque ideas of the beautiful relationship ahead. You know the type — the commercially inspired snapshots of how it is to be in love, which bear bugger all resemblance to any real relationship I've ever seen.

Jack and I, wrapped up in matching robes beside a roaring fire, a prettily decorated Christmas tree twinkling in the foreground . . .

Jack and I cosily tucked up together under a big, fluffy, white duvet, looking ridiculously perfect despite having just woken up . . .

Jack and I cooking a spectacular haute cuisine meal and laughing with our super-attractive couple-friends in a dreamy "entertaining" scene . . .

Jack and I shagging rampantly right here on the bar . . .

It was much later that day when Jack finally appeared. I had spent the preceding several hours in a foggy state of apprehension, mixing up people's orders and staring into space for long periods with a blank expression on my face. I had no idea how I was going to address the situation, and my nerves were on permanent alert every time somebody walked through the door.

When, after countless false alarms, it actually was Jack who entered the empty bar on a howl of wind, I was so strung out that I felt a little sick with anxiety.

"Jaysus," he yelped, oblivious to my discomfort as he forced the door shut against the tempestuous Irish weather. He peeled off his jacket and shook raindrops from his sodden hair like an excitable puppy, regarding me with twinkling eyes. "It's a fairly wild one out there, Miss Potter. I think you'd be best off camping here for the night!"

As usual, there was only the slightest hint of suggestion in his tone. His smile was wide as he watched me, waiting for the dry rebuff that usually came his way when we bantered like this. Instead, my mouth went dry and my stomach rolled agonisingly as I allowed myself to consider his offer.

Jack registered my serious expression and immediately backtracked. "Sorry, sorry, I'll control myself!" he joked, slapping himself on the wrist exaggeratedly.

Still, I couldn't bring myself to respond. It was like the cogs of my brain had suddenly all jammed up and all I could think of was curling up in this man's arms and inhaling his scent. I just stared at him unblinkingly as he moved through the bar towards the back door.

He was starting to look a little uncomfortable now (well, who could blame him?). He held aloft his numerous shopping bags and explained slowly and clearly, as if addressing somebody with questionable mental health, "I'm just going to put these out in the back store. We can get stuck into the decorating next week?"

I think I managed a slow nod as he edged out the door, regarding me with some concern. As soon as he was out of sight, I returned to my usual, relatively sane state of mind.

What the hell was that? I berated myself.

I'd spent the entire day mooning around, thinking of all the things I'd like to say to Jack, imagining all the romantic ways I could let him know that I felt the same way he did, anticipating the moment we finally gave in to our desire. And then, when he was right there in front of me, what did I do? I stared at him like he was dinner and gave him the makings for some fairly grisly nightmares. If I continued with this sterling work, I'd succeed in putting him off me completely by morning.

"*Dammit!*" I slammed a hand down onto the counter-top, which hurt considerably but spurred me into action. I would just go out there and tell him how I felt. Of course, I wouldn't mention the whole Jenny thing, out of loyalty to her. I'd just let on that I had only just noticed that he was keen on me.

Trying not to think too much about what I was doing, I took a deep breath and strode purposefully out the back door. In my puffed-up state of nervous energy, I kicked the door quite hard and got an almighty fright when it crashed into something on the other side, juddering back in my direction slowly. It was only when I heard an ominous crumpling sound and a slight whimper of pain that I realised that that "something" was Jack's face.

"Shit!" I yelped, peering into the half-light of the back hallway, where sure enough, Jack was sitting, both hands cradling his face.

"Oh Jack, I'm so sorry! What can I do? Will I call an ambulance? Do you need some ice?"

He raised watery eyes and shook his head very carefully, holding up one hand to silence me. Thankfully, there didn't seem to be any evidence of the bloodbath I was expecting.

"Help me up, you crazy wench," he muttered between clenched teeth.

"Oh, yes, okay."

I hauled him to his feet, registering as I did so that he really didn't weigh much at all. Despite the somewhat tense circumstances I couldn't help wondering if I'd crush him in bed. If I ever got him there, which wasn't currently looking the likely end to this evening's events.

We staggered into the bar, where he collapsed into one of the booths while I busied myself loading a handful of ice cubes into a tea towel. By the time I brought it over to him, I could see a pronounced dark line forming across the bridge of his nose and shadows spreading over both eye sockets. I gulped, as I handed him the makeshift ice pack.

"Sorry," I whispered again. "I think it might be broken."

To my surprise, Jack started to chuckle softly. Shaking his head, and wincing in pain as he did so, he spoke gently. "Rosie Potter, you've been nothing but a headache to me since I first set foot in this bar."

Hmmm. Not exactly an opening for me to declare undying infatuation.

"I'm sorry!" I repeated, an irritating whine creeping into my tone. "I was just —"

But I didn't get a chance to explain anything. Jack pushed away the rapidly melting ice pack, reached out and buried a hand deep in my hair. He pulled me to him with surprising strength, and kissed me hard.

It was a good kiss. A very good kiss. Unfortunately, it didn't last long.

"Ah, fuck," he exclaimed, only moments into it. "That hurts!"

We both laughed then. A heady mixture of excitement and relief.

"At least it'll be a good story to tell our grandkids," he said, with a soft smile, his rapidly blackening eyes fixed on mine.

From that night on, we were a couple. And once his nose healed up a little, we did a lot more of the very good kissing.

CHAPTER
SEVEN

"Jack?" Lydia Smith's voice trills from the bar. It seems to pull him out of the trance he's been in for the past few minutes. He takes a deep breath and gets to his feet. I stay close beside him, wishing I could just pat his shoulder or something equally simple and comforting. I don't really want to make him shudder in revulsion right now though, so I refrain from putting my ghostly hands anywhere near him. Together we exit the snug. The bar is still empty, which isn't unusual. It usually doesn't see much action until after twelve, when the lunch rush starts. Poor Jack, I hope Lydia and Roger will see fit to give him the rest of the day off. The last thing he needs right now is to be working my shift in the bar. He walks round behind the counter and reaches for a bottle of vodka, pouring himself a stiff measure and throwing it straight back.

"What is it, darling?" Lydia simpers.

Who's she calling "darling"?

My hackles go up instantly, but then my attention goes back to my poor boyfriend, who's pouring himself another hefty measure.

"Rosie's dead." His tone is flat, muted, matter of fact.

Lydia's mouth forms a perfect "O" and her eyes open wide. Something about the genuine shock in her expression, and the tender way she reaches out to touch my boyfriend is just too intimate by far.

Eh? My spine begins to prickle as a feeling of complete dread comes over me. *Something doesn't feel right about this.*

Jack turns a dark gaze on the blonde as she reaches out towards him. There's something emanating from him that is truly disturbing. Not grief, that's for sure. No, I've seen that look in his eyes before. Usually just before he . . .

WHAT THE HELL IS HE DOING?!

My boyfriend; my poor, mourning, grieving lover, has just grabbed Lydia Smith around the waist, dragging her close against him. As I watch the grotesque tableau unfold before me, while he kisses her deeply and violently, and she squeals and writhes like some kind of horny kitten, my stomach churns. She's offering no resistance. This turn of events comes as no surprise to her. It looks like I'm the only one not in the loop here.

"What the HELL are you doing?" I can't help myself pointlessly roaring at the pair of them.

Predictably, they pay no attention whatsoever.

"Stop that! Stop it right now!"

They don't stop it.

Instead, Jack grabs a handful of one of those awful breasts and Lydia whimpers in ecstasy. I feel sick to my stomach. I can't take this. Waking up to find myself

54

dead? Piece of cake, compared to the shock and horror of this debacle. I have to get out of here.

I stumble through the front wall, barely registering the chalky, muddy flavour that fills my mouth. Blinded by the bright morning light and my own tears, I stagger around in small circles for a few dizzy moments, before I feel cold metal under my hand and gratefully bend double, leaning on the bonnet of Lydia's silver MG. I dry retch a few times, trying hard to get the disgusting scene I have just witnessed out of my mind, choking emptily on a potent mix of grief, rage, loss and humiliation.

What on earth is going on between Jack and Lydia?

How long has it been going on?

Why am I here?

And how exactly am I leaning on this car?

As quickly as the thought enters my mind, I find myself falling straight through the shiny silver bonnet to the ground, tasting metal and oil.

Bollocks.

I lie prone for several long, painfully drawn-out minutes, looking up into the dark and twisty undercarriage of the nifty vehicle, fantasising about cutting the brake cables or something equally damaging. I would be sorely tempted, except that I couldn't tell a brake cable from a fan belt, and even if I could, I probably couldn't physically lay my hands on them to do the dirty deed anyway.

My bottom lip quivers. I feel so sad and lonely and scared and miserable. At a time like this there's only one place a girl wants to be. I roll out from under the MG and clamber to my feet, setting off at a gallop.

I want my mum.

The Potter family home is a ten-minute drive from the heart of Ballycarragh. There, down a barely noticeable little lane, nestles the cottage my mother fell in love with when she first arrived in town in the late seventies. It's very different now to how it must have been then, when it was barely more than a run-down cow-shed. She set about renovating it with all the enthusiasm in the world (but none of the expertise). Over the years, there have been several interesting extensions built onto and around the original building, which huddles in the midst of these large, exotic-looking structures like an embarrassed relative hoping nobody notices it's with them.

My mum is a little exotic herself, you see. Born in New York City to a pair of madly-in-love lawyers-turned-hippies ("Happies", as Granny Pip and Granddad Robin liked to call themselves), she grew up a real city girl, throwing herself into the booming hippy life-style from a tender age. At the age of twenty-one, she decided to skip out of university for a gap year. Packing a small bag and her hairy, besotted boyfriend of the moment, Stuey, she took off for the green shores of Ireland to see where she really came from.

How they ended up in Ballycarragh remains a bit of a mystery. Any time Mum talks about it, she feels compelled to use words such as "fate" and "destiny", but I suspect the truth is a little less romantic. Whether

56

they were dropped here by a low-flying UFO or stumbled upon the village by accident, they arrived and my mother pretty much instantly declared herself in love with the place. That was even before she met my dad. The local blacksmith's son and aspiring apprentice, John Potter, was three years my mum's junior and never stood a chance once she set her sights on him. Poor Stuey was packed off back to the USA before you could say "free love", and Lucy McGuiness, New Yorker, set about becoming Mrs Lucy Potter.

She bought the run-down cottage a few miles out of the village with some of the "Happies" money; willingly donated, on the condition that they have their own appointed room to stay in should they ever choose to visit. She took to wearing tweed and rain-gear and wellies and being enthusiastically "local", and to this day her assumed Irish accent and phrases sound more Cork by way of Pakistan than regular old West of Ireland. But, folks around here being by and large a friendly and hospitable bunch, she was welcomed into the local community, albeit as a "blow-in". It certainly helped that her chosen husband was as steady and level-headed as they come.

My dad is a typical, quiet Irishman. He has a quick mind, but he's slow to voice his thoughts unless he sees fit to do so. He's tolerant and patient, utterly smitten with Mum, and one hundred per cent content. He enjoys his work, and will probably never retire or change direction in his lifetime, unlike Mum, who is as changeable as the weather and twice as unpredictable. He and Mum couldn't possibly be any more different, but their relationship truly works and always has done. Despite the fact that a typical conversation between them goes something like this:

Mum: "John, that stool is in the relationship corner of the kitchen. It's completely stagnating the flow of chi, I simply have to get rid of it!"

Dad: "The cat looks fairly comfortable there, love. Maybe you could wait till she's finished her nap."

Mum: "The cat be damned, the future of our marriage could be at stake here! We need to get something green and leafy in there, pronto. Maybe I could move the yukka from the bathroom — but no, that's absorbing the negative energy from the drains . . ."

Dad: "Ah, the drains are grand, pet."

Mum: "What? Oh, I know! I'll install a water feature right there! It'll do wonders for our sex life! Now, what can I put there in the meantime?"

Dad: "I'll move the cat, will I?"

That's my parents in a nutshell. Completely crazy in their own ways. Totally lovable and loving and in love with each other. Their combined eccentricities have produced a pair of fairly normal children in Chris and me, which often causes my poor mum some consternation. We had our clashes growing up, but behind it all there's always been a very solid bond between my brother and me.

Most days, we'd be herded outside, rain or shine, to play in the garden or the surrounding fields, or later, in Walker's woods. We had a pond full of koi fish for a while, as well as several chickens, a goat called

Morrison, a couple of donkeys and a half-blind old dog called Benny, who Mum swears came with the cottage. These were the best friends of my early childhood. For some reason, other children struck me as boring and dull. Until I met Jenny, I would regularly kick up a fuss when I was forced to go to birthday parties or spend time with "screaming kids" as I deemed anyone my own age. I was much happier in my own little fantasy world with my animal friends and the infinitely more entertaining mysteries of nature.

When I had had enough of solitude in those days, I would simply seek out Chris and his best friend Charles Walker. I spent many happy hours with the two boys, despite the fact that most of the time they weren't actually aware that I was spending time with them. I learned to be very quiet and developed some rather useful tracking skills. On the odd occasion that they would actually need me for one of their wildly violent games, I invariably ended up lying in some long grass covered in ketchup, playing the role of Victim, while Good Guy (usually Charles) chased Bad Guy (thoroughly method-acted by Chris) through the fields. I never got to play an active role in these shoot-'em-up games because, as was impatiently explained to me many times, I was a *girl* and a girl can't be a *guy*, good or bad. To this day, just the smell of ketchup makes me feel simultaneously sentimental and nauseous.

When I wasn't on bloody corpse duty, I fancied myself as another character: The Secret Agent. I saw a long and illustrious career ahead of me and considered all the long hours spent spying on my brother and his friend as training. I learned a lot about how men think during those surveillance sessions. I also had to sit through some interminably dull conversations about football, BMX bikes and cars. But, resourceful child that I was, I deduced that these long, seemingly pointless discussions were actually code for Top Secret Missions. I worked on breaking that code for years. As a matter of fact, I still occasionally have to stifle a chuckle when someone mentions the offside rule or the word "wheelie" in my presence.

When I found my own best friend in Jenny, I rapidly lost interest in Charles and Chris. Funnily enough, it was around then that they started seeking me out more, so the four of us did end up spending some time together when Jenny and I didn't have Girl Stuff to attend to. I always harboured a suspicion that Chris had a bit of a soft spot for Jenny, to be honest. She always drooled over Charles though. She still goes a little gooey when his name's mentioned. I don't really get what the appeal is, but then again they're practically both my brothers, and both still irritate and delight me in equal measure.

So that's my family. And, boy, am I desperate to see them.

CHAPTER
EIGHT

Opening the rusty gate at the bottom of the garden, I tread the narrow, well-worn path that meanders up to the house with a heavy heart. They must have heard the news by now, which means they're likely to be in shock. I'm not relishing the thought of bearing witness to this, but I can't help myself. All I really want is to be at home, even if that means I have to watch my poor family suffer.

An excited barking fit breaks out from the direction of the house as the gate creaks shut behind me. Benny will be along any minute, half-blind, smelly little wannabe guard dog that he is. And suddenly it hits me.

I just opened the gate.

Again, I've made contact with a solid object without even realising it. I turn back and determinedly grab at the rusted metal, but I touch nothing other than thin air. This is so frustrating!

I'm still trying my damnedest to get a grip on the gate when I notice a snuffling noise somewhere around my ankles. It's Benny, wet little muzzle sniffing circles around my feet.

"Hey, boy," I sigh, giving up my pointless struggle. "How's everyone doing up there?"

The scruffy black-and-tan mongrel sits back and starts gnawing intently on his own back leg.

"That good, huh?"

I cast one last baleful look at the stupid gate before setting off up the path towards the house. A few steps on, I realise that Benny's following me. I turn to face him again.

"Are you looking at me?" I enquire of the poor animal, then in my next breath mutter to myself in disgust, "Why, yes, Rosie, thank you for noticing!"

He *is* looking at me though. His head is cocked to one side, as if he can hear me too. Under my scrutiny, he gives his tail a little half-wag/half-droop, as if unsure exactly what's expected of him.

"You can see me, can't you, Benny?" I say, with mounting excitement, though what I intend to do with a half-dead canine sidekick is anybody's guess. "Who's a good boy?"

Now his tail is wagging in earnest and I can't help myself crouching down to give him a cuddle. This time it registers almost immediately that I'm actually scratching the dog's ear, that my hand isn't passing straight through to tickle his kidneys. Instinctively, I try to keep this realisation in the back of my mind, kind of like when I used to try to do the meditation exercises my mother promoted wildly throughout my teen years. I was never any good at that, but this seems to be working. It's a strange sensation, like splitting my brain in two; the intention to touch and the awareness of touching having to stay on separate levels of consciousness in order for the actual touching to take place. Honestly, I have no idea how I'm doing it, but at least I'm making some progress!

I spend a wonderfully soothing half hour with Benny. It's nice to actually get some attention. Today has been all about me on the one hand, yet nobody has paid me even the slightest heed. I feel so much better when I finally stop petting the (by now delirious) dog, I guess I'm ready to see my family. I can't help wishing they could see me too though.

With my loyal companion trotting along beside me, I make my way up to the house. The crooked metal chimney is belching out plumes of smoke, more than likely releasing the odd puff into the kitchen below too. Chris's car is parked haphazardly in the driveway. Good. I'm glad he's here with Mum and Dad. I sneak up to the kitchen window, peering through to survey the scene inside.

Mum, who has her back to the window, is stirring a large pot atop the Aga. Her greying hair is caught up at the back of her head with a series of feathery hair clips and she's wearing what looks like a burlap sack, cinched in at the waist with a thick, elaborately decorated leather belt. Dad sits facing me, his ruddy face looking amused. As usual, his white hair is standing up at several different angles from his balding head, giving him the appearance of a charmingly nutty professor. Chris stands in the doorway, leaning against the door-frame, wearing a very familiar trying-to-make-Mum-see-sense expression.

It takes a few moments for the warm fuzzy love buzz of seeing my lovely family to wear off before, with perfect timing, I hear a car approaching and realise all at once that:

1) They haven't heard the news yet, and

2) I cannot begin to face seeing them interrogated by Ballycarragh's answer to CSI.

That's absolutely not what I came here for. I came here for comfort . . . Panic sets in as I watch all three familiar faces turn to the window to check out the unexpected visitors. Seán and Seán are waving in an incongruously casual manner, and time seems to have slowed down for me as I try to figure out my next move.

Then I snap into action and do the only reasonable thing.

I run away.

Several hours later, and after a lot of hopeless meandering, I finally creep back to the house. The worst must be over and I'm sick of feeling so alone. I return to the kitchen window, and resume my watch. They don't seem to have moved an inch from their previous positions, but all three now share an identical grey pallour of grief and shock. The Gardaí are thankfully long gone.

Noticing that my nose is feeling peculiarly cold, I go a little cross-eyed trying to check it out. It's probably because instead of being pressed up against the glass like it should be, it's actually hovering *in* the glass. Will I ever get used to this weird ability to put bits of myself inside bits of other things? Ah, hell, may as well go all the way now.

I step through the window, right into the kitchen. It's as if somebody has just turned on the sound in the scene before me. I register that my transition through the glass was actually quite pleasant, with a cool, minty flavour, and am resolving to always try to enter and exit through windows in the future, when my brother's voice jolts me into the moment.

"It's just not appropriate, given the circumstances. And it's certainly not what Rosie would want."

"How do you know what I want?" My sibling buttons firmly pressed already, I can't help demanding to be involved in the conversation. As usual though, Chris and Mum simply ignore my contribution.

"How do you know what she wants?" My mother's tone is shrill, indicating that she's very upset. Usually her voice is low and husky, same as my own.

"Yeah. You tell him, Mum!" I'm enjoying this a bit, I must admit. Dad, on the other hand, has picked up an old copy of *Surfer* magazine, and is pretending to be absorbed in an article called "Monster Barrels on the North Shore", which is absolutely his usual style during any kind of familial conflict.

"It's an ancient and beautiful way of celebrating the life and death of a loved one and releasing them into the next realm with the best possible send-off," Mum continues.

It dawns on me just what she's talking about. "Oh, God, no. Chris, stop her, please!" I do an abrupt about-turn, hoping Chris has the ability to actually make my mother see sense on this occasion.

"Rosie wanted to be cremated —" he attempts to cut in, but Mum is still in full flow.

"It *is* a form of cremation! Honestly, the way you're going on, you'd swear I wanted to stuff her and put her on display in the entrance hall!" Stirring frantically at what, from the delicious smell wafting through the kitchen, is a perfect steak and Guinness stew, Mum's voice breaks a little as tears fill her already puffy, red eyes. "How could she possibly have told you how she wanted her body disposed of, anyway, Christopher? She was only a . . . a child!"

Chris has crossed the kitchen in two long strides, taking her into his arms and squeezing her tight, his own eyes welling up a little. My mum talks into Chris's armpit (we both long ago outgrew both our parents. There must be a long-forgotten Viking giant in our family history).

"I just want what's best for my little girl."

"I know, I know," says Chris in a soothing voice. "Mum, Rosie and I did discuss this, not in a morbid, horrible way, but only because you always told us how *you* want to be sent off. We agreed that we'd do whatever you wanted whenever that day came, but we also made a pact that if it was one of us, we'd make sure we had a say in the matter. Rosie had an organ donor card, and that was really important to her. She also wanted a small, intimate cremation ceremony."

My mum pulls her head out of his armpit for a moment, looking up at him with bleary eyes. "You swear I'll get my pagan bonfire ritual? And all the rest?"

"Mum, I swear, I will personally bedeck your dead, naked body with flowers atop a pyre of ash or beech or whatever wood you declare appropriate, douse you in whiskey, set you alight, and dance the night away with all our family and friends until the last embers have gone out and the wind has carried away whatever remains of you in this world. And Dad will help me too, won't you?"

Dad shrugs and nods as if he's being asked if he wants sausages for tea, then returns his gaze to the magazine.

"All right then," Mum relents. "She can have her boring old cremation. But I'll be watching when my time comes."

I can't help snorting at this. From my own experience with this whole death malarkey she's not wrong there; these two men better do what she says or she'll haunt the hell out of them. She throws a challenging look at my brother, then my father.

Dad finally puts down the magazine and pats his knee. "That sounds lovely, Lucy. Now come sit down here a minute and take the weight off your wee feet."

Mum snuggles into Dad's embrace as Chris takes over stirring the stew. They stay like this for some time, with silence all around except for the sound of the wood crackling in the stove and the bubbling of the pot. It's very comforting for me to see them all supporting each other like this. Even though I'd desperately love to be able to spill my guts to them about what a wanker my boyfriend is being and get some support of my own,

I don't feel too hard done by. I can see they have bigger things to deal with at the moment. Namely, my death.

It's good to see that they're coping. I couldn't bear it if they were wailing and beating their chests and cursing the heavens. But then, that wouldn't be our style. We've been brought up with a healthy respect for life and death. My mother isn't a religious woman, but she is deeply spiritual, and her beliefs are comforting and uplifting. My father has his own ideas, but they both accept and understand each other's points of view. Chris and I grew up with the opportunity to form our own theories on life, the universe and everything, which led to interesting religious education classes if nothing else.

I can't say I ever bargained on this being the way it worked though. Even if I always semi-believed in spirits and energies and maybe (at a stretch) ghosts in theory, I never really gave any thought to the possibility that I might actually become one. And now look at me. Lurking around this kitchen, unable to provide any comfort to my loved ones, and really bloody wishing I could scoff a bowl of that stew.

I lurk a while longer, taking some comfort in their unity, but there's still a lingering sense of something sour within me. It strikes me as unjust that there's no place set for me at the table, even though I know that's ridiculous. While their togetherness is beautiful, it's really made me start to grieve for my own loss, which isn't a nice feeling at all.

My mind just keeps going round and round in the same circles: Why am I here? Am I being punished? Is there some lesson I'm supposed to learn, a key I have to turn in some metaphorical lock? What comes next? This can't be it, can it?

Can it?

And every time I get to this point, I feel the panic start to rise within me and I shut down that line of thinking and focus on something else for a while. Eventually, I make my excuses to deaf ears while Mum, Dad and Chris are clearing away the dinner plates and head up to my old bedroom, with the intention of curling up in a ball and finding out if ghosts sleep.

My room is somewhat the same as I left it when I moved out eight years ago. Apart from the fact that all the furniture has been pushed against the walls and there's a hot-pink yoga mat, several velvet cushions, a large wooden Buddha with burnt-out incense sticking out of his armpits, and a large ring of candles in the centre of the floor. As soon as I moved out, Mum declared that this was going to be her "meditation studio" and unveiled great plans for a complete overhaul. Somewhere along the way she must have got distracted, though, because around this little central plane of calm there are still hairy rock stars snarling down from tattered posters, one bright red wall (one of my own ill-advised ventures in interior design), garish leopard-print curtains (me again, I'm afraid) and a clashing zebra-print bedspread.

"Meditation studio"? Methinks not.

I've just plonked myself down in the centre of the yoga mat to indulge in a hearty little weep when the front doorbell chimes. There's a flurry of activity downstairs, some doors opening and closing, then muffled greetings float up to my super-sensitive ears.

I sniffle a bit more, but I've been distracted now, the tears have stopped coming. A shout of alarm echoes up the stairs:

"Oh, bugger! Grab him, he's all wet and dirty!"

Then my mother's voice:

"Wet and dirty is the least of our problems, he's utterly incontinent too!"

What the . . .?

It all comes clear though, as Benny pokes his raggedy little head around my door, panting. He bounds over joyously and starts licking my elbow with all the enthusiasm of a playful puppy.

"You little brat!" I whisper, my heart swelling with love for our canine buddy. "You know you're not allowed upstairs!"

"I'll get him!"

A male voice, which I assume is Chris, accompanies the sound of heavy footfalls sprinting up the stairs.

"Benny?" Outside the bedroom door. The dog's ears prick up, but he stays where he is, nestled into the crook of my arm.

"Benny?" A dark, shaggy mop of hair appears around the door.

That's not Chris.

Deep-set, dark brown eyes scan the room and come to rest on me.

70

I swear he's looking straight at me.

"Charles!" I exclaim, my face breaking instantly into a huge smile, a tingle of surprise and delight passing through my whole body. He's been away for so long . . .

But then I remember, I'm dead. And invisible. I slump and break eye contact with him. After all, he's looking at the damn dog, not me. I poke Benny — not without a hint of malice — in the butt.

"Go on, Benjamin. Go with Charles."

Benny casts a hurt look in my direction and waddles reluctantly over to where Chris's best friend hunkers in the doorway, filling most of the frame with his bulk. I'd forgotten how big he is. He's always towered over me, even when I'm in heels.

"Hey, boy," he says, his voice a little shaky. It must be weird for him to be looking in at my old room, where Jenny and I used to secret ourselves away and deny entry to pesky Chris Potter and Charles Walker. He looks around one last time, his eyes flicking over me as if I'm not even here, then stands up, knees cracking, Benny tucked under his arm and held safely in place with one giant hand.

"Let's go sit by the fire, eh?"

The stairs groan one by one under his weight as he retreats. After a couple of seconds of feeling dejected, I spring to my feet and follow him.

"Yeah!" I snap, feeling snarkily rebellious for absolutely no good reason. "Yeah, let's go sit by the bloody fire."

It's only when I've barged in and made myself at home on the hearth rug, once more spying on the two boys just like the good old days, that I have a sudden, mortifying flashback.

The last time I saw Charles Walker. Oh, no. Make it stop.

CHAPTER
NINE

One of my mother's dearest friends is Maggie McCarthy-Wilson, an impossibly eccentric artist who lives in the wilds of the Cork countryside. Visits to Maggie's house in my childhood should have had their very own set of vaccinations; more often than not they devolved into several-day-long parties, where children ran wild in the heather and grown-ups may not have been at their most vigilant. Maggie is in her early seventies now and shows no signs of slowing down. A couple of years ago she returned from a month-long holiday in Jamaica with more than a tan. Much to the distress of her partner of twenty years, Arthur — a handsome and charming Welshman in his fifties — Maggie brought back a little souvenir from her travels, in the shape of a twenty-nine-year-old Jamaican called Gordy. She moved Arthur into the studio at the bottom of her garden (in fairness, it's a very luxurious "studio" with its own kitchenette and en-suite, and our whole family stayed there several times in complete comfort) and despite having always declared marriage "an anachronistic mechanism of patriarchal control", wed her toy-boy lover in a rushed ceremony at the local registry office.

They had a happy marriage, if a short one. Three months after the wedding, Maggie divorced Gordy (she kept the "Wilson" in her name though, saying it was far more pleasing to the ear than plain old McCarthy) and packed him off home to Jamaica with much fondness and friendship and promises of keeping in touch. She then proposed to Arthur, but didn't let him move back into the house, saying she wanted to do it right this time, that they couldn't live together until they'd taken their sacred vows.

And so my whole family set off to Cork in the middle of August last year to celebrate the union of two people who had been together for pretty much as long as I could remember, barring the three-month period Maggie had taken to referring to as her "little bout of sunstroke".

It was to be an extravagant affair, taking place in a beautiful old country manor situated right at the edge of some dramatic cliffs overhanging the surging Atlantic Ocean. I couldn't wait. From the moment we received the invitation (in fact, we received several, to be distributed to Maggie's favourite Ballycarragh residents like golden tickets from Mr Wonka himself), I harboured delirious fantasies of how romantic and glamorous it was all going to be. I googled the manor house and pored over photos of the stunning gardens and beautifully decorated interiors, with their freestanding antique baths and four-poster beds.

I pictured myself tripping through the gardens in a floaty gown, sniffing huge, fragrant roses, while perhaps a hunky gardener watched from afar . . .

Or lounging in an overfull bubble bath (the type you never really have the guts to actually indulge in, because what if the overflowing water leaked through the floorboards, causing the bath to drop through the ceiling of the room below?), a glass of champagne in one hand, fresh strawberries in the other . . .

Or walking elegantly down the sweeping staircase with a handsome, be-suited man at my side, my hair swept up in an effortlessly chic (and impossible-to-actually-create) chignon . . .

Or standing by the bar, surrounded by debonair young chaps, my head thrown back in gales of laughter as they clamour for my attention . . .

Yes. I may have been getting a little carried away. But don't we all when we've been single for a while?

It certainly didn't work out the way I had wishfully predicted it would. The manor house was utterly gorgeous as promised. As was the scenery, the setting, the atmosphere, etc. However, any thoughts of lazy hours spent soaking in the tub went out the window when I discovered that we were only going to be staying for one night, which of course meant arriving with little or no time to spare, because no-one in my family can ever be on time, *ever*. Hence, when I got to my room (actually, *our* room, the place was wildly overbooked with Maggie's guests, which meant I was actually sharing a room with my big brother — oh, the joy) I had only fifteen minutes to frantically get ready. Thankfully, my canary-yellow silk dress was floor length, so the fact that I didn't have time to shave my legs wasn't such a big deal. Not so easy to hide was the hair on my head, which was completely untameable and impossible to twist into any kind of style without a halo of frizz puffing up all around my face. My only choice was to leave it down, where it bounced wildly about my ears, taunting me with stray curls whipping into my eyes every so often and generally doing an excellent impression of Sideshow Bob.

I needn't have worried about my appearance though. There was a distinct lack of debonair young chaps in tuxedos, apart from a couple of disappointingly young waiters. There didn't appear to be a hunky gardener lurking anywhere nearby either. In fact, the mean age of all the other guests appeared to be somewhere around fifty. Well, what did I expect? It was hardly the wedding of someone I went to school with, was it?

Still, I was finding it hard to hide my disappointment as I looked around the function room, desperately trying to seek out anyone of approximately the same generation as me. Amid a sea of crêpey cleavage and wildly sprouting eyebrow/nose hair, my options weren't hard to spot. Aside from Chris and Charles, there were maybe two other guys who fit the criteria, but they were both clearly not in the market for fun, with their partners firmly velcroed to their sides. Then there was gorgeous Gordy, flown over from the Carribbean as a guest of honour, his white teeth flashing bright against his lusciously dark skin as he flirted outrageously with several older ladies at once. Somehow I didn't think I was in his target age range.

A pretty Polish waitress floated by with a tray of champagne. *Aha!* There was one aspect of my fantasy that wasn't going down the Swanee. I deftly reached out and grabbed two flutes, smiling dazzlingly at the waitress to indicate that my date would be along any minute and of course I wasn't being just plain greedy. And I proceeded to follow Plan B. Which involved drinking plenty of champagne and thoroughly getting into the spirit of things.

Several hours later, I was certainly spirited. The DJ had just started playing and I was eagerly dragging people onto the dance floor to swing their (replacement) hips. I was the life and soul of the party, or so I thought. There is always "One" at these occasions, and unfortunately this time it was me. I'd already managed to spill red wine down the entire left side of my dress, but was insisting that this was okay because it made it look "more designery" to anyone who would listen. I'd been flirting outrageously with one of the younger male guests, while his girlfriend looked on in mute rage, until finally (mortifyingly) he actually asked if I would mind going back to my own table. I had "hilariously" knocked over a huge, antique vase in the entrance hall while smoking a ridiculously large cigar with an old man with a big moustache whose name I was convinced was Castro (it was Fred). Thankfully, a passing waiter caught the bloody thing or I would have been paying it off for the rest of my living years, but not before it rained pungent-smelling water and slime on another guest, who I then insisted on taking up to my room and giving a makeover. Actually, at that point of the night, I think I was still in "charmingly intoxicated" mode, as Lily (the slimed lady in question) came quite willingly and spent the remainder of the night showing off her perky arse in my Diesel jeans. Lily, being in her late sixties, received her fair share of congratulations on having such a fine derrière, and I was so taken with my handiwork that I insisted she keep the entire outfit. Which was a pretty dumb thing to do as it was the only change of clothes I had for the next day. But I wasn't thinking ahead at that point, was I?

No. I was living in the moment and full of the wonder of it all.

It gets hazy after that. I remember standing lopsidedly at the bar with Chris and Charlie, having a heated debate about whether whiskey affects women in a different way to men (i.e. they were suggesting that ladies can't handle their spirits and I was hotly debating this sexist view) while I demonstrated my point by enthusiastically slugging some lip-smackingly good Glenfiddich. I also remember waking up with a start after I dozed off on the loo in the Ladies. And lots of dancing. Lots and lots of dancing. I started to think the DJ was maybe quite cute despite his bulging gut, balding, pony-tailed hair and "trendy" hornrimmed glasses.

I was happily jungle-boogying the night away with a man called Ernie, who had a smelly fisherman's beard and wandering hands, when a large, dark shape stopped me in my tracks. Mid-twirl, I face-butted a solid shoulder and looked up, dazed, to see Charles looming down at me with a slightly condescending smile.

"Oi! Charlie!" I said, my dented nose causing a slight nasal twang to creep into my voice. "You coulda jus' ask'd f'r a dance, 'stead of beatin' me up!"

It had been a while since I'd attempted to make conversation, thanks to all the dancing, and it was just sinking in that I might have moved on to the stage of "hopeless inebriation" when Charles said (quite pompously, I must point out), "Come on, Rosie, it's time for bed."

How rude! I was incensed. Indignantly in denial in the way that only the truly smashed can be, I railed at him. "Wassamatter wi' YOU?! Bed meyarse."

A firm hand gripped my elbow in what must have been some funky martial-arts move, as I was powerless to resist moving through the now crowded dance floor with him. Up the stairs, straight to my room, halting only briefly for me to retrieve one of my shoes as it bounced down the stairs. All the way I was hissing abuse at Charles, telling him I was FINE and that he was a PARTY POOPER of the highest order. When we arrived outside the door I had a flash of brilliance.

"I los' my key." I smirked up at him, focusing on his slightly crooked nose when I couldn't manage both eyes at once. Now we'd have to go back down and I could leg it. Little did he know the key was safely tucked into my bra. My smug "checkmate" expression faded as he pulled out a small silver key from his top pocket.

"Nevermind," he said, mildly, "I'm sure it will turn up in the morning. Chris's will do the trick for now though."

BUGGER IT. Time to bring out the big guns.

"*Charles Walker!*" I roared belligerently, concentrating very, very hard on my pronunciation to prove how not drunk I was. "How dare you drag me "way from all my lovely new frien's an" try to put me to bed like you're my big ol'daddy?"

Charles remained infuriatingly unruffled. "Because, Rosie Potter, your own father retired to bed quite some time ago, as did your mother, and so the task falls to me. Your brother was more than willing to accompany you up here himself, but I managed to convince him that it would be more convenient for all involved if I did so in his place."

He paused and regarded me quizzically as he slid the key into the lock and half opened the door. I nodded sulkily. Despite myself I could see his point. My clashes with Chris had been known to come to some quite messy ends, especially since we'd been old enough to indulge in the demon drink. This situation would doubtless have caused a doozy of a row. I started to mutter a stubborn denial that *anyone* should be taking it upon themselves to put me to bed, but Charles continued regardless, "You've had your fun, and frankly you were starting to make quite a tit of yourself in front of all your new 'friends', so suck it up and get some sleep. I'll talk to you in the morning."

He pushed the door wide and ushered me through. I took a few unsteady steps, like an ungainly foal, before my legs just gave in and I crumpled to the softly carpeted floor with some surprise. Ooh. Maybe I was a little tipsy after all.

"Dammit, Rosie!" Charles's voice was harsh with concern. He stepped in after me, and took my chin in one of his giant paws, pulling my head up to peer into my eyes.

"Focus now, good girl." He was talking to me like I was one of his bloody veterinary patients; a lost heifer, a crippled bunny rabbit. For some reason, my eyes filled up with hot tears and my lower lip started to wobble.

"Ohhh, Charlie, 'm ver'drunk." I sniffled up at him, pulling my chin out of his grasp and feeling it drop down onto my chest with no resistance at all from my somewhat useless neck. "I though' there'd be a gar'ner for me, anna bubble bath . . ." A fresh wail issued forth from my lips. "An' looka THIS! My lov'ly dress's ruined with re'wine!"

Charles didn't respond. Instead, he hunkered down and hefted me into his arms, standing up swiftly and carrying me over to the fluttering four-poster bed like some kind of conquering hero. I must admit, through my drunken haze of self pity, I was pretty impressed by how easily he lifted my considerable mass. Very few men have ever been able to manage that. In fact, I usually really, *really* hate it when guys try to pick me up. I don't look all that heavy, but the curves plus the height mean that I end up feeling like a big old lump of a thing and the fella is left embarrassed and winded.

Maybe it was the surprise that made me go all funny in the head — added to the soft feather eiderdown beneath me and the romance of the setting, with the breeze blowing the soft drapes all around the bed and the scent of honeysuckle in the air.

And the fact that I was the ever-so-dangerous combination of drunk as a skunk and horny.

Whatever it was, I made a snap decision as Charles laid me on the bed. I deliberately made my body a dead weight, trapping his arms beneath me for a moment. His face was inches from my own and I could feel his breath on my face. It was warm and I could smell the sweet spice of whiskey.

"Well, since we're both here . . ." I whispered in my sauciest voice, lifting my head and closing the distance between our lips. I didn't close my eyes, so as our mouths crashed together (a little harder than I had intended, I'll admit) I saw his eyes widen in shock. And horror? He pulled away abruptly, whipping his arms out from under me as if he'd been burnt.

"Jesus, Rosie!" he spluttered. "What a way to —"

He saw the look on my face and stopped short. I was so mortified, I could actually feel the blush burning up my throat. Oh, hang on, that wasn't a blush.

"*Shit!*" I squeaked, hauling my legs over the side of the bed and making a sideways stagger for the bathroom, where I just about made it to the toilet bowl in time. Not pretty, or clever. Not something you want anybody to witness, let alone someone you've just unsuccessfully hit on.

Understandably, I've been trying to avoid him ever since. Which has been surprisingly easy, seeing as he's been on some kind of strange veterinary retreat in

Africa for almost a year. Saving poverty-stricken goats or something like that.

I didn't actually *see* him for the hour that my head was buried in the toilet bowl, but he was there, holding back my hair and rubbing my back. I would have asked him to leave me to it, if I'd only been able to stop retching for long enough. I don't even remember at what point he did eventually leave. But that was definitely the last time I saw Charles Walker.

In fact, I now realise with some despair, that was literally the last time Charles Walker would ever see me.

What a fabulous final memory to have of a gal.

CHAPTER
TEN

For the first time since I woke up dead, I find myself thrilled to be a ghost and invisible to my company. The mortification of that night is burning as hot as the fire behind me as I revisit the memory. What was I *thinking*?

Well, we all know what I was thinking really. I mean, look at him there, all too-big-for-the-armchair. Crinkly eyes, broad smile, nice sturdy nose (oh I do love a nice sturdy nose) and big, strong Man Hands. On a purely physical level, hell yes, it makes sense. But that's Charlie, one of my favourite (annoying) darling people in the whole world. Imagine if he had submitted to my evil seduction . . .

A momentarily sexy image floats through my mind, but is rapidly interrupted by the far more likely scenario of my actually vomming *on him* instead of making it to the bathroom. I shudder, and turn my attention to the real-life scene before me. Judgementally, I offer my tuppence of wisdom to Chris and Charles.

"Easy on the whiskey there, lads. It's a cursed spirit." I chuckle at my own wit, elaborating purely for my own benefit, "Takes one to know one! Mwahahaha!"

They don't get it. But at least I crack myself up a little bit.

Chris is listening to Charles, who's describing his time in Uganda; in particular, a disturbing shower scene where he had to be accompanied by an armed guard even as he cleaned himself. Those must have been some valuable poverty-stricken goats. I've missed the guts of the story, so by the time he gets to the dénouement ("All right, all right man, just don't point that thing at me!"), I'm completely lost.

Chris laughs quietly though, so he must be in on the joke. Then they lapse into a few moments of silence while they both stare into the flickering light of the fire. It feels kind of nice, like I'm actually in the room for once, as their eyes appear to be on me. The comforting, flattering light of the flames casts shadows along the strong lines of Charles's face, emphasizing his rugged handsomeness. Chris, by contrast, looks like a twelve-year-old boy, with his short cropped ginger hair and clean-shaven jaw. I feel another stab of grief as I regard my brother affectionately. He must feel it somehow as he ruins the moment in typical big-brother style by saying suddenly, "D'you remember when we chucked her in the rainwater barrel and she couldn't haul herself out and she thought she was going to drown?"

Charles barks out a trademark loud guffaw as I make a sour face and swear at them both under my breath. Yes, I remember that. I finally managed to escape only by rocking the barrel back and forth with my body weight till it fell over and shattered. Despite my awful bruises and obviously traumatised state, it was *me* who got in trouble for smashing Mum's lovely big wooden wine-barrel, which she used to collect rainwater to water the garden on dry days. ("My flowers don't drink nasty, fluoridey, tap water!")

And then they're off.

Charles: "What about that time you cut a chunk out of her hair while she was sunbathing and then convinced her that she'd fallen asleep and your dad had accidentally lawn-mowed it?"

So mean!

Chris: "Remember the first time she got drunk? And we made her get up really early and come on a hike with us and she thought she had some kind of weird disease that was going to kill her because we kept telling her they weren't hangover symptoms . . .?"

I actually cried myself to sleep that night.

Charles: "Did she ever find out that it was us who warned that spazz Jimmy Rossa off when she was fifteen?"

NO! I really liked him.

Chris: "No, but he was kissing Suzie Gallagher on the sly, so that was actually us doing Rosie a favour."

Much as the hilarity has all been at my expense, I'm enjoying being a fly on the wall while these two talk about me. It's a nice trip down memory lane, and their obvious fondness and affection towards me is showing through, so I'm disappointed when Charles suddenly changes topic.

"What about this Jack Harper character she'd been dating? What's he like?"

I butt in. "From the sounds of it, he's just like fecking Jimmy Rossa."

But, as usual, Chris is talking over me. "He's okay, I guess. I don't really know him. They kept it real quiet at the start for some reason and that kind of set the tone of the relationship. They kept themselves to themselves. She didn't bring him round here much or involve him in family stuff."

Well, now. I never even noticed that myself. But he's right. We really did keep ourselves to ourselves. I suppose we had to, given the circumstances.

Chris continues, "One thing that always struck me as a bad sign was that Jenny *hated* him. I don't know why — she just said he's bad news and then clammed up when I asked her more about it. I was keeping an eye on them from a distance, but there didn't seem to be any real problem, I suppose."

Charles is looking into the fire again. I self-consciously straighten my pyjamas, I can't help it; it really does feel like he's checking me out.

"Sounds like he wasn't good enough for her, if you ask me," he says gruffly, his eyes resting somewhere in the region of my left nipple. I feel a little glow of pleasure (from his words, not the fact that he's perving on my boobs. Well, not entirely).

"Awww, thanks Charlie," I smirk up at him like an adoring kitten. It's great not to have to play the tough-little-sister card, or worry about embarrassing myself at all, or even vie for attention in this scenario.

"She had really shit taste in men, didn't she?" Charles finally shifts his gaze back to my brother, who enthusiastically agrees with this libellous statement. The self-satisfied smirk has been properly wiped off my face, as tough-little-sister blood rushes to my head.

"Bollocks!" I blurt out, pointlessly. Meanwhile, they've moved on. The new topic is my parents and how best to support them through this difficult time.

"I'm going to bed." I stand up abruptly, eliciting absolutely no response from these two gossiping fishwives. Infuriated, I wave and swivel and shake my booty like a madwoman, right in their faces. Still nothing. They don't even pause to draw breath.

"Goodnight, fuckers." I whistle for Benny and exit the room, half hoping one of them will notice the dog following me and come to get him, but they're too absorbed in each other. As always.

I throw myself onto the zebra-print bedspread when I reach my room, Benny leaping up delightedly beside me. What is it with these people and their opinions on my love life? First Jenny and now Charles.

What's most irritating is that they're *right*. But I've only just come to this conclusion myself, after discovering the truth about my own relationship being a farce. Which doubles the sting. They all knew long before me.

I've been an idiot. I should have listened to Jenny all along.

Some of her choicest words come floating back to me:

"You'd do well to stay the hell away from him."

"If you get involved with him, you'll end up very fucking sorry."

"Be careful, won't you Rosie?"

And of course, the clincher, this morning to the Gardaí: "Jack Harper did this."

Icy fingers wrap around my spine and pull hard on my intuition.

Oh, boy. What if Jack Harper did do this?

CHAPTER
ELEVEN

Jack and I didn't go public with our blossoming relationship straight away. Partly because Jack wasn't entirely sure how the Smiths would take their two senior employees hooking up right under their nose (and their roof, for that matter) but mostly because I just didn't know how to break it to Jenny. For all my bravado when I'd been reasoning to myself that she'd only want what's best for me, I was somewhat less convinced once faced with the daunting task of actually putting it to the test. I still didn't understand her unflinching animosity towards Jack, though he seemed to take it in his stride. He said she'd always accused him of being a bit of a womaniser when they worked together, so was probably just looking out for me. He tried to console me by telling me that once she saw how serious we were about each other, and that he was a changed man, she'd soften up.

I just didn't want to upset my best friend — even though I had made a decision that was inevitably going to upset her — so I put off telling her for as long as possible. She must have known something was going on though. Suddenly I was staying out overnight with no explanation, leaving the room to take phone calls, and generally mooning about the place with a big goofy grin on my face.

The only fly in the ointment was the fact that I had nobody to share my joy with. I could have told my mum all about Jack and me — she would have been more than willing to hear all the juicy details — but the only person I truly wanted to talk to was Jenny. I felt like it would be a further betrayal of her trust if anyone else found out before her, so I hugged my blossoming new relationship to myself like a secret that was burning a hole in my heart.

One night when I was staying in Jack's flat above the bar, I woke with a terrible thirst on me in the middle of the night. I extricated myself from Jack's tight embrace with great care, surprisingly managing not to wake him. I slid out of the bed and padded as quietly as possible into the tiny kitchen-cube, where I filled a pint glass with water. Stealthily, I made my way back into the bedroom, only to stub my toe on Jack's bedside dresser in the dark.

I yelped loudly, my knee reflexively shooting up and hitting my elbow, which in turn jerked hard, causing the hand holding the glass to quite literally *throw* its contents halfway across the room.

"*OW! Owww! Ow!*"

I was trying to be quiet but some sounds refuse to stay down, especially when one has quite possibly broken a couple of toes. A light flicked on and temporarily blinded me as I hopped crookedly on one foot, stark naked, an empty pint glass clutched in one hand and what felt like a couple of glowing, throbbing cartoon toes held in the other.

As my eyes adjusted to the light and the pain began to subside, I realised Jack was sitting up in bed, looking at me with a quite peculiar expression on his sleepy face. I ceased my hopping immediately, staring back at him in horror as I realised that he was soaking wet. He had unfortunately been on the receiving end of my pint of water. A long moment passed as we stayed frozen in that tableau of disaster.

"Rosie," Jack finally said, in a very, *very* serious tone of voice, which made me gulp as if I were being addressed by the headmaster after doing something exceptionally naughty, "I am completely, utterly in love with you."

It was the first time he had said those magic words to me and you could have knocked me over with a feather right then and there.

I dried him off as best I could, which led to a delightful little encounter on the bedroom floor, after which we simply pulled the duvet off the (rather damp) bed, snuggled up where we lay and drifted off to sleep. My last thought that night was a firm decision to tell Jenny everything the next day. I was in love, my gorgeous man felt the same way, and I wanted the world to know.

She didn't take it as badly as I expected. That is to say, she didn't let loose a diatribe of hate and tell me that I could burn in hell with my devil boyfriend for all she cared. Instead, she just looked sad and disappointed, which made me feel even worse. She sighed and said resignedly, "Okay, Rosie, it's your life and I won't keep going on at you. I love you no matter what. Just be careful, won't you?"

I gave her a big hug and tried to reassure her by telling her all about how madly in love with me Jack was, and how I just knew this was so right, et cetera. She smiled tightly. I could tell she was really trying to be supportive, but there was such an emptiness in her eyes I resolved not to go on too much about the details of my love affair just yet. In time, I hoped she'd come to accept Jack and me, and see that it was all for the best.

Despite my best intentions to give her time, I was impatient for Jenny to come around. I harboured fantasies of the three of us palling around cosily like she, Tom and I used to years ago. Which is why I did what I did next, despite the voice of reason screaming in the back of my mind that it was *NOT A GOOD IDEA!* All I can say in my defence is that happy love hormones may have caused my powers of reason to be temporarily suspended. Any idiot could see that Jenny was struggling to accept even the idea of me and Jack being an item, but I was just so desperate to have my cake and eat it too that I cooked up a plan whereby I could *trick* her into seeing how good we were together and how lovely he really was.

Yes, I know. Hardly genius.

So, I invited Jack around for dinner one Thursday night, neglecting to tell Jenny that he was coming. Instead, I asked her if she'd like to have an evening in with me with some home cooking, wine and gossip. I felt slightly guilty when she responded with great enthusiasm, but hastily pushed any doubts to the back of my mind. This was all for the best. For all three of us. The sooner we could just put our issues behind us, the better. I have to admit that the only person I thought actually had any issues was Jenny, so this ambush wasn't quite so selfless as I tried to convince myself it was.

Jenny got home from work as I was prepping the ingredients for her favourite slow-cooked lamb hotpot. She had a clinking bag in hand, signalling that she was prepared for plenty of the wine part of our plan. She plonked herself down at the table, uncorking a Pinot Noir, and releasing a satisfied sigh as she stuck her nose deep into the glass and inhaled happily.

"I needed a night like this!" she said, a big smile on her face.

We spent an hour or so catching up, sipping on our wine, giggling and generally just carrying on the way we always had. It was lovely, and I realised that I too had needed a night like this. I'd almost forgotten entirely about the real reason I had arranged this meal, so when I glanced at the clock and saw that Jack would be arriving any minute it came as quite a shock to me. I knew I had to give her at least a little advance warning.

As casually as I could, with my heart hammering in my throat, I asked Jenny to set the table. She set to it immediately, still chattering away about a difficult customer she had had to deal with that day. I handed her an extra setting and, with a catch in my throat, asked her to lay three places at the table.

She twigged immediately what I was up to, looking up at me with wounded eyes, a touch of panic evident behind the hurt.

"Oh Rosie, no!"

I instantly regretted my decision. I wished that we could just keep going the way we had been. Her reaction kicked me in the gut; the sheer disappointment and sadness written all over her face. My hand was moving towards the back pocket of my jeans to call Jack and cancel, but it was too late.

A sharp rap at the door signalled that the third member of our little dinner party had arrived. Jenny swiped a hand against her cheek, under the pretence of brushing her fringe aside, but I didn't miss the sudden reddening of her big brown eyes.

She busied herself straightening the mismatched wooden chairs around the table for a moment, while I stood frozen to the spot. Then, drawing her shoulders back and lifting her chin defiantly, she strode over to the door. She looked me in the eye as she reached for the handle.

"We need to talk later, Rosie," she said, ominously.

Before I could respond, she had wrenched open the door, admitting our not-so-welcome guest.

"Jenny McLoughlin!" Jack exclaimed as he stepped through the front door, smiling broadly and throwing his arms wide in the invitation of a hug. "How lovely to see you at last!"

"Hello, Jack." Jenny said stiffly, looking anywhere but at him and neatly side-stepping his embrace.

I took advantage of it, though, stepping into his arms for a hug before helping him out of his jacket and taking the bottle of cheap Chilean red he proffered.

Despite Jenny's chilly reception, I was glad to finally, in some way, have our relationship out in the open. We'd been secretively carrying on behind closed doors for so long that I was beginning to wonder if I'd slipped into some kind of half-mental dream-world. While I served dinner I kept up a steady stream of chatter. Jenny was pretty much silent, but she stayed in the room, which was all I could ask for really. The wine was flowing and all in all I thought things were going pretty well. Jack stayed chipper in the face of Jenny's obvious dislike, knowing how important it was to me that she see there was nothing to worry about. I sent him lots of warm and grateful smiles as he told funny stories about how hard it had been for him to adjust to life this deep in rural Ireland after all his years of being a cityslicker.

"It must have been a real culture shock for you to move to Dublin straight from here?"

This question, he directed at Jenny. I turned in my seat to observe her reaction. She barely looked up from her plate.

"Not really," she replied, flatly, taking another long gulp of her wine.

"Ah, but you still ended up running back to the country when city life got too tough, didn't you?" he asked, his tone lightly teasing.

Jenny paled a little, her mouth tightening even further, but she didn't respond.

"Then again," Jack continued, seemingly oblivious to her discomfort, "I don't blame you. Ballycarragh certainly does have a lot to offer."

As he said this he shot a long, lingering look my way, practically stripping me with his eyes. With a shriek of wood on wood, Jenny pushed her chair away from the table forcefully.

"Toilet," she uttered hoarsely, before belting from the room.

Jack turned an innocent gaze on me as I rose to clear the table, troubled by her extreme reaction. "What was *that* about?" He seemed as bewildered as I was.

"Actually, I was going to ask you the same question."

A brief silence passed between us as I ran hot water over the dinner plates. As I turned to grab a couple more pieces of crockery, I discovered that Jack had risen from his seat and was standing right behind me.

"Oh!" I squeaked, as I found myself nose to nose with him. "You gave me a fright!"

He didn't reply, instead crushing me back against the sink and planting a hard, demanding kiss on my mouth. Much as this display of manly dominance was a turn-on, I couldn't help being aware that Jenny might walk in at any moment and that this was perhaps not the most sensitive way to deal with her upset. I tried to pull back from his embrace, but he had my arms pinioned to the counter and my hips trapped by his own. His considerable hard-on was pressing insistently into my upper thigh and his kiss was growing ever more passionate. While a part of me would gladly have melted into the moment and to hell with the consequences, thankfully I still had a semblance of reasoning power left in me. With a Herculean effort, I stopped kissing him and turned my face away.

"Stop it, you bad man!" I joked, trying to lighten the sexually charged atmosphere. I saw a flash of something close to anger in my boyfriend's eyes, which unnerved me, and certainly helped dampen the flames of my arousal. But then it was gone and he was wrapping his arms around me in a comforting hug.

"Sorry, sweetheart," he said, his voice husky with desire. "I just can't control myself around you sometimes."

With that, he finally released me and returned to the table to top up our glasses. He shot me a little smile as he held out my wine. I took it and clinked it against his before taking a large mouthful.

"Thanks for making such an effort with Jen," I said, shaking my head sadly. "I really wish I knew what the problem was. I just can't work out why she's so hostile towards you."

Jack didn't reply immediately. He seemed to be trying to find the right words. He sat with his mouth working but no sound coming out. Finally, he just blurted out, "Do you think maybe it's possible that she has feelings for me herself?" Wincing as soon as the words had left his mouth, he didn't give me a chance to respond. "Bloody hell, sorry. I knew that would come out sounding completely poncey. What I mean is . . ." He made a few more pained-looking faces, then continued. "Well, I always thought she might have had a bit of a thing for me in Dublin, and now she's acting so jealous of your happiness. It just strikes me as a bit unfair that you have to work so hard to get her approval."

I was torn. Part of me was in complete agreement with Jack. After all, it had been a long, uphill battle with Jenny and she was still freaking out for no apparent reason. I was deliriously happy and there wasn't anything to be upset about unless she did indeed have a thing for my man. On the other hand, that was my best friend he was badmouthing and I couldn't help feeling pretty cross with him. He was right, he did sound completely poncey.

Before I'd figured out quite how to respond, Jenny reappeared. She looked much calmer as she took her seat at the table and drained her glass in one go. I felt another sharp stab of sympathy. This was obviously hard for her whatever the reasons. And if she did have feelings for Jack, I could see why. I just couldn't understand why she hadn't simply told me that in the first place. Perhaps she was ashamed that she'd had a crush on Jack in Dublin while she was still with Tom? That would be just like Jenny. I resolved to insist on a full and frank discussion about it all when Jack was gone. For now, though, as he topped up her glass and I busied myself serving some slightly limp-looking lemon-meringue pie, I would just try to keep things on a slightly less fraught level.

I wouldn't describe that evening as a roaring success, but for a while after dinner things seemed to be going pretty smoothly. We popped a few more bottles of wine, which eased the flow of conversation considerably. We stuck to the safest topics: work, crazy Irish weather, repairs needed on the cottage and gossip about mutual acquaintances. Jenny had downed a large quantity of wine (the majority of it, in fact) and seemed to have relaxed considerably, which made me very happy, especially as I'd been bursting to use the loo for at least an hour but had been reluctant to leave the two of them alone in case I came back and found a fork in Jack's eye.

I was preoccupied with plans to escape and relieve myself when the tone of the conversation changed, almost imperceptibly at first.

What were we talking about?

I traced back the last few sentences in my mind, trying frantically to catch up with the other two, who suddenly had an icy silence crackling between them. Ah, yes, hadn't we been speculating on Lydia Smith's most recent surgical procedures? Jenny had been giving out about Botox and the increased pressure women were under in this day and age to stay young-looking, blah blah blah, familiar rant which we indulged in regularly. Jack must have made the mistake of giving a male perspective. Dammit, why hadn't I been concentrating?

"All I'm saying," he suddenly piped up again, as I tried to shoot warning vibes at him using the power of my eyeballs alone, "is that I don't see any problem with a woman wanting to look good for her man. Why is that such a controversial thing to say?"

Oh dear. I was going to have to side with Jenny on this one. We both stared at him in stony silence. Good Lord, was my lovely boyfriend going to launch into one of those awful caveman diatribes on how too many women "let themselves go" once they've bagged their man? I couldn't stand it, my discomfort magnified by the overwhelming urge to pee.

"Perhaps we should just drop —" I tried to be the voice of reason, but there was no room for reason at this table.

"Why aren't we considered good enough in our natural state, hmmm? Why is it considered so unnatural that a woman should age at all?" Jenny's voice had taken on the low, aggressive tone that always put me in mind of some kind of rattlesnake warning before an attack.

"Oh, come on!" Jack snorted, "You want to be desired, don't you? You want your man to want you sexually."

The way he said that word was enough for me to ignore the basic nonsense I thought he was talking and just start wishing he'd drag me off to bed by the hair, club in hand. But it didn't seem to have the same effect on Jen.

She waved her wine glass dangerously in his direction. "What about a woman wanting her man "*sexually*"? Don't we have that right too?"

Her eyebrows raised so high they almost disappeared under her short fringe, as she regarded Jack with thinly veiled distaste.

"Or don't you go in for that sort of thing, Jack?"

She grabbed the near-empty bottle of red from the table and up-ended it into her glass, her point seemingly made. I was thoroughly confused and so was Jack from the bewildered expression on his face. Thankfully, it didn't look like she was waiting for a reply anytime soon. As a matter of fact she was lost in the depths of her wine glass, swaying gently in her chair.

I couldn't defy nature any longer, so I jumped to my feet and shouted, "Loo!", realising that I was far from steady on my feet as I dashed for the bathroom. And Jenny had drunk a lot more than me — no wonder she was rambling incoherently. I stayed in the bathroom for a little while, partly to clear my head and partly to scrub some of the violet-tinged wine stains from my lips and teeth.

On my way back, I paused momentarily outside the kitchen door (just to catch my breath, you understand, not to eavesdrop or anything sneaky like that) and eavesdropped.

It wasn't easy to make out exactly what was being said through the heavy old wooden door, but there was definitely a hushed conversation going on in there. Jenny's voice was high pitched, though quiet, and sounded very strained, as if she were holding on to the last vestiges of control.

". . . trying to torture me?"

Then Jack's voice, very low, very intense muttering, of which I could only catch snatches of words.

"Blah blah blah . . . What's best . . . blah . . . Rosie . . . blah di blah . . . Tell her . . . blah blah blah blah . . . SORRY!"

I thought I heard a muffled sob at that point, but it could just as easily have been a sneeze. My conscience got the better of me and I decided that I'd heard enough. I had, in fact, heard bugger all, but I certainly didn't want either Jenny or Jack to be drunkenly crying over me in my own kitchen. So I breezed through the door trying very hard to convey the careless nonchalance of a non-eavesdropper.

Thankfully, no-one was in tears. Jenny's eyes were a little red, but that could have been due to an excess of alcohol (after all, her lips were a distinct shade of purple too). She sat crookedly slumped in her chair, while Jack crouched in front of her, supporting himself with one hand on the table and the other gripping the back of her chair.

They both looked up at me, and Jack gave an easy smile. Shifting his weight slightly, he squeezed Jenny's hand and got to his feet.

"I'll leave you girls to talk," he said, concern evident in his voice as he slipped through the door behind me. "Back in a minute."

I pulled a chair up next to Jenny and looked closely into her eyes. "Are you okay, Jen?" I asked, smoothing down an unruly lock of her hair to no effect.

Her big, soft eyes filled with tears.

"Oh, Jenny, what is going on with you?" I asked desperately, wrapping my arms around her as she sniffed against my shoulder. We stayed like that for only a moment before she stiffened again and pulled away.

"I just want to tell you that I'm sorry for upsetting you and behaving like a jealous bitch," she said, the words sounding strange, tripping out like a script.

"I really do want you to be happy, Rosie. I love you so much."

This last part was said with conviction, but there was still something in Jenny's tone that made me uncomfortable. From what I'd heard outside the door, it was clear that it had been Jack's suggestion that she apologise, but I still didn't quite understand why she was so visibly shaken. I didn't have time to ask her any questions though, as Jack reappeared at that moment. So I hugged her tight, and whispered that I loved her too and that she didn't have anything to worry about at all.

We busied ourselves tidying up after that and then went our separate ways to bed. Jack told me that he'd had a few quiet words with Jen, and I told him about her apology. He said that was very good of her and that it must have taken some courage to do, without ever mentioning that he had suggested it. I remember feeling a great surge of love for him, being deliriously happy and somehow convinced that he'd managed to smooth things over with Jenny. I was sure that her odd behaviour was down to too much wine and that we'd all taken a big step forward that night.

Clearly, I was completely delusional. The three of us never spent any time together again after that night. Jenny ensured that she was always out when Jack was round at ours, and Jack seemed quite content for us to sleep at his place most nights. She didn't actively criticise him anymore, but then again, she didn't speak about him at all.

Until now, I had put that awkward night behind me; wiped it from my memory because it sat uncomfortably with my idealistic view of Jack.

Now that I'm dead, it all seems a tad more suspicious.

CHAPTER
TWELVE

I wake up with a start, blinking against the bright light that's pouring through the open curtains of my old bedroom. Well, there's that question answered: ghosts *can* sleep. And I feel better for it. Clearer. More focused.

The question of why I'm still lingering here remains at the forefront of my mind, but I think I've come to a conclusion about what needs to be done. I fell asleep last night remembering the events of that awful night and seeing it all from a whole new perspective. I still feel slightly sick as I remember how Jenny's face looked when I came back into the room. She looked scared, pale, clammy, panicked. Jack could have been threatening her, bullying her, emotionally blackmailing her . . . Who knows what the slimeball was up to? And I, blinded by infatuation, completely denied what I saw, stubbornly putting it down to too much wine instead of opening my eyes and listening to my gut. I can't help wishing in hindsight that I'd pushed harder, taken heed of her initial warnings, perhaps even put Jack under a bit of pressure to get to the bottom of it all.

But I didn't and I can't change that now. There is something I can do, however.

A creepy grin (I just know it's creepy, even though I can't see it myself — it *feels* satisfyingly creepy) spreads across my face as a thoroughly suitable plan of action finally takes form in my mind.

I am going to haunt Jack Harper.

I'm going to haunt him till he's a blubbering mess.

He's the prime suspect in the case of my untimely demise, and even if by some strange twist of fate it turns out he didn't kill me, he still deserves to suffer a bit. The way he upset Jenny. The way he's philandering with the overblown pout that is Lydia Smith. The way he used to spend longer in front of the mirror than me.

My blood starts to boil again as I fantasise about all the brilliant ways I can harass Jack. He won't know what's hit him. Even better, he'll eventually figure out that it's me doing it and then I can really make him squirm.

The radio downstairs is switched on, interrupting my rather enjoyable moment as an evil genius in my own mind. I can hear my mum clattering about in the kitchen in the most familiar manner. For just a few blissful seconds, I forget that I'm dead and jump up to join my family for breakfast. It's one of our traditions. Whoever is in the house, whatever the antics of the night before or the plans for the day, we all sit down for a cosy, nourishing half hour of breakfast together before going about our business.

To hell with it, dead or not, I'm not missing breakfast.

The news has just come on when I enter the warm, inviting kitchen, hot on the heels of my sleepy-looking brother. I wonder if they're going to report my death?

A young woman's body was found yesterday in her own home in Ballycarragh. Gardai have stated that foul play is suspected, probably by her rat-fink boyfriend, Jack Harper. In other news, Lydia Smith is a vile slapper.

Now that would be some quality news reporting, right there. Instead, they focus on some boring bank trouble and an armed raid on a sweet shop in Westmeath. What is the world coming to?

"Did Charlie stay over?" Mum asks Chris, as he takes his seat at the table and stares blankly into his empty coffee mug.

"Coffee?" he grunts, like a baby silverback gorilla.

She dutifully plunges the cafetière and pours him a hefty measure before asking him again about Charles.

"Oh, sorry, Ma. I'm knackered — we stayed up talking till about four."

Mum snorts. "Talking! And guzzling the good stuff too."

Chris looks sheepish. "Yeah, sorry about that. I'll replace that bottle today . . ."

She ruffles his hair. "Don't be silly, love. Just answer my question so I know how many rashers to put on. That man eats like a ravenous beast."

"No, he went home. Had an appointment early this morning."

I feel a funny twinge of disappointment. Irritating as he is sometimes, it was nice to see Charles last night.

Then my dad comes in and breakfast starts in earnest. They all make small talk, not really mentioning me at all until Chris finally asks, "So, what's our plan then? Regarding Rosie?"

Dad instinctively reaches out and puts his hand over Mum's, where it lies on the table. Her eyes well up a little, and she says in a quiet voice, "Your father and I were just talking this morning about how surreal all this is. Everything just continues as normal even though it's all changed irreparably."

Chris nods. "Me and Charles too."

"And there's all this talk of 'suspicious circumstances'," Mum's voice wavers as she continues, "I mean, how could that even be possible? In this town? Our little girl never hurt a fly."

Chris shakes his head. "Ma, there's no point even thinking about that right now. The Gardaí have her body, and we'll hear soon enough what the results of the autopsy are. For the moment, we just have to keep living, I suppose. Take it as it comes. And if somebody did hurt Rosie . . ."

His face is stony, his expression dark and almost scary. Which is generally a very hard thing for a freckly ginger fella to pull off.

Dad clears his throat and speaks. "Lucy would like to hold a traditional Irish wake today. We were thinking that there will be a lot of people coming as Rosie was such a popular girl, so we'll call McMorrow's today and talk to Roger about having it there."

And they think this is surreal for them? I'm sitting here listening to my folks planning my wake.

109

Chris looks a bit perplexed, and is about to open his mouth to speak when my mother's phone starts trilling Vivaldi's *Four Seasons* and buzzing around the tabletop like an angry, crippled bee.

She picks it up and peers myopically at the screen, holding it close to her nose and then at arm's length, regarding it like it's going to bite her. There's nothing unusual in this display — this is what Lucy Potter does *every single time* her phone rings. She looks up as the annoyingly loud ringtone cuts out mid-note, and exclaims, "That was a Dublin number!" as if surprised such a thing exists.

The phone starts ringing again almost immediately, giving her a bit of a start, and she turns to Chris in a panic. I watch in amusement as she presses the green button and then in a sudden change of heart practically throws the phone at my brother. "You talk to them!"

There's a tinny voice on the other end of the line going "Hello? Hello . . .?" as Chris gets a grip on the phone.

"Yes, hello," he finally manages to croak into the receiver. "No, this is her son, Chris Potter . . . Yes, she is, she just can't come to the phone right now . . . All right . . . Ah . . . I see . . . Well, we were told . . . Yes, I do understand . . . Do you have any idea when it *will* be released then? . . . Okay . . . Right . . . Well, there's nothing to be done really is there? . . . All right then . . . Keep us informed, won't you?" Chris hangs up and passes the phone back to Mum, who looks like she's going to burst a blood vessel with curiosity.

110

"Well?" she blurts, eyes wide. "Who was it and what did they want?"

"It was someone from the lab where they're examining Rosie's body." Chris's voice is sympathetic but resigned.

"I thought this might happen. Despite what we were told yesterday, they won't be releasing it today after all. Apparently it's not as clear cut a process as they'd initially thought."

There's a long silence around the kitchen table. Mum looks like she's chewing on a wasp. Finally, Dad blurts out a suggestion. "We could just wait a few days —"

"No freaking way, John," Mum cuts him off with her strongest swear word. The woman means business. "Rosie needs her send-off. We need the body for the cremation obviously, so we have to wait to do that. But our poor, beautiful daughter is at this moment probably floating about somewhere nearby, just waiting to be released and set free on her journey to the next life."

Well, now. She might be onto something there.

"So we will proceed with our decision to wake Rosie this evening at McMorrow's. We can build a little altar to her, something special and befitting the occasion, so that friends and family can say their farewells." Her voice breaks a little and my father pulls her chair closer with one good tug, nestling her into his armpit. She steels herself visibly, then continues, like a commander about to go into war. "Christopher, you get on The Face Book and invite everyone. And print off some nice pictures, and we'll buy a few glitzy frames, and I'll get some flowers and candles and that will do just fine rather than a damned morbid coffin anyway." She turns up her face to Dad, giving him a swift peck on the cheek. "John, we'll spin into town and pick up a few bits. I'll have to make a few sandwiches. And I'd like some of that jasmine incense too. You know, Rosie's favourite."

Little does she know I just burned that stuff when I was a teenager to hide the fact that I was —

"The stuff she used to burn when she was smoking out her bedroom window, the brat," Mum adds wryly, making my brother and Dad laugh, and softening up the sad atmosphere a little.

They all get to their feet and bustle around, clearing up the breakfast table and preparing for their appointed tasks. I feel like I'm in the way somehow, especially with my mum's theory of me just hanging around in limbo going round and round in my head. Could it be as simple as that? That I'm just awaiting my send-off? Not that I'm here to avenge my death, like I was kind of thinking might be the case?

Well, we'll soon see, if this wake is going to go ahead today. In the meantime, I may as well get started haunting Jack.

Unfortunately, when I get to McMorrow's after a speedy shortcut through the fields, leaping over walls like they're little kids' hurdles and generally pretending to be a superhero, Jack is nowhere to be found. I rifle half-heartedly through a few cupboards in his flat, but all I find of any interest is a pair of unidentified

112

women's knickers, much to my disgust. I contemplate hanging them off the beer tap down in the bar, but the idea of actually touching them makes my skin crawl too much, so I just kick-flip them into the bin and leave in a huff.

Where is he? How is he getting away with going AWOL at a time like this?

I get my answer as I pass a harassed-looking Roger Smith talking on the phone while he paces outside the pub. "I just need someone to come in and help me for a few hours tonight . . . There's a wake on, and you know how that kind of thing can get in this town . . . Yes, but it's my bar manager's wake, that's what I'm trying to tell you . . . Well, he was going out with the girl in question, and he's taken some time off to go home and do some mourning in peace! I'm telling you, there's nobody else . . . NO! Lydia is staying with her mother this weekend!"

Oh dear, poor Roger. I can't help feeling a small stab of pleasure that he's finally having to deal with the headache of rostering staff himself.

Not as easy as it looks, eh?

I ramble off down the road in the direction of Honeysuckle Cottage. May as well go and visit Jenny. I feel pretty lonely really. Even Jack the creep has someone to comfort him in his hour of need (obviously, despite Roger not putting two and two together, those two are off "Rogering" each other somewhere. *Mourning, me arse*).

To compound my gloomy mood, I find Honeysuckle Cottage empty too. Dammit, where is everybody?

What's a ghost gotta do for some company around here? I perch myself on the garden wall and wait for my housemate to come home, feeling fantastically sorry for myself. It's a nice day with the snap of winter in the air; wispy white clouds and cold, bright sunshine making the countryside look extra pretty. Across the neighbouring fields I can see Walker's woods rolling on the horizon. And just beyond that is Charles's house. I could go there, I suppose.

I wonder what he's doing right now?

CHAPTER
THIRTEEN

When I was ten years old, Charles found me sitting in the raspberry patch in my back garden. We were ostensibly playing a game of hide and seek, but to be honest I wasn't very interested in the game, more in the handfuls of juicy, ripe fruit I was stuffing into my mouth.

Besides, Chris was "it", and he would more than likely completely forget about me once he had found all his friends. It was his twelfth birthday and seven hyperactive, rambunctious boys had been marauding through our house for several hours, much to my disgust. It appeared that my mother felt the same, as half an hour previously she had suddenly roared, "Right! Out with you! It's a fine soft day!" despite the fact that it had been drizzling greyly all morning. When met with a few whimpered protests, she threw her eyes skywards as she ushered all of us out the back door (the injustice in my eyes was that I had to go too — these savages were nothing to do with *me*, surely she should be able to see that!). "Ah, sure, it's only a spot of rain, aren't you all fine strong Irishmen?"

With that, the door slammed behind us. I stood there for a moment, glaring at the solid oak, then stamped my foot and shouted as loud as I could, "No! *I'm* not!"

It was no use though. Mum had obviously had her fill of children for the day, thanks to my brother and his sugar-fuelled buddies, and now I was condemned to share their fate.

Making the best out of a bad situation, it was me who suggested the game of hide and seek. I was well aware that Mum had expressly asked Chris and me not to eat too many raspberries as she was planning on making a nice batch of jam any day now. However, under the current circumstances, I saw my chance for a justified raid of the precious booty. I didn't care if she got cross with me. *I* was cross with *her*, anyway.

So there I was, munching away righteously, when a rustle in the bush beside me made me jump nearly out of my skin. Much to my relief, it wasn't Mum catching me literally red-handed (and -mouthed and -cheeked and -shirted), it was Charles Walker.

"You can't hide here," I told him bluntly. "There's not enough room and Chris will find us in no time."

Not to mention that I didn't want him eating what was left of the raspberries. After all, I was quite fond of Mum's jam and I didn't want to put the kibosh on it altogether. I needn't have worried though, Charles didn't seem the slightest bit interested in the sweet, ripe fruit that so tempted me.

"*Shhh!*" he hissed, crawling in beside me and shaking his head in warning. "Chris is just over there!"

"Humph!" I rolled my eyes and spluttered through another handful of raspberries. "Don't care."

Charlie didn't respond and we sat together like that for quite some time, the wet Irish afternoon silence punctured only by my scoffing sounds and the occasional gleeful yelp in the distance, presumably when my brother discovered another victim lurking somewhere in the garden. When he was sure the coast was fairly clear, Charlie turned to face me. "I may as well stay in here now, Rosie," he said, his head to one side as he kept an ear out for any suspicious noises. "You picked an excellent hiding place, I must say."

"Flattery will get you nowhere," I responded, huffily, but I didn't kick him out either. So long as he wasn't poaching fruit, I didn't care what he did. Besides, of all Chris's friends, Charlie was always the nicest to me. Nicer than Chris, in fact. Grudgingly, I offered him one squashed raspberry from my haul.

"Oh lovely, thanks!" He popped it in his mouth and smacked his lips with exaggerated relish. "They're perfectly ripe, aren't they?"

A few minutes later after another long silence, he appeared to be getting restless. "Have you seen *The Matrix* yet?" he asked me, causing my eyes to pop wide open.

"No! Have you?" I demanded, excitement making my tone shrill.

"Sorry." I lowered my voice several notches as he held a finger to his lips in admonition. "I *love* Keanu Reeves. Did you know his name means 'Cool Breeze Over The Mountain' in . . . er . . . some Indian language?"

I paused to try and remember the specifics, then gave up and reiterated the most important point instead. "I. Love. Him."

Charles cocked an eyebrow at me in what I thought privately was a very grown-up way. I resolved to go practise that in front of the mirror later. "Really?" he said, in that particularly infuriating tone that can be taken to actually mean: "You can't be flipping serious?"

"What?" I demanded, instantly defensive.

"Well, I don't know," he said, thoughtfully, "I mean, how do you know you love somebody when you've never even met them?"

"Pah!" I shrugged off the question, partly because I thought he was being deliberately annoying, but partly because I didn't have an answer to that. "Well, because I'd marry him if he asked me!" I finally blurted out when Charles just kept looking at me with that ridiculous expression of superiority.

"Oh," was his less than impressed response. "Right."

After another few seconds, he looked up and grinned at me. "And there was me thinking I might ask you some day."

"What?!" I was perturbed beyond belief, all pretence of hiding forgotten as I scrambled to my feet. "Don't be so mental!" I squeaked. "You're just a . . . a . . . silly little boy!"

Charles didn't look too bothered by my outburst. He just shrugged and said in a very irritating, know-it-all-tone: "Well, it's just as well I haven't asked you yet, isn't it?"

At that moment, a cold, firm hand shot through the bushes and grabbed me by the forearm. "Gotcha!" my brother's voice rang in my ear. "What a silly place to hide. Oh, Rosie, look at your face! You've been at the raspberries again, haven't you? I'm sooo telling on you!"

CHAPTER
FOURTEEN

I didn't go over to Charles's house in the end. Instead, I sat on the wall at Honeysuckle Cottage for a few hours revisiting many happy memories from my short life, wondering some more about the purpose of my ghostly presence here and doing a little bit of therapeutic mourning of my own.

Then I got bored and decided to check out the preparations for the party being thrown in my honour this evening.

So here I am, swinging my legs on a stool in McMorrow's, watching Chris and Jenny trying to erect the Altar of Rosie to my mother's very detailed and rigid specifications: there must be eight pictures, eight roses with eight petals each, eight candles *and not one of them may be allowed to go out at any time.* Apparently eight is a very significant number in terms of life and the afterlife. Infinity, the cycles of nature, et cetera. I didn't really pay much attention to what she was guffing on about to be honest. I was more interested in the warm and gently supportive dynamic between my brother and my best friend. I suspect something might be developing there, which makes me a happy little spy.

In the meantime, I've had plenty of time to make myself comfortable in the bar and have another quick snoop around for Jack in case he's returned. No sign, the rat-fink. In fact, it looks like despite his best efforts to call in some help, the only person behind the bar is Roger Smith, which I've never seen in all my years working here. I allow myself a nasty little smirk as I anticipate his shock when the entire town descends upon him in approximately twenty minutes. That'll teach him to leave me to tend the bar alone during the World Cup.

My parents arrive with what seems like a never-ending supply of sandwiches to be carried in from the car. The lights are turned down, the fire is roaring in the corner, and for some reason Bruce Springsteen is crooning over the sound system. We're ready to greet our guests.

It's a strange scenario for all involved, not just me. A confusing blend of a festive occasion and the formality of grief. As people begin to straggle through the door, the sadness becomes palpable. While I wouldn't exactly love it if nobody was bothered at all by my untimely passing, it's still very hard to see and hear everyone quietly talking about me and feeling quite obviously uncomfortable.

I remain at a safe distance and watch proceedings, half-entertained, half-horrified by what I witness. For the most part those closest to me are in reasonably good humour, considering the circumstances: smiling, hugging, a little teary-eyed now and then, but sharing happy memories and warm support all the same. It's the others who seem to be most ill at ease; the typical funeral-crashers, the old school "friends" who I haven't seen since Leaving Cert results night, and plenty of nosy distant relatives. They stand together in little clumps, mourning my passing by tut-tutting and shaking their heads at some of the less conventional aspects of the gathering.

Granted, my mother's red shoes are the brightest thing in the room and the magnificently bedecked altar is a bit glitzy with the last-minute addition of eight peacock feathers and a gigantic sparkly gold Buddha, but I agree with my mother on this one: it's better than a grisly open casket any day.

Thankfully my family is well used to being disapproved of. If anything, it's always been a bit of a spur to behave even more eccentrically in public. Most of the mourners are enjoying the unusually upbeat atmosphere to the best of their ability, but it's clear that there's a prevailing feeling of loss and sadness too. That, and a slightly nasty undercurrent of fearful gossip. I hear whispers all around, growing louder as more and more people arrive.

"Well, they couldn't possibly display the body, could they? Shot in the head, they say."

"I'll be locking my door tonight, sure, couldn't it be a serial killer in our midst?"

"You never know what kind of stuff people are messed up in in their personal lives — could be drugs or black magic or anything at all these days!"

"These sandwiches are a bit dry for my tastes really."

And so on. Thankfully, my folks are oblivious, showering attention on everyone as they arrive and settle in, sharing around sandwiches and hugs, and generally just being wonderful human beings. The more people arrive, the more the atmosphere softens, until most of the awkwardness and discomfort have dissipated and there's simply a gentle hum of chat in the room.

It's only when I hear somebody asking after him that it dawns on me that Jack isn't even going to turn up for my wake. Why, the arrogant little slug! Wouldn't that be a sure sign of guilt? I mean, if I were trying to cast off any suspicions anyone might have about my own involvement in a suspected murder, I would certainly show up for a public display of grieving.

Or would I? Hmmm, is Jack smart enough to pull a double bluff like that?

An elaborately coiffed blonde head appears through the front door, causing my stomach to do a loop-the-loop. Is it Lydia? Is Jack with her?

But it's not Lydia.

No, I realise, with an even sharper jolt. It's actually Suzie Gallagher. Two more similarly hued heads come in behind my old classmate, pausing to the left and right of their leader in a well-practised wing formation, giving them several seconds to make the desired impact with their entrance. Three heads swivel as one in all directions, surveying all possible individuals of interest, the rest completely discounted, before the blonde trio moves off towards the bar.

It's been a long time since I saw that display. "Suzie and the Floozies", as Jenny and I had not so affectionately termed them back in high school. Back in high school, when they had smiled to our faces as behind our backs they venomously spread a rumour that lasted the duration of our school life, which even some of the teachers were said to believe. They haven't changed a bit. In fact, I'm pretty sure I remember that silver mini-skirt Siobhan is wearing from the nineties.

What the hell are they doing here? These girls *hated* me. They masked it well at first, but when Jen and I confronted them about the slanderous shite they were talking, their true feelings had come out. Precisely, I believe the words used were "freaky skank-midget" and "fat ginger bitch". Jenny and I left them to it after that, but the very fact that we ignored them seemed to enrage them further. They waged their own little war on us. Primary attack appeared to be the active and enthusuiastic pursuit of any boy we might take the slightest interest in. Sometimes we'd pretend to fancy some really horrendous ones just to see if they'd act on the false information. And they usually did, much to our amusement. Mean girls? Yes. Clever girls? No. They used every trick in the book: scrawling derogatory graffiti in all the loos in the school, making bitchy comments at every opportunity, sometimes even deliberately banging against us with sharp little elbows, or sloshing a drink "accidentally" onto a white shirt here and there. Just being your average evil teenage wenches.

124

Which leads me back to the question, what in God's name are they doing here? Are they actually using my funeral as a social event? It appears so. Suzie barks at Roger with her distinctive nasal twang, "Three Bombay Sapphire and Slim, two cubes of ice, lime twist."

I can't help wondering if she might be a bit nicer to him if she realised that far from being a sweaty old barkeeper, he's actually one of the wealthiest men in the area. But Roger doesn't seem to care that she treats him like a lackey. He fumbles to get her drinks while one eye keeps darting back and forth to the door with every new pair of feet that walks through. He's really sweating at this stage, the poor bastard. I almost feel sorry I can't jump in and help him out.

I glance over my shoulder to see who Roger has just nodded at absently as he tries to slice a lime into the delicate slivers Suzie is demanding, and a lump instantly forms in my throat as I see Jenny sitting at the bar, flanked by her parents, looking drawn and exhausted as she waits to order. Oh how I wish I could comfort her, make her laugh, tell her that it's really not that bad to be dead as a dodo and that she oughtn't worry. I can absolutely imagine how she must be feeling though. I would be just as bereft if the roles were reversed.

I watch closely as her gaze is drawn to the three blondes further down the bar. For a split second I catch a glimpse of the fire I so love in Jenny's eyes as her mouth tightens into a grim line and her brows arch furiously. But just as quickly the wind seems to go out of her sails. She drops her gaze and looks away, ordering two pints and a glass of red, and ignoring our high-school tormentors.

They don't ignore her though. I see Suzie spot Jen, dark little eyes lighting up with malicious glee. I could swear I almost see a pair of horns sprouting from her shiny forehead and a flicking forked tongue lick her lips. She-devil!

"Oh my *goodness!*" she squeals, drawing her two sycophantic clones' attention to Jenny, and attracting the notice of pretty much everyone else in the pub too while she's at it. "Jenny McLaughlin, you poor thing!" she says, her excitement making her breathless as her hypocritical words pierce the quiet atmosphere of the bar. "You girls remember Jenny, don't you?" She turns to Sorcha, then Siobhan, lowering her voice to a stage whisper as she needlessly reminds them, "She was Rosie's *very best* friend, you know."

My jaw drops as I watch the three of them turn malevolent eyes on Jenny. I cannot believe this vile creature is still singing from the same hymn sheet. I can see from Jenny's expression that she's well aware what's coming next. From the slight twitch in her left eyebrow, I can also see that she's getting very, very cross. Oh, yes. Very cross indeed. This could get quite heated actually. I take an instinctive step backwards, but the three Floozies aren't as wise to the signs. More fools they.

"My goodness," Suzie repeats with glaringly false sincerity, "how awfully tragic for you to lose such a *special* friend so young. You must be heartbroken, you poor dear. Especially since there aren't all that many of your sort around these parts either."

There it is. At my own wake, in front of my family, my friends, my boss and who knows who else, Suzie Gallagher is once again trying to out me and Jenny as lesbians. It would be funny if it weren't so unbelievably nasty. What a piece of work. I have a good mind to . . .

Oh, hang on, here we go. Jenny has flushed a deep shade of pink. Not from embarrassment, though from the satisfied glint in Suzie's eyes, I can see that she certainly assumes it is. I know the real cause though. The real cause is adrenaline. Any second now, my little lesbian lover is going to explode.

Through gritted teeth, Jenny speaks clearly and evenly in a sing-song tone that makes the hairs on the back of my neck stand up. "Oh, I wouldn't be so sure about that, Sue," she says, standing up and smoothing down her pencil skirt. She takes two swift steps forward and hooks the startled blonde's thick gold necklace around two fingers before she has a chance to react. I'm bracing myself for a headbutt, but instead Jenny pulls sharply, bringing the pouty over-glossed lips of our long-time enemy to her own in a very hard, very sloppy kiss. She reaches around Suzie's back and grabs a handful of ass, which she clearly squeezes very, very hard, judging from the muffled squeal that issues out from the midst of the girl-on-girl action.

I'm as shocked as everyone else, but it seems our wits catch up with us all at once as the entire bar erupts in laughter and catcalls. Jenny finally releases her squirming victim and exaggeratedly smacks her lips together. "Mmm, you know, I always knew you wanted me for yourself, Suzie. Why else would you have been such a fucking *bitch* to Rosie?"

With that, she turns on her heel and stalks off, head held high, to enthusiastic applause from almost everyone in the place. It's a spectacular moment, made all the better by the fact that as soon as Suzie begins spluttering abuse and making as if to follow Jenny, my darling brother steps in front of her and says politely, "I think you and your pals should leave now, Miss Gallagher. This is a private party, you see. Friends and family only."

Several hours later and the details of the show-down are still being told and retold to those who missed it. People are hugging Jenny and congratulating her on her performance, making giddy reference to concepts such as "love thine enemy" and "turn the other cheek". My own mother (after quietly enquiring if we were indeed an item — bless her, she would have loved that) tells Jen that I would have been ever so proud of her. That brings tears to both our eyes. I *am* ever so proud of her, the gorgeous little creature. I just wish she wasn't in so much pain.

It's pretty frustrating watching everyone hugging and drinking and sharing stories about me, most of which are vastly embellished or just plain made up at this point, what with all the drinking. And there's still no sign of Jack, which, infuriatingly, nobody seems to care about. It's really grating on me that no-one finds it the slightest bit strange that my boyfriend isn't here. I'm getting more and more edgy as the pub fills to bursting point with people, none of whom pay me the slightest bit of attention. It's getting difficult to avoid being walked through and I seriously don't want to experience that right now. Or ever, for that matter. The very thought of what passing through a human body might taste like is enough to make me want to retch. I'm frantically dodging a herd of American tourists who seem to have got caught up in the festivities of my wake when I spot Lydia ducking through the back entrance of the bar. Her hair is messy and her cheeks are flushed. Dammit she's smiling, glowing like she's just been having a great ride. I hope Roger notices and denounces her as the adulterous slut she is.

Instead, he's pathetically grateful to see her and obviously doesn't have the time or the inclination to ask her any questions. He gives her a swift kiss on the cheek (can't he smell Jack's Dolce and Gabbana on her, the cuckolded fool?) and presses a tea towel and a bottle opener into her hands as braying customers press forward for service.

"Bloody idiot!" I roar, losing control once and for all. "She's been off shagging my boyfriend while you've been breaking your back down here! You hear me? They've been at it like rabbits for God only knows how long, you silly old plonker! LISTEN TO ME!"

But he certainly isn't listening. Nobody is.

"*Aiii!*" I kick out in a moment of blind rage, sending a bar stool flying across the crowded room. Miraculously, it doesn't hit anybody in its path, but it does shatter against the wall with astonishing force.

Another shocked silence descends on the bar as the patrons momentarily freeze in place. It's certainly been an eventful night so far. Then everyone starts moving again at normal speed.

"Jaysus, love, are you all right?"

"Mary, what on earth happened there?"

"Have you had a few too many, pet?"

For a couple of bizarre seconds I dumbly gaze around at all the concerned faces, thinking they're talking to me. But then I follow their eye-line to the floor and discover that they're addressing my Great Aunt Mary, who appears to have been sitting on that stool when it bore the brunt of my frustration. Oops.

Bloody great, now I'm beating up old people. This day just keeps getting better and better. I look up in exasperation and there's Charles, dead ahead, staring at me with that particular expression of disapproval he seems to save for me and me alone. I stop dead and stare back, like the proverbial bunny-about-to-be-roadkill, afraid to move in case I discover that he's a mirage.

How come he keeps looking at me like this?

Tentatively, I lift an arm and wave a tiny little wave in his direction. He doesn't respond, but his gaze doesn't falter either. Although, now that I really look . . .

Deflating already, I turn and look over my shoulder. Sure enough, directly behind me there seems to be some kind of scuffle going on between Lydia and Roger behind the bar. Probably arguing about the best course of action to take to avoid being sued by poor old Auntie Mary over inexplicably exploding bar furniture. I look

130

back at Charles and it appears his attention has returned to my brother beside him. Somehow I don't think he'd be standing there so casually if he really had just spotted the ghost of his best mate's recently departed little sister. Nevertheless, I make my way over to where they're standing. I guess I still have the urge to eavesdrop on them whenever the opportunity presents itself.

It felt nice to be seen, even if it was a mistake on my part. For that one short moment, I felt a surge of hope. Now I just feel lonely again. So I distract myself by harassing Charlie a bit.

"*Oi! Big fella!*" I bellow in his ear. "What you lookin' at?"

I walk around and around his large, solid frame, bouncing up and down before him and making a series of strange faces and animal noises. Hell, I have to entertain myself somehow, and at least this feels like human interaction. Besides, I've always enjoyed tormenting Charlie. It's like bear baiting, except with a large, stuffed teddy bear who just shoots you the odd disdainful look in retaliation.

I'm starting to get bored when he moves off, letting my mind wander to who I'd most like to be able to communicate with from beyond the grave if it really were an option, so I absent-mindedly follow him through a nearby door. It certainly wouldn't be Charles anyway. When I was alive, I would have voted for Jack, of course, but now I know better than that too. I guess it would have to be Jenny or my mum. Ah sure, why not both? It's never going to happen anyway.

"Whoa!" I leap out of the way just in time as a rather pissed young fella reels by me, doing up his fly. That was a close one — I nearly tasted teen. Then again, I'm pretty sure he would have had an overwhelming flavour of beer if we had collided, which wouldn't be the worst. Blinking stupidly, I suddenly snap out of my twisted train of thought and realise where I am.

Ah, the Gents. Last time I was in one of these forbidden areas was in a nightclub in Bundoran when I was absolutely bursting for a wee and the queue for the Ladies was just too ridiculously long to consider. That one was full of men and I lasted only a couple of seconds before I was escorted off the premises by a couple of burly bouncers. I didn't even get to do my wee, in spite of my loud protestations.

In this men's room, however, there are no bouncers to be seen. Only Charles, standing at a urinal with his hands hanging limply by his sides. I'm absolutely not perving or anything of the sort, but I can't help noticing that he's just standing there like a lemon; he hasn't unzipped or anything, which strikes me as somewhat odd.

And then he speaks. "I know it must be quite tempting to catch me with my pants down, so to speak, but honestly, Rosie, you're causing me some considerable stage-fright." With that, he turns and looks me straight in the eye.

"*Yeearghh!*" I spin wildly on my heel, losing my balance entirely and landing in a heap in one of the open cubicles. My head, it takes me a few seconds to realise, has come to rest smack bang in the centre of the toilet bowl.

Thank God the last person flushed. The thought comes unbidden to my mind while I'm struggling to regain my composure. As I sit up, dazed and confused, another unwelcome thought flashes through my mind.

So here I am in the loo with Charles Walker, my head stuck in the toilet bowl.

Again.

CHAPTER
FIFTEEN

It vaguely occurs to me, as I hurriedly remove myself from the undignified heap I've landed in, that the toilet bowl doesn't taste half as bad as wall. In fact, it's somewhat reminiscent of the over-chlorinated taste of the water in swimming pools, and so long as I don't think about exactly what passes through it . . .

What? Come on, Rosie, pull yourself together, woman!

I pull myself together, staggering to my feet and staring at Charles through disbelieving eyes. Did he really just talk to me?

"Did you really just talk to me?" I ask.

"Yes," he replies simply, in a tone that suggests speaking to dead people is something he's entirely comfortable with. In fact, that it might even bore him slightly.

I'm a little speechless, but I needn't worry as he then says somewhat impatiently, "Really, Rosie. I could do with some privacy."

"But . . . But . . ." I can't help it, I'm so excited and happy to be talking to him that my eyes fill up with tears. "But, Charlie, it's so good to see you! Even better that you see me!" I'm grinning like a loon, bubbling over with questions for him: "Is it weird? Am I sort of see-through or anything, or do I just look normal? Have you ever seen a ghost before? Are you *a psychic?* How come —"

Deadpan Charlie cuts me off mid-flow. "Look, Rosie, I really am desperate for a whizz. You can stay here and watch if you must, but I'd rather have this chat under different circumstances."

"What?" I splutter, getting annoyed now. "But this is unbelievable! You can see me — WE ARE ACTUALLY COMMUNICATING — and all you can think about is taking a piss? I'm dead! You're obviously going to be my living sidekick, we're going to team up and solve the mystery of my brutal murder, and —"

I abruptly stop jabbering as Maggie's husband Arthur staggers in, obviously a little worse for wear. He squints sideways at Charles, who's standing at the urinal with his arms crossed, glaring into what appears to be an empty cubicle. The newcomer is fumbling about inside his trousers before I finally twig what I'm about to witness.

"Oh, God. No!" I blurt, squeezing my eyes shut and making a blind dash for the door, a wall, anything that will separate me from this disturbing scene. "I'll wait out here!" I manage to squeak to Charles, as I feel the cool brick of the dividing wall melting away around me.

The bar has filled up even more since my little trip into the Gents. At this point, several drinks have been imbibed by the mourners and the atmosphere is, predictably, taking a more boisterous turn. In fact, there seems to be a large, motley crew of complete

135

strangers milling around all of a sudden. I find myself face to face with a very strange-looking creature indeed. She's almost as tall as me, with a fluorescent pink tee shirt which appears to be several sizes too small for her and short, spiky, fire-engine-red hair. Her make-up is quite startling too. Up this close, I can almost see the brush strokes and count her spidery stuck-on lashes. Certainly not a local, that's for sure. So caught up am I in my examination of this bizarre-looking woman, I almost miss Charles as he brushes past me, muttering out the corner of his mouth like some kind of James Bond wannabe, "Meet me outside in five."

Pink-top's eyes light up. "Cor, yeah I will 'andsome!" she says, in the gruffest cockney accent I've ever heard. Charles's expression makes me choke with laughter. His jaw drops and uselessly flaps a few times as he tries to figure out the nearest escape route.

"Get your coat, love, you've pulled!" I roar at him, laughing even harder when his eyes flick to me, wide with barely disguised panic.

"I, um . . ." he splutters, as Pink-top grins up at him through lipstick-stained teeth.

"I was actually, ah, talking to myself," he finally stutters, pathetically. "Terribly sorry for any confusion!"

With that he dashes off into the safety of the crowd, leaving Pink-top shaking her head in disappointment. "Now, that is a shame," she informs her companions, with the look of a lioness who has let a particularly juicy springbok through her claws, "I coulda shown him a fing or two 'e ain't learned in Cafflic school!"

136

I join in the raucous laughter this elicits before setting off through the throng towards the front door. That little exchange has certainly put me in better spirits than I've been in since I died. A spirit in high spirits! My good humour is short-lived though, as it's such a struggle to make my way through all these bodies. I still refuse to just start walking through them, but when you're invisible you can't exactly start shoving people without causing an almighty row, so it's pretty hard to get anywhere at all. I find myself gingerly wading through tables and hopping point-lessly into any free space that appears, which is frankly getting me nowhere.

Just as I'm getting really fed up and considering a vicious poke to the ribs of a skinny brunette who just wont get the HELL out of my way, a piercing whistle silences the bar. "Right, you lot!" a heavy Dublin accent bellows. "It's time for us to move out. Back on the wagon with the lot of yiz!"

Suddenly it all becomes clear. All these extra people are from a PartyBus tour. The big green, white and gold coaches full of drunk (and often rather confused) international tourists rarely stop here, but when they do, it's always an interesting night to be working. Jack and I used to keep each other entertained for hours with tales of the goings-on on various PartyBus nights.

Pink-top is among those who form a disorderly queue to exit, which I conveniently tag along with. In no time at all, I'm breathing in the fresh night air, watching the big, bass-booming bus roll off to its next destination. There's no sign of my date, so I hop up

137

onto the wall and entertain myself flicking small pebbles at Lydia's precious car.

I look up with a start as a body swings out of the front door on a burst of music and chatter. It's not Charles but Jenny. She still looks pale and miserable; clearly she's had enough. She's never been the type to drown her sorrows, preferring instead to retreat into her own space and recover quietly in her own time from any set-backs she has encountered in her life. I can only imagine how hard it's been for her to stay in the crowded pub this long. She casts a wary glance over her shoulder; clearly making a quiet escape to ensure nobody tries to "take care of her", which is textbook Jenny behaviour. I watch her sadly as she trudges off into the darkness in the direction of the cottage, and resolve to follow her as soon as I'm finished with Charles.

Where is he anyway? I would have thought talking to me might be a little more important than propping up the bar in McMorrow's. Then again, he seems to be taking this all a little too much in his stride; perhaps he's convinced himself that he's imagining things and he's not even going to come out to meet me at all.

My thoughts continue to go round and round in this dizzying manner so that when Charles finally does step outside, I do the only logical thing and yell at him. "*What were you doing in there?* Why did you make me wait so long? Are you not in the least bit shocked that you can see me? I swear, I was about to have a heart attack out here!"

138

Charles looks a little bit cross at first to be greeted in such a manner, but then a small smile plays across his lips and he points out, "I should think that shouldn't really be a worry under present circumstances, Rosie."

"Humph!"

"Besides, I've had some time to get used to you lurking around, during which I have come to terms with the fact that either I've lost my mind or you're haunting me. Neither of these options particularly suits me, but one has to work with what one's given, eh?"

Charles is leaning on the wall now, looking up at me with his direct, wolfish gaze, and still being infuriatingly calm about this whole thing.

"I'm certainly not haunting *you* in particular. In fact —" I break off as something suddenly strikes me. "WHAT?" I yell, finally causing him to jump a little. "What do you mean *some time?* Are you telling me that you've been able to see me all along?"

He nods, barely moving his big old head, but nevertheless acknowledging the fact. My tone becomes even more shrill as this information sinks in. "You could see me last night, couldn't you? Even when you came up to get Benny — *I knew it!* And you didn't think at any stage that I might like to know this? You just ignored me, blithering away and flapping round like some kind of mental case? How could you? Don't you realise how desperate I've been to talk to somebody, *anybody?* And now I'm stuck with you, someone who just doesn't give a toss . . ."

"*Rosie!*" Charles barks sharply, causing me to bite my tongue mid-rant. "Can you please shut up a minute? I realise that you've probably had a pretty difficult time of late, and that you may be somewhat distressed, but honestly, you're being a squawking nightmare. Settle down."

I inhale, feeling my face contort into pure-rage mode, but he holds up a finger and says in a much more patient tone, "Just let me explain?"

Sulkily, I do as he asks, although I do fold my arms petulantly in a minor show of defiance.

Charles ignores my pre-school behaviour. "Yes, I saw you in your room last night. You gave me the fright of my life. I thought I was losing my mind. Then you came into the sitting room and plonked yourself right in front of me and I had to pull myself together and deal with the situation as best I could. I kept waiting for you to disappear, or for myself to wake up, but neither of us was obliging. Admittedly, I thought it might be the booze, or perhaps the mind-altering state of shock and grief. Also I noticed that Chris quite obviously wasn't aware of your presence and, thankfully, despite being in a state of shock, I resisted blurting out to him that his dead sister was hogging the fire in her ugliest pyjamas." He pauses and looks at me unblinkingly until I give him a begrudging nod of acceptance. As if as a reward for my compliance, he smiles a little and adds, "Looking cute as a button, as always."

I roll my eyes and snort derisively, but of course, I relish the compliment. He knows how to charm the girls, this one.

140

"I also went ahead and made the judgement call — and by all means correct me if you think I was wrong here — that it may not have been appropriate to strike up a conversation with you at any point during your wake in a bar full of your nearest and dearest, despite your quite exceptional harassment techniques. Believe me, I was very close to speaking to you at that point, but once again, your brother's presence was somewhat of a deterrent. Besides, as was becoming increasingly obvious, nobody else could see you, so if I had expressed precisely what I wanted to tell you to do, there would surely have been some kind of misunderstanding among the surrounding punters." He shudders perceptibly and I'm pretty sure he's thinking of old Pink-top at this point. I can't help smirking a little. Charles grins suddenly, his eyes twinkling with mirth, "Oh yes, you liked that, didn't you, you little minx!" he says, as we both start to laugh.

"She was hot!" I splutter, through my giggles.

"I'm not even sure she was a she!" he retorts.

I put on a shoddy attempt at a cockney accent, "Cor, yeah, 'andsome!"

We laugh even harder when the same teenage lad I nearly ran through in the Gents comes outside for a smoke and then thinks better of it when he spots Charles hanging onto the wall and guffawing away to himself. He does a hasty about-turn and retreats back into the safety of the bar. Most likely he's gone back in to tell everyone who'll listen that Charles Walker has completely lost it.

Our giggles die down and splutter out eventually, leaving me feeling much more relaxed than I have in ages, a feeling of companionship and relief flooding through me. Oh well, maybe it's not such a disaster that Charles is the only one who can see me. At least someone can. I smile at him fondly, but he's looking at me with a funny expression on his face.

"How did it happen, Rosie?" he asks softly, all humour gone from his tone, his eyes flicking from mine to the sticky patch at the side of my head that I've been trying to forget about.

"Oh, my wanker of a boyfriend killed me so he could run off with another woman." I try to be flippant about it, but even as I say the words, my eyes well up again with hot tears.

Charles doesn't say anything, but his eyes narrow and his big hands curl into some rather dangerous-looking fists. A good minute passes, during which he seems to be regulating his breathing with effort. Eventually he hisses between clenched teeth, like the air escaping from a punctured tyre, "*What?*"

"Err . . ." I hesitate to repeat my melodramatic statement. Charles looks as if he might blow his lid at any moment. "Well, you see . . ." I stammer under the ferocity of his gaze. "I mean, I don't have any proof or anything."

"What proof do you need, Rosie?" he barks. "You were *there* weren't you?"

"Well, yes, um . . ." I'm not quite sure what the answer to this is. "Well, no. Not really, no."

Charles's white-hot-rage look has downgraded to a just-plain-irritated look now, thankfully. "Rosie?"

"Well, I just can't quite remember what happened the night I died. It's not that it's blurry or muddled up, it's literally just a big black hole."

I get a little defensive when I see his expression change to a more familiar one. His "Oh, Rosie Potter, you little fool" face.

"Look, I've just got a hunch, okay? I know for a fact that he's been cheating on me with Lydia Smith. God only knows how long that's been going on. And Jenny's sure he did it too. I don't know, I just kind of *know*, you know?"

"No," Charles says abruptly. "You have a hunch. We can look into it, but Jack remains innocent until proven guilty, do you understand?"

"Since when were you a flipping lawyer?" I mutter sulkily in response.

I'm simultaneously relieved and disappointed that the murderous look has gone from Charles's eyes. I definitely want him on my side, that's for sure. He's like a great big hulk of a thing when he's all steamed up like that. Big, strong, manly . . .

"Rosie, I think I've had enough excitement for one day," he startles me out of my funny turn. Looking at him again, I can see that he is indeed showing signs of exhaustion.

"I'll just take you home now, and we can talk more about this tomorrow, all right?"

I feel a sudden stab of panic.

"You will help me, won't you?" My voice comes out sounding shrill and needy even to my own ears, but I can't help myself. He's the only one who can see me; he *has* to help me.

"Of course, Rosie," Charles says wearily, as he yanks open the passenger door of his clunky old Land Rover for me. "I just don't know if you're barking up the right tree at the moment."

I clamber into the weathered old vehicle, explaining as I do so that I could probably outrun him if I chose to, seeing as I have some pretty nifty superpowers now, but eventually I realise he's not listening. He's off in his own little world, and I have no idea what's going on behind his dark eyes as we trundle off down the narrow, dark road towards the cottage. The rest of the short journey passes in silence, until we reach the gate and stop, the engine idling noisily. The house looks like it's been gift-wrapped in yellow tape. But the lights are on in the kitchen, which means Jen has completely disregarded the Crime Scene warnings and stickers everywhere. Good on her.

"Are you sure you're okay to stay here alone tonight?" Charles asks, still staring with the same vacant expression out the windscreen

"I won't be alone," I reply. "Jenny's in there."

"Okay."

"Well, goodnight then," I say feebly, reaching for the door handle. Before I can stop myself, I blurt out, "I will see you tomorrow, won't I?"

Finally Charles looks at me, his eyes full of some emotion I can't quite place.

144

"Yes, Rosie. Of course. I'm sorry, it's been a long, hard day. I have to get my thoughts together and get some rest. But I will help you, I promise you that."

"Okay."

I can hear him laboriously trying to turn his great big machine in the tiny space offered by our driveway as I step through the sitting-room window. The moment I'm inside, I can feel that there's something very wrong. Every hair on the back of my neck is standing to attention and I have a wild churning sensation in my gut. Like adrenaline, but amped up a thousand times. Then I hear a very familiar voice.

I dash into the kitchen, where a horrible scene awaits me. Jenny is pinioned against the kitchen counter, her back bent at a painful-looking angle as she tries to pull away from the man whose face is only inches from her own.

"What the fuck are you doing setting the Gardaí on me, you crazy bitch?" Jack is practically spitting in fury.

I don't stop to think. Instead, I leap out through the front wall and race after the retreating vehicle.

"*Charles!*" I scream, "*Charles, come back!*"

CHAPTER
SIXTEEN

With a screeching of brakes, Charles reverses at speed back down the lane. He's out of the car and halfway up the path before I've even managed to grunt out "Help Jenny!" like some kind of monosyllabic cave-woman. He barrels through the front door, slamming into it with his shoulder to force it open (he didn't actually need to do that, he could have just turned the handle like a normal person, but I guess he's caught up in the moment).

I dive back into the kitchen just in time to see him burst in and grab a surprised-looking Jack by the scruff of the neck, hauling him across the room like a rag doll. Next to Charlie, Jack looks like a scrawny teenager; all over-styled hair and skinny jeans. Suddenly I wonder why I ever thought he was gorgeous. I guess that's always been my type — pretty, image-conscious, boy-band-a-likes. He goes for regular sun-bed sessions, for goodness' sake! Not to mention that he's a nasty, adulterous bully.

"Kick his ass!" I can't help myself blurting, like an over-excited cheerleader. Fortunately, Charles seems too wrapped up in the task at hand to take any notice of me. He slams Jack up against the fridge door, twisting one arm behind his back in a move I've seen him and Chris practise more times than I can count.

"What *exactly* do you think you're doing, mate?" Charles's tone is even, almost friendly, but in a marvellously scary way. Jack makes a series of gurgling noises, his nose squashed against a photo of me and Jen that's Blu-Tacked to the fridge, his eyes wide with shock.

"What?" Charles is speaking through clenched teeth now.

It looks like his patience is wearing a little thin, so I helpfully point out, "Um, I think Jack may be having a little difficulty speaking, what with you trying to push his face through the fridge door."

Charles turns his gaze on me, surprise slackening his jaw somewhat. "*This* is Jack?"

Jenny, bless her, thinks he's talking to her, and utters a hoarse "Yes" from where she sits on the floor, rubbing her bruised-looking wrists. She's looking up at the scene unfolding before her with a disturbingly blank face, skin pale and clammy, eyes red-rimmed from crying. The poor thing is in shock, I reckon. Now if I remember correctly . . .

I tweak open the cupboard to the left of where Jenny is sitting, and yes! There it is. Jenny gazes in confusion at the cupboard door for a moment, clearly trying to convince herself that she didn't just see it open all on its own. And then she spots the glint of gold. My secret stash of brandy for emergencies such as this (and, as is more often the case in our house, emergencies such as running out of booze at a party).

"Good girl!" I encourage, as she grabs it and takes a hefty swig straight from the bottle. "That'll calm your nerves."

I return my attention to Charles, who now has his face very close to Jack's and is whispering quite intently in his ear. Jack looks a little green around the gills, nodding every now and again in the small amount of space Charles has given his head to move.

"Righty ho then," Charles says at normal volume, releasing Jack and stepping away swiftly, like a wrangler releasing a snake back into the wild, "You'd better get a bloody move on before I change my mind."

Jack needs no second bidding; he scuttles out the door like a rat escaping a sinking ship.

"*Oi!*" I bellow, "What are you doing? You're letting him get away!"

Charles fixes me with one of his very grown-up looks. "He's not our priority at the moment," he says, breaking my gaze to look down at Jen with an expression of such tender concern I feel a momentary stab of jealousy. I'm bloody well dead, and he doesn't look at me like that! But then I look at my friend, mascara smudged all over her face, regarding Charles quizzically through puffy eyes, and all I can feel is a surge of love for her. The poor thing, she's having a hell of a time of it.

"Who are you talking to, Charles?" she asks, her voice shaking a little.

"Oh, don't worry, it's just a bad habit of mine, talking to myself."

148

Humph. I can't help noticing that he uses a much softer tone with Jenny than he does with "himself".

"Now then, let's get you up off the cold floor." Charles crouches down and sweeps Jenny into his arms, transferring her as delicately as if she were a piece of fragile bone china onto one of the kitchen chairs. I'm sure somewhere deep down she must be enjoying this despite all the trauma. She's always raved about how Charlie is a "Real Man" and found it hard to believe that I don't fancy him at all.

Charles flicks the kettle on and turns back to Jenny, who's gazing up at him blurrily. He gently prises the bottle of brandy out of her white-knuckled grip, crooning softly as if talking to a baby, "Give me that here now, Jenny, and I'll make you a nice cup of tea."

"*Hey!*" shouts Jen, when he finally liberates the bottle from her grasp.

"*Hey!*" I shout simultaneously at the meddlesome bugger.

Charles just shakes his head as he busies himself making a pot of tea.

"Two peas in a pod, you two. Medicinal brandy is all very well and good, but just a drop. Anything more than that and you risk getting yourself into an even worse state, trust me."

Jenny grunts her reluctant agreement and accepts the steaming cup of tea without putting up a fight. If it were me, I'd be screaming blue murder by now, along the lines of him being a condescending, know-it-all teetotaller. Instead, Jenny bursts into loud, shuddering tears, tea slopping messily all over her hands and onto her jeans.

"Oh dear." Charles removes the teacup in a hurry and then stands there looking bewildered while Jenny continues to wail. Yes, that's a "Real Man" for you.

"Kitchen roll," I suggest, blithely. Charles shoots me a grateful look, grabs a couple of sheets from the counter-top and starts uselessly patting at Jenny's thighs.

"No, no!" I rebuke him, crossly. "Give her the whole roll and stop pawing at her like that!"

"Right, right!" he mutters, obediently doing just that.

"And a hug," I add, glowering at him when he looks at me reluctantly.

"It's not that bloody hard to hug a crying woman, trust me! She's not going to explode or anything!"

Hesitating for just a moment before pulling up a chair, Charles awkwardly wraps one large, heavy arm around Jen's shoulders. She immediately collapses into him, making a cosy, comforting space for herself in the nook of his shoulder. Very soon, her sobs become less hysterical and her breathing starts to return to normal. Eventually, she speaks. Just a few disjointed words at first.

"Bastard."

Yes, quite.

"Poor Rosie."

Indeed.

"I should have told her."

Abso — Huh? Told me what?

"Told me what?" I demand, earning myself another disapproving look from Charles (*quelle surprise*).

He rubs Jenny's shoulder with one of his shovel-like hands, "Go ahead, let it all out."

Jenny sits bolt upright and fixes Charles with a steady, dark-eyed gaze. "No, you don't understand," she says, her voice stronger now, a glimpse of the tough Jenny I know and love showing through. "I let her go out with him. I let her put herself at that vile scumbag's mercy, because I was too ashamed to tell her the truth. And now he's gone and killed her and it's all my fault!"

"Told you so." I can't help myself. Charles looks up at me with a stunned expression on his face.

"But how can you really know for sure that he killed Rosie?" he asks, reaching for the brandy and pouring himself a stiff measure.

"Oh, trust me. I know Jack well," she says, her voice sharp with bitterness. "In fact, it's about time I told someone the truth about Jack bloody Harper."

And so, she does.

CHAPTER
SEVENTEEN

"I knew Jack when I lived in Dublin. Rosie knew that much. I was working in the Laramie Hotel as a receptionist and living with Tom in Rathmines. I was happy. Jack was involved in the organisation of a big music festival that was coming up in a few months, which was basing a lot of its events at our hotel.

"I didn't pay much heed to him at first, he was a bit show-offy and OTT flirtatious, but I didn't mind at all because I'd grown so used to ignoring that kind of carry on I barely noticed it anymore. But then he started really paying me attention. Lots of attention. He'd bring in my favourite coffee every morning, he tried to make me laugh all the time, he always told me how well I was looking and that kind of thing. I'm pretty sure it was the exact same kind of stuff he used on Rosie. I can't say I hated it; he's a charmer when he wants to be. But I did tell him in no uncertain terms that I was engaged to a wonderful man who I was bonkers about and that I would never even consider cheating, so his efforts were wasted on me.

"He used to fix me with this look that was half-injured, half-knowing, and clasp a hand to his heart, asking me 'How could you think that of me? I'm just buying my friend a coffee!' I actually started to think it was funny. He'd do it all the time, 'I'm just bringing my friend some flowers!', 'I'm just asking my friend out for dinner!'. So it became like our own little private joke. Looking back now, I suppose, that in itself was the first sign of danger.

"He insisted that we call each other 'J' and started hanging round the front desk all the time. I couldn't complain, he was becoming quite the bright spark in my days. In fact, with all the attention he was giving me, and all the glamorous stories he had of his own life, not to mention the ones he would playfully make up about what our life together would be like if only I would give him a chance, my own life with Tom started to look a little bit dull. Coming home in the evening was like entering an old black-and-white movie set, where the action is slowed down and there's just no colour at all. I started to wonder if this was what I really wanted after all.

"In other words, I started to fall for Jack's shite.

"The minute he saw me starting to question whether I was happy with Tom, Jack started to up his game. He would talk to me at length about my feelings, about what he felt I deserved from a relationship, telling me 'as a friend' that I should never, ever settle for anything less than fireworks and butterflies. I saw it as his genuine care for me. His desire to be with me was very flattering, but his kindness and willingness to just talk for hours about my doubts and dreams and feelings was what started to turn the tide for me. I thought it was amazing that he was trying so hard to be there for me, to help me analyse and potentially escape my not-so-satisfying relationship with another man so that he could make me happy himself. I was, of course, at this stage completely oblivious to the fact that my dissatisfaction had pretty much been created solely by him and his insidious, manipulative crap. All I knew was that he wanted to whisk me away and live together blissfully in a little cottage here in Ballycarragh with chickens and lots and lots of babies. He wanted what I wanted! My dreams of settling down in the country sounded like heaven to him! Tom, on the other hand, was being a bit cagey about moving back to Ballycarragh in the near future. He insisted that the work was in the city, and that if we were going to have all those kids I was hoping for, he was going to have to get together enough funds to buy a bloody big cottage before we started.

"He was right, of course, but Jack's impulsive desire to do everything and anything I wanted was intoxicating. So things started to spiral out of my control. We were basically acting like a couple in every way except physically. We'd sneak off for long lunches, where we'd get drunk and flirt outrageously until the restaurant was empty and the staff were hinting around setting up for the next shift. We'd stay after work and whisper together in a quiet corner of the bar, not caring what my co-workers thought. I'd sneak out for walks at the weekend and he'd meet me round the corner with a takeaway coffee and a smitten smile.

"And all the while, Tom just pottered along, never noticing that I was becoming increasingly distant and distracted from our own relationship. That made it even worse. We were already behaving like an old married couple, bored of each other's company, just going through the motions. To be honest, I know now that it only seemed that way because Jack made things seem so new and exciting. I fell into the biggest cliché trap of them all. In truth, what Tom and I had was a relaxed familiarity with each other, complete trust and friendship, and a solid base for something long term and real. Which I was flagrantly disregarding. But making excuses that the relationship had gone stale helped me to ignore that part, especially with Jack encouraging me and steering me that way all the while too.

"So the day inevitably came where I finally decided that I would cut my losses and give it a go with Jack. I told him one evening that I was planning to break up with Tom when I got home. He smiled this funny little smile; his eyes lit up with what I thought was delight, but now, picturing that expression, it could only be described as victory. I was finishing my shift on the front desk, and he held out his hand to me and led me all the way up to the penthouse suite. I was a little uncertain — I had wanted to go home to Tom first and get the hard part out of the way before I let things move any further with Jack. But he opened the door and revealed a room full of roses, with a bottle of expensive champagne chilling in an ice bucket, and two crystal glasses ready to be filled. My heart melted. What harm would it do to stay a little while and celebrate with this wonderful man who only wanted to spoil me? After all, I had already made up my mind to leave Tom.

"It never occurred to me to ask Jack just how he knew I'd make up my mind that day. How he had the room ready to go before I even told him my news. It's ridiculous really that I was so naive. There must have been some poor girl sitting in a bar somewhere, waiting for her charming date to arrive and sweep her off her feet that evening. Instead, I was getting his full attention.

"He had barely kicked the door closed before he was kissing me. I didn't complain, he was a good kisser and this was something I'd been looking forward to doing for quite some time now. But right from the start I was worried about how I was going to stop this going too far. I had a sense that something wasn't quite right, but like most women, I didn't want to cause a scene or hurt his feelings, or seem like I was overreacting.

"That said, I definitely didn't want to do anything more than kiss Jack. I couldn't justify that level of betrayal of poor Tom, I still loved and respected him as a person and wanted to do the right thing. I needed him to know where we stood before I let anything else happen. So I broke off the kiss, a little reluctantly, I must admit, and jokingly suggested we make a toast to being able to be together tomorrow, hoping that Jack would hear the subtle emphasis on the word 'tomorrow' and get the message.

"He didn't. Instead, he lifted me off my feet and tossed me onto the bed, making me squeal and giggle. But when he pinned me down and started kissing me

156

again, harder this time, I started to feel a little bit uncomfortable. I turned my face away from him and told him to stop, playfully at first. The look in his eyes was one I'd never seen before, but it's all I can see when I look at him now. It was angry, determined and utterly cold.

"All my desire left me in that moment. But we still had sex. And it was awful, because I really didn't want to, but I was scared not to.

"Afterwards, he popped the champagne cork and poured us each a glass. He kissed me and said 'To tomorrow!' and then he just got up and left me there. I sat on that bed for half the night, with my head spinning round and round. Then, in a daze, I walked the six miles home, watching the dawn break. I got home just as Tom was leaving for work. He laughed when he saw me. Told me I looked like I'd had a fight with a pack of hyenas, and that he'd be home early to cook me some hangover-recovery food, but that for now I should get some sleep.

"I told him in a flat, dead voice that I was leaving him. I went inside, packed a bag, and drove straight home to Ballycarragh. I never explained it to him, never actually spoke another word to him, even though he begged and pleaded with me while I packed. It completely broke my heart, but I knew the pain I felt was what I deserved after betraying him like that. I knew he deserved better and that he would eventually get over it.

"And so I came home and I didn't tell anyone what had really happened. I was so ashamed of myself for falling for that bastard and then letting him use me like that. I know I should have told Rosie. I tried to tell her without actually telling her, but that was pointless as she just thought I was being unfair. I was on the verge of spitting out the whole sordid story a couple of times, but it never worked out and it just got harder and harder the longer I left it. Besides, they were actually in a relationship and she seemed happy, so maybe it was just me.

"I even felt . . . It's so weird and makes me feel sick, but sometimes I even felt jealous. Why did he do that to me and not to Rosie? Isn't that awful? And now he's gone and killed her and it looks like he's going to get away with that too, and I feel like it's all my fault and there doesn't seem to be anything anyone can do."

CHAPTER
EIGHTEEN

Jenny stops talking, her eyes almost closed as she leans into Charles's barrel chest. Her breathing isn't quite so jagged anymore, but it's clear that fatigue is taking the place of panic now. In my case, pure rage is taking the place of any semblance of reasonable thought.

"THAT SWINE!" I screech, finally letting out the emotion that's been building up inside me throughout Jenny's heartbreaking story and earning myself a sharp look from Charles.

"He's actually been *torturing* her the whole time he's been here, Charlie! Telling me she 'had a bit of a thing for him' in Dublin! And all the time he knew that he had . . . he had . . . Oh, bloody hell!"

I'm vibrating, fizzing, consumed by so many conflicting feelings it seems I might shatter into a zillion pieces at any moment.

"*Shhh.*" Charles's tone is soothing as he strokes Jenny's hair, but he's still looking at me, clearly trying to communicate without freaking her out any more.

"I can't *Shhh!* How can I *Shhh?* Poor Jenny. My poor, poor Jenny." The pitch of my voice is rising to a level only dogs could register at this point. "Oh, Jenny, why couldn't you tell me?"

"*Shhh!*" Charles repeats, slightly less gently. I pay him no heed.

"Right!" I declare, pacing the tiny kitchen. "I'm going after him. Somebody needs to teach him a lesson!"

Charles stands up abruptly, Jenny cradled in his arms like a little sack of potatoes, stopping me in my tracks. He fixes me with a very serious gaze and whispers in the same soothing tone he's been using with Jenny all night,

"It's been a rough day for you, Jen, I'm just going to take you off to bed, and *we'll talk this over in the morning, all right?*"

It's quite obvious that this last bit is directed at me, especially since Jenny is clearly half asleep already, worn out from the combination of shock, brandy and confession.

"Subtle as a sledgehammer, Charlie," I grumble, side-stepping his bulky frame and stalking off into my bedroom, which still looks like a small bomb went off in it. The pathetic single strip of police tape across the door passes through my belly like a ghoulish finish-line. Thankfully, my dead body is no longer centre stage, so I can fling myself onto the bed without having to share it with anyone.

This just keeps on getting worse and worse. I can't believe how rotten to the core Jack is. How could he do that to Jenny and then turn up here out of the blue and pretend it never happened? And to think that I actually considered the possibility that she might have a crush on him. I shudder, horrified at myself. God, I wish I

160

could comfort her. Instead, Charles is playing knight-in-shining-armour, while I'm banished to my bedroom like a grumpy teenager. What qualifies him to march in here and start ordering me around anyway? I seethe away to myself, conveniently forgetting that it was me who went running after him for help in the first place.

I mean, tucking her into bed, for goodness' sake, she's a grown woman!

"I think you need to calm down a little, Rosie."

I sit up abruptly as Charles enters the room. For such a big lump of a man he sure can move stealthily when he wants to. Even my super-sensitive spidey-senses didn't pick up his approach. Then again, I was rather occupied with my righteous huffing, wasn't I?

"Oh, so you're talking to me now, are you?" I demand.

Somewhat unreasonable, I know. He could hardly chat away to me in the presence of a traumatised Jenny, could he? He doesn't answer me, and just as I draw breath to berate him some more, I realise why. It's the first time he's seen the crime scene that is my bedroom. His eyes are fixed unblinkingly on the dark-red bloodstain that spreads across my pillow like a particularly ugly birthmark. He looks a little pale as he grips the door-frame with a white-knuckled paw.

"Ah, look, don't get all freaked out, Charlie, it's just a bit of blood. I don't exactly need it anymore, eh?" I try to joke him out of his stupor, but he doesn't even look at me. He picks his way gingerly through the debris scattered across the floor and sits down heavily

161

in the armchair beside my bed, his head in his hands. When it becomes apparent that he isn't going to snap out of it anytime soon, I bounce up and down on the bed impatiently a few times before enquiring awkwardly, "Are you okay?"

He doesn't lift his head. Instead, I get a muffled response aimed down at his feet. "Not really, Rosie."

We sit in silence for a few minutes before he speaks again, his face still hidden behind the vast expanse of his spread fingers. "It's a lot to take in. It's been a difficult day and I'm just knackered."

Yeah, yeah. Try being the dead one, you big wimp.

I don't voice my uncharitable thought, but that doesn't mean it's not niggling at me as I try to be as comforting as possible. "Well, it could be worse, couldn't it? I mean, at least you've got me to entertain you from beyond the grave!"

Light-hearted doesn't work. In fact, what it elicits is a long, loud moan of what sounds like utter despair.

"Wow." I throw myself backwards and bounce horizontally a few times on the springy mattress. "Why don't you tell a gal how you really feel."

He tuts loudly, but there's no apology forthcoming. I engage in a short-lived silent treatment; a battle of the wills, which in reality is probably very much one-sided, before I finally give in and sit bolt upright again, scooting over to the edge of the bed and regarding him impatiently.

"Charles. Charles. Charlie. Charlieee . . . CHAA-ARLES!"

162

It's a tried-and-tested technique from years of little sister-dom.

Sure enough, he eventually looks up at me, his glassy eyes taking a moment to focus.

Was he . . . crying?

Then he raises his eyebrows and wiggles them, as if to say, *Yes? What do you want, you annoying little woman?*

But I don't know what to say, because I think he might have just been crying and Charles Walker isn't supposed to cry, it just doesn't feel right. So I sit and stare at him, with what must be a horrified and simultaneously dumb-looking expression on my face, until he speaks.

"Yes? What do you want, you annoying little woman?"

But he cracks a small smile. And the tension in the air dissipates again, and we're on safe ground. I push any thoughts of Charles crying over me to the back of my mind, because that's just *way too much* responsibility right now, and I can't bear to see him sad. Also, he's absolutely no use to me *wah-wahing* like a big baby, I need him to help me get to the bottom of all this ghostly stuff after all.

"How come you can see me and nobody else can?" I blurt out, surprising myself. But it's as good a way as any to steer the subject in a helpful direction, I suppose.

He shakes his head, "Buggered if I know, Rosie, my sweet."

"No theories?" I push it.

"Well, I don't know, maybe I had a fit of psychosis and killed you myself, because you were asking me annoying questions all the time, but then I was so traumatised I blanked it from my memory in one of those self-induced amnesia cases, so you're here to haunt me and harass me until suddenly my memory is jigged and I can repent."

I've been laughing since he got to the annoying questions part. I can't help it, he's got this dry humour which a lot of people don't understand at all, mainly because he delivers almost everything in this deadpan voice with a straight face, but I always find him hilarious.

"Hahahaha!" I'm chuckling away, but he just raises one eyebrow a tad, in that old-school way of his, and for a moment I falter. Gosh, he does look very serious. I gulp out the last of the laughs and regard him with sudden suspicion. "You *are* kidding, aren't you..?"

The grin that breaks like dawn across his oh-so-serious face is both playful and self-satisfied.

"You arse!" I swat at him, carefully aiming not to make contact at all.

We chuckle together for a few blissful moments, eyes crinkled and locked together, sharing a lifetime of friendship and understanding, and thankfully shedding some of the horrible badness of the past twenty-four hours.

"Seriously, though. You might not be far off, with the haunting and harassing idea." I begin, intending to share with him my idea about haunting Jack. "It might even be the reason —"

But he cuts me off, with a sharp "Don't even think about it, woman."

I splutter, indignant. The warm fuzzy feelings of just a moment ago are rapidly dissipating. *How dare he!* I can hear the argumentative edge in my own voice as I enquire self-righteously, "Well, what *are* we going to do about all this, Charles?"

He responds in his most dictator-like voice.

"Until we have our facts straight, Rosie, we are going to do absolutely nothing."

"WHAT?" I explode, dropping to my knees directly in front of him so I can eyeball him close up.

"Did you not *hear* Jenny in there? Did you not see the state she's in? Are you suggesting that we just let him get away with it? That we stand around like useless lumps while he merrily shags Lydia Smith and God only knows who else, and Jenny suffers in silence? He's got the whole bloody village charmed, the slimy shit, even the Gardaí's finest!"

"Well, he certainly had you charmed, didn't he?" Waves of distaste are radiating from Charles as he says this quietly, not meeting my eye.

I open and close my mouth a few times, like a gasping fish out of water, before suddenly and unexpectedly bursting into tears. Great, heaving sobs pour out of me as if a dam has burst somewhere deep inside.

Charles looks on in horror. "Oh dear, oh bugger!" he stammers, knuckling his forehead forcefully as I blubber away. "Rosie, I'm sorry, that was really rather insensitive of me. Of course, this has all been very hard on you too."

"I didn't exactly know that he was a nasty, murderous, rapist BASTARD when I decided to go out with him, you know!" I wail, feeling simultaneously guilty about Jenny, angry at Charles and humiliated by my own lack of judgement. "I didn't really have all the relevant information in front of me, did I? And besides," I snuffle ferociously into the sleeve of my ghostly pyjamas, "don't you think I've suffered enough for my *horrible taste in men?*"

"Oh, Rosie, I'm sorry."

Charles has assumed the same quiet, comforting tone he used on Jenny. He reaches out to pull me into a hug, but of course his great big arms go straight through me, causing me to shudder in revulsion and scuttle backwards out of his reach.

"UGH! Don't *do* that! Have you any idea how disgusting it feels?" I yell, feeling a stab of vicious satisfaction when he flinches at my reaction. He retreats back into the armchair like a puppy whose nose has been smacked. "And you don't have to treat me like I'm some kind of delicate flower either!" I snap, swiping away the last of my tears crossly. "It's sexist nonsense. I'm just having an emotional moment, allright? I can look after myself, you know."

If Charles picks up on the irony of a ghost sitting in the exact location of her gruesome death and declaring that she can look after herself, thankfully he's wise enough not to point it out. Instead, he just looks at me with an unreadable expression and nods mutely.

"Good." I turn my back on him and curl up in a little ball. "You can turn the light off on your way out. I'll talk to you in the morning and goddamn it, we'll come up with a plan then."

I listen as he gets up and turns off the light. I hear his careful footsteps as he finds his way back to the armchair and eases himself into it. His bulky presence is there as I close my eyes, his quiet breathing breaking the silence of the dark November night.

And though I'd rather chew off my own left arm than admit it, I'm glad he's there.

CHAPTER
NINETEEN

I'm too restless to sleep. Uncomfortable memories are floating very close to the surface of my conscious mind, which I really don't want to remember. How was I supposed to know that Jack was dangerous? How was I to know?

Well, there was that one time in Bronco's.

Early on in our romance, Jack and I took a spur-of-the-moment bus ride to the nearest real nightclub, "Bucking Bronco's", located several miles away in the next town.

We had been perched on a couple of bar stools in McMorrow's, trying to come up with something a bit more risqué to do with the rest of our evening. To be honest, I was just about to suggest a spot of cow tipping (a typically rural sport, which involves finding sleeping cows — they sleep standing up, just like horses — and prodding them with a big stick. This topples them over, usually with a wonderfully confused expression on their bovine faces, eliciting great hilarity among the "tippers"). I was eyeing up a likely-looking broomstick in the corner when Jack suddenly sat up a bit straighter, holding one finger aloft as if he were checking what direction the wind was blowing.

"What?" I demanded, excitedly. Jack pointed through the window at the mini-bus chugging outside in the frosty January night air.

"Isn't that the bus into town?" he enquired, a mischievous glint in his eye.

"Yup," I replied, not yet catching his drift. I can be a little slow, but in my defence it was at least ten years since I'd last set foot on that bus. Several spotty youths who had been drinking soft drinks — no doubt spiked with something from their pockets — in the cubby were making a dash for the door.

"What are we waiting for then?" Jack was on his feet and dragging me with him before I had time to protest. He bundled me onto the bus, choosing a seat smack bang in the middle of the squalling teens. When I weakly protested that I hadn't even had a chance to grab my coat, he wrapped me up in his leather jacket and assured me he'd keep me warm. Once the bus pulled out onto the road, I accepted my fate, taking great pleasure in telling Jack just how awful our destination was and that he didn't know what he'd signed up for. He just grinned, and declared, "If you can't beat 'em, join 'em!"

So join 'em we did, necking like horny schoolkids all the way to the club. By the time we arrived, we were both desperate for a wee. After a brief delay, while the bouncers ID'd all our fellow travelers, we finally got past the threshold and dashed off in our separate directions, agreeing to meet back at the bar when we were done.

I made a super-fast round trip to the Ladies, eager to impress my date with how little faffing about I was capable of, then raced back to the bar to find Jack. Hopefully he'd be impressed with my speedy return. But when I got to the bar he was nowhere to be found. Brilliant, I was faster than a man; brownie points for me as a girlfriend.

I bought us a couple of beers from the extremely camp barman and pasted a smug look on my face in anticipation of Jack's arrival. It was still fairly empty in the club. There were a few young things dancing self-consciously on the small, disco-ball-bedecked dance floor, busting some bizarre stripper-esque moves with their barely formed booties.

I glanced at my watch. Where was Jack? I took another long slug of beer as a young fella of around twenty approached the bar beside me.

"Howaya?" He nodded at me politely before ordering a selection of suggestively named cocktails.

"Hi," I responded, as himself behind the bar started flinging bottles around with surprising skill.

"D'you come here often?" I enquired out of sheer boredom, after a long silence spent watching the barman. The young fella turned to face me with an expression of mixed horror and embarrassment. I couldn't help laughing out loud. "I'm not coming onto you, you big eejit! I'm waiting for my boyfriend!"

"Oh, thank fuck." His relief was palpable, if rather insulting. "My girlfriend would kill me!"

We laughed, successfully past the minefield of the initial, awkward stage of male/female nightclub interactions.

"I'm Rosie," I said, extending my hand.

"Seamus."

We chatted away inanely for a few minutes about nothing much. Seamus was good craic and obviously delighted to have the opportunity to get off the dance-floor. At one point his girlfriend, Dervila, joined us long enough to take a huge gulp of her glowing purple beverage. She had on a very short, very tight, white dress that was glowing radioactively under the ultraviolet lights. Her hair was scraped tightly back from her face, creating a DIY Botox effect on her high forehead. Unfortunately, the lights also made her clip-in blonde extensions stand out like weird alien antennae which held my fascinated gaze as they flipped around the back of her head. She stayed only long enough to give me a mildly disinterested "Howaya?" and land a sloppily proprietary kiss on Seamus before a Beyoncé song came on and sent her dashing back to her friends, squealing excitedly. He watched her go with an expression of sheer adoration on his young face, and I felt all warm and happy that I had someone to look at me like that too. And I didn't even have alien hair.

"Wait till you meet my fella," I told him. "He's *lovely!*"

However, it wasn't quite the introduction I'd been expecting when Jack finally appeared. Seamus had just made a comment about the barman being "the only gay in the village" or something equally hilarious to me in my inebriated state, and we were both hanging off the bar in gales of laughter. I was initially delighted to see Jack as he loomed in between Seamus and me, and I started to introduce the two. But something in his stance stopped me.

"Jack?" I put my hand on his arm warily. He looked completely freaked out. Shrugging off my hand roughly, he pushed his face right up into poor Seamus's.

"What the *fuck* do you think you're doing with my woman?" he demanded, his voice high pitched with rage.

"Jesus, Jack!" I exclaimed, in complete shock. What the fuck was *he* doing? And then, unbelievably, before I had a chance to stop him, my boyfriend had grabbed the almost empty beer bottle out of my hand, and was brandishing it under the nose of the petrified-looking young fella.

Everything slowed down in that instant. With perfect clarity, I saw that this was not a man to fall in love with. I knew in those long, drawn-out seconds that Jack was bad news and that I absolutely had to break up with him. And then the bouncers rushed in and dragged him off, still screaming obscenities at Seamus, and everything speeded up again, and all I wanted to do was make sure he was okay and explain to him that he had it all wrong about me and Seamus. I wanted to tell him off and for him to be sorry. I wanted it all to be fine and I wanted him still to be my boyfriend and I really, really wanted to forget that moment of clarity I'd just had.

I rushed outside, pushing past the bouncers at the door and demanding they tell me where Jack was. One of them, an old fella who'd worked there for pretty much as long as the club had existed, took hold of my arm gently.

"He's on the bus, love, but maybe you should think about waiting for the next one."

"What?" I demanded, crossly. Who was this big brute to tell me what to do? But when I looked up at him there was only kindly concern in his eyes.

"He's off his head, love. He was out here earlier on the phone, calling up all sorts, loitering about waiting for a 'friend'. You know what I'm on about."

Well, actually, I didn't, but I nodded anyway, squinting up at him and trying to take in what he was telling me.

"He's not in a reasonable mood, love. He's in an *altered* state, you know?"

My mouth made a little "O" as I realised this guy was trying to suggest Jack was on drugs. But there was no way. We'd already had that conversation. I *hated* drugs and all that went with them. Jack had completely agreed with me. Why would he lie? This old guy had my best interests at heart but he must have been mistaken. Working in such a job, he must expect everybody to be at that stuff.

"Ok, well, thanks." I said, smiling weakly up at the big bouncer and making to leave. His expression hardened a little as he saw that I was still intending to get on the bus.

"Ah well, it's your life."

Damn right it was my life. I got on the bus and found Jack glaring out the window in the back seat. I was expecting him to be repentant, but I faced a stone wall of silence all the way home. By the time we pulled into Ballycarragh I was so desperate for him to talk to me, I apologised for talking to Seamus. Finally Jack looked at me. He was scowling, but when I gave him a little kiss his eyes softened.

I kissed him again and said quietly, "There really was nothing going on there though, Jack. I love *you*."

He didn't answer me, but he did put his arm around me and let me snuggle into his shoulder. Somewhere in the recesses of my mind a little voice was shouting that this was definitely not fair, but I didn't listen. Once again I ignored that creeping feeling that all was not as it should be.

We didn't talk as we got off the bus, let ourselves into the flat and climbed into Jack's queen-size bed. I whispered a final "I'm sorry" as I curled around the cool flesh of his back and closed my eyes.

"It's okay," he said, eventually, as we were drifting off to sleep. "Just don't pull that kind of shit again, all right?"

How was I to know?

Well, there was that one time at the party by the lake.

During the summer and on bank holiday weekends Ballycarragh is, for some strange reason, a bit of a tourist hot spot. Probably something to do with its unspoilt beauty and rural charm or some such guidebook diddly-aye nonsense, but for this reason we have quite a large caravan park and a little cluster of pretty wee holiday homes down by the lake. Hen parties in particular rent out the holiday homes, often for whole weeks at a time, all year round.

One such hen party had been terrorising the village all weekend — the June bank holiday weekend of last summer — and were having a giant bash on the Sunday night. I had to work, but arranged to meet Jack there when I finished up. The parties thrown in those houses are legendary around Ballycarragh, and nobody wants to miss out on the opportunity to let loose somewhere they don't have to help with the clean-up.

It wasn't an almightily busy night in McMorrow's, so after several hours of listening to me whinging in his ear, Roger finally relented and agreed to close up the bar and let me go early. I dashed off, planting a smacker of a kiss square in the middle of his forehead, prompting him to point out grumpily that if Lydia hadn't been on a night out with the girls, he most certainly wouldn't be doing me this favour.

I grinned at him, slapping on some lippy and a coat of mascara before heading out the door. After a moment's consideration, I decided to drive down. I wasn't sure I felt like having a drink, and it was a drizzly auld night.

As I turned onto the tree-lined lane that led down to the lakeside development, I could already see the signs that a party was in full swing. Several revellers were making their way by foot at the sides of the road and a couple of worse-for-wear young ones looked to be making an early (and shaky) departure. When the houses came into view, it was clear which one I was headed for. With all the lights blazing and cars backed up out the driveway and down the street, not to mention the small bonfire blazing in the front garden, number six was clearly the place to be.

I parked a safe distance away and hurried into the throng. Several locals greeted me enthusiastically, thrusting drinks my way and enquiring after mine and Jenny's well-being. I accepted a can of beer from my old flame Jimmy Rossa and chatted for a few minutes to Carl Curran, who I went to speech and drama classes with (and dated from October '97 to February '98. We broke up because he didn't get me a Valentine's card).

It's true, I had probably lip-locked most of the men at the party at some point in our past, not because I was a prolific teen slut or anything, but simply because they were all that was on offer and we all needed some way to spend our days. As I looked around at the familiar, barely-changed faces around me, I thanked my lucky stars that I'd met Jack. That he had chosen me out of all the girls in Ballycarragh who would have given their left tit to hook up with him.

I asked a few mutual friends where I would find him and got several different answers.

"I think he's in the bog."

"He went to get me a beer half an hour ago, the fecker!"

"He's on the decks in the conservatory, love."

I set off on a mission to find my boyfriend, checking every corner of the ground floor before moving upstairs. It was time-consuming, as every second person was drunk and happy and wanted to chat. I put down my beer after a few sips, realising that I didn't want to drink at all. I'd only be playing catchup with everyone else here who had obviously been on it since the early hours of the afternoon. In fact, what I really wanted most of all was to find Jack and drag him home to snuggle up with me in bed and have our own little party.

I must be getting old! The thought occurred to me as I checked the door of one of the bedrooms upstairs. *That or I'm madly in love.*

I scanned the queue for the toilet that was winding its way down the stairs, and waited for whoever was occupying it to come out, but none of them was my man. I ventured into another bedroom and was enthusiastically invited to join a game of "Strip Twister" with what looked like at least ten more players than recommended by the rules. I was actually quite tempted by that, it looked like a lot of fun, but my desire to find Jack won out in the end, and after staying to watch until the half-dressed tangle of bodies collapsed in a hysterical heap, my search continued.

I finally opened the last bedroom door, finding it dark and empty. It was a small box room, and appeared to be uninhabited. The hens were probably all sharing the other three larger rooms, this one having just a tiny single bed squeezed into it and not much room for anything else. I closed the door behind me and breathed a deep sigh of relief. Maybe I really was getting over this whole scene. Maybe my wild days were behind me once and for all. Maybe it was time I started thinking about settling down and making babies.

A silly grin plastered across my face as I flopped onto the tiny excuse for a bed and gazed out the window. Not quite there yet, I reckoned, but some day I could certainly picture me and Jack and a little brood of our own, blissfully happy and settled.

It was still drizzling away outside, I noticed, as I looked out over the back lawn. Someone had put fairy lights into the branches of the tree right outside the window, and they twinkled prettily at me through the rain-streaked glass. Just as I was wishing that Jack could be beside me in this quiet little oasis of a room, I caught a flash of movement through the branches of the tree. I pressed my nose up against the glass and tried to peer down at an impossible angle. Yes, there it was! A familiar-looking, stripey, blue-and-red jumper. Jack! What was he doing out there in this weather? I couldn't quite see his face, but I'd looked everywhere else. I was about to leg it downstairs and catch him before he disappeared again, when I realised there was someone else under the canopy of branches too. A blonde, wearing an awful lot of sequins. Again, I couldn't see much what with the branches and the fairy lights and the rain, try as I might to swivel my head against the glass. Maybe it wasn't Jack after all. It looked like whoever these two people were, they were having a rather heated discussion. There was lots of arm waving and head tossing going on, which is probably why I spotted them in the first place.

I was trying to decide what my best course of action was when something genuinely shocking happened. Through the swaying foliage, I clearly saw the guy in the stripey jumper draw back his arm and slap the blonde woman hard. She staggered backwards, landing in a crumpled heap in the mud. I yelped out loud, instinctively drawing back from the window and the awful scene I'd just witnessed. When I looked back just moments later neither of them was to be seen.

How awful! I thought to myself. *That poor woman.*

But it couldn't have been Jack, I reasoned. There must have been hundreds, thousands of that very same jumper sold in River Island stores across Ireland.

I didn't go looking for him.

I hurried out of there, shaken, got in my car and drove straight back to McMorrow's, where I crawled into Jack's bed with one thought going round and round in my mind.

Please don't let him be wearing that jumper tonight. Please don't let him be wearing that jumper tonight.

Jack arrived home several hours later. I heard him come through the back door of the bar, and the clink of glasses as he helped himself to a pint of Mi-Wadi (he always insisted that it was God's hangover cure of choice). I listened quietly as he flicked on the telly and fluffed about down there for an interminable time. When his footstep finally sounded on the stairs I thought I might wee myself with nerves. I kept telling myself I was being silly and that there was no way that had been my boyfriend out there battering some strange woman tonight. But until I could be sure he wasn't wearing that jumper I felt there would always be a doubt in my mind.

He came through the bedroom door and took off his leather jacket and I actually burst into tears with the relief of seeing a plain-white tee shirt under it. Jack, of course, was completely bewildered at my state, and spent ages telling me how much he'd missed me and asking me why I had left in such a rush (Carl Curran told him I was looking for him). He begged me to tell him what was wrong, but I just held him tight and went to sleep berating myself for doubting my man even for a second.

In the morning, I kissed him gently without waking him and slithered out of bed, silently mooning over how cute he looked with his wee eyes closed and a little dribble of saliva pooling on the pillow by his mouth. I set off downstairs with a spring in my step, once again counting my lucky stars that I'd found myself one of the good ones.

But on my way through the bar, I stopped dead as I saw what was slung casually across the back of one of the high stools. It was only a stripey blue-and-red jumper, but it made my blood run cold. I worked very hard to erase that image from my memory for weeks and weeks afterwards.

And yet I'm still asking myself: how was I to know?

CHAPTER
TWENTY

I open my eyes, coming out of my half-dream state with my skin crawling and my jaw clenched so tight it hurts. It's still pitch black in my bedroom, but I don't think I'm going to get any more sleep tonight. Not with such awful memories resurfacing like that. I can't believe I was such a blind fool. In fact, I can't believe I *chose* to be so blind. Sure, women turn a blind eye to small faults in their chosen fellas all the time, but I managed to ignore the fact that mine was a complete PSYCHO.

I never brought up the stripey-jumper issue with him. In fact I'm ashamed to say I just threw it in the bin so I never had to look at it ever again. Much the same as the Seamus incident, I put it in a special box in a dark part of my mind and kept on viewing Jack through Rosie-tinted glasses. I'm pretty sure there were plenty more signs that all wasn't well, but I stubbornly refused to address them. I probably had an inkling that Lydia Smith was talking about herself being the apple of Jack's eye that day in the bar, and that she was the blonde he was arguing with under the tree, but I managed to ignore any intuitive intelligence that may have pricked the surface of my mind. In fact, I have the awful, sneaking suspicion that even if Jen had mustered up the courage to tell me her story, I may well have tried to explain that away too.

I feel ashamed of myself, but that shame quickly morphs into dark, hot anger. Some of it is directed at myself, but thankfully most of it has a different target. And I don't reckon I can lie here doing nothing for much longer, no matter what bloody bossy Charles Walker says.

I prick up my ears and peer over at his bulky frame where it's hunched in the armchair. Steady, heavy breathing, gentle rise and fall of the chest. Yes, he's fast asleep. I don't have a problem slithering out of the bed silently, eluding my prison-guard, Mr Walker. In no time at all, I'm galloping off down the lane towards McMorrow's. With any luck, I can get in a bit of paranormal activity and be back in bed before he even misses me.

My blood is boiling and adrenaline coursing through me like quicksilver by the time I get up the stairs to Jack's flat. I slip through the interior door (plasticky, chemical, vile) and lurk in the hallway for a moment, taking in my surroundings. All clear. No sign of movement anywhere.

I walk through the open bedroom door and my heart leaps into my throat. Of course I knew about Lydia and him, and besides, he's a bastard of a cold-hearted villain, but it's still an awful shock to see her lying beside him in the bed where I spent so many cosy, contented nights. I used to feel so safe there, lying wrapped around my future murderer, our breath in sync, our skin warm and soft to the touch. I creep over and sit on the edge of the bed, looking down at the sleeping adulterers with a heady mixture of regret and disgust.

Right there used to be my absolute favourite place to be. I used to stay awake as long as I could just to enjoy the feeling. Jack twitches three times before he's fully asleep. The first time is barely noticeable, the second, a slightly more forceful jerk, and the third an astonishing, bed-shaking jolt, which bizarrely indicates not that he is waking up in fright, but that he's actually sound asleep. I told him about it once, and he told me off for telling tall tales. He tried to convince me that I say the rosary in my sleep in retaliation. As if! I don't even know the full —

Yeeeeaaarghhhh!

I nearly fall through the bed as Lydia suddenly sits bolt upright inches from my face. She stares straight ahead for a long, unblinking moment, and as my fright subsides I'm quite intrigued to note that her perfectly applied slap is still intact. I wonder if it's that tattooed-on stuff they do in high-tech salons nowadays.

In another sudden flurry of movement, she gets out of bed and pulls on her shoes and dress, scuttling out of the room like some kind of wild-haired robot woman. I would guess from her rush that she didn't intend to sleep over, she probably just fell asleep after they . . .

Nope. Still can't go there.

A door slams in the distance, signalling that the blonde has left the building. I allow myself a creepy grin and lean down close to Jack's simple-looking face.

In my best Hannibal Lecter voice, I rasp menacingly, "Alone at last, my love!"

Without further ado, I reach down and whip the pillow out from under Jack's head. No sooner has his skull bounced rudely onto the mattress, his eyelids blearily shooting open on bloodshot eyes, I slam the pillow back down on top of his face and enjoy the frantic struggle that ensues.

I have no intention of smothering him to death in the manner of some jilted soap-opera character (okay, so the thought does cross my mind momentarily) but I do want to give him the most effective scare possible, so I leave it just a fraction longer than would be considered playful.

Letting go suddenly, I step back to admire the after effects of my first attempt at haunting. The pillow flies across the room, as the pressure I was exerting is suddenly lifted, and all Jack's strength is released into the innocent, feather-filled cotton sack. I can't help laughing gleefully at the panicked expression on the poor bastard's face. He casts about frantically, his head flying this way and that in the dark room. Obviously his night vision isn't quite as good as my own. Well, I can help him in that regard.

I reach for the wall switch and flick the top light on, twisting the dimmer to its brightest setting.

"There we go, pet," I croon, "don't want you getting all afraid of the dark."

While he's still blinking in the blinding light, clearly wondering how the hell the lights have just turned themselves on, I really get the party started, setting off the alarm clock, switching on the telly and pressing "play" on the stereo in quick succession. Volume levels all at full, I hop around the room, delighted with my handiwork, as Jack cowers against the headboard, silently mouthing what could be curses or prayers, neither of which are going to do him any good.

Giddy with power, I flit around the room, turning everything off again. It's had the desired effect, and frankly the noise levels are giving me a bit of a headache what with my supersonic hearing and all. Back in the dark silence, I grin evilly when Jack says in a shaky whimper, "Hello..?"

"Hello, lover!" I boom, plonking myself down on the bed as hard as I can, making it bounce noticeably. Sure, he can't hear me, but I'm fully in character now.

He leaps away from the sudden indentation in the mattress, repeating a little louder and more high-pitched, "Hello? Who's there?"

I follow him across the bed, in a parody of the flirty kiss-and-chase lover's games we used to play right here.

"It's me, Jack," I snarl, pointing one finger and prodding him hard in his ribs, "Or have you forgotten me already?"

My finger makes extremely satisfying contact with his flesh. It's the first time I've managed to properly touch a living person and I'm very satisfied with the result. He leaps off the bed like there's a rocket up his arse, hauling open the bedside locker and pulling something out. He waves the object around with shaking hands, and my jaw drops as I realise what it is.

Jack's got a gun!

Undoubtedly the very same gun that put this hole in the side of my head. That right there is *evidence* on a large scale.

I leave him waving around his precious murder weapon, terrified out of his wits by things that go bump in the night. It's clear as day now to even the most dubious of observers that he killed me. And he's not going to get away with it for a moment longer.

"What do you mean, he's already gotten away with it?" I demand, glaring at Charles with a dumbfounded expression on my face, where he sits bleary eyed and just awake in the armchair by my bed.

"Are you seriously telling me we're not going to do anything about this?"

"No, Rosie, I'm not saying that," he says, grimacing as he runs his tongue around his teeth and scrunches his eyes open and closed once or twice. "But I do seem to recall saying very clearly last night that we should wait and rationally discuss our next move very carefully. Entertaining as your little terror mission sounds . . ." Charles cracks a smile, obviously enjoying the mental image of Jack leaping around the bedroom like a perma-tanned poked pig in tartan boxers I painted for him as soon as I came hurtling into the bedroom several minutes ago. "And although it does sound very entertaining, it still doesn't remove us from our somewhat precarious position. We don't have any way of *proving* Jack guilty, or even giving the Gardaí sufficient evidence for them to investigate him further."

186

"*But he has a bloody gun!*" I roar in disbelief. "Probably the one that made all this mess!" I gesture wildly at my bloodstained bed and the small, gory hole in my head simultaneously, making Charles wince.

"Unless the Gardaí have reason to search his flat, they won't know that, will they? And he does appear to have an alibi for the night in question."

Charles's expression darkens visibly as I draw breath to complain.

"Look, Rosie, I'm not saying that I don't believe Jack did this. After hearing what he did to Jenny, and from my own limited experience of him, it's clear he's a nasty, dangerous, cowardly piece of work, and I want him to pay for it just as much as you do. Just as much as your family would want him to. It's just a matter of going about it through the correct channels and getting every step right. Life and the law are unfortunately not as simple as they make out in the movies. We have to be a bit more realistic."

I raise my eyebrows and slowly, deliberately pass my hand through the wall a few times. "Realistic. Riiight."

Charles chortles, shaking his head. "Yes, well, as realistic as we can be in these somewhat unusual circumstances."

I let loose a dramatic sigh. "So what do we do then? Can't you just go to the Gardaí and tell them he has a gun?"

Charles snorts inelegantly. "Just tell them! Sure, why didn't I think of that? And how would 'we' explain the circumstances in which we discovered this, exactly? I don't know how it'll go down if I call them up and tell them that Jack Harper's dead ex-girlfriend goaded him into such a state of fear that he pulled it out in self defence. Oh, and that I know this because for some ungodly reason she's hanging around talking to me!"

"No need to be a smart shite," I huff mildly.

"I like how strongly he reacted to you and your shenanigans though," Charles says thoughtfully, after a short pause in which we both consider our position. "He's quite obviously got a hell of a guilty conscience. I wonder how he'd hold up if you were to keep at him."

"Well I'm planning on haunting the fecker anyway!" I declare gleefully. "That's what I was trying to tell you last night when you shut me down. I think maybe that's why I'm still hanging around here on the mortal plane. To avenge my death and drive him mental. Do you think he'll start to crack up pretty quickly?"

Charles is regarding me with a combination of amusement and admiration, which makes me preen self-consciously. "I think the sooner other people notice that he's acting strange the better." He nods thoughtfully, and continues, "The more people start to see Jack as a suspicious character, the more the Gardaí will consider him a likely suspect again and investigate him a bit more closely. What do you reckon, are you up to the job?"

"Am I ever!" I whoop excitedly. "I haven't had that much fun in ages!" I raise my hand for a high-five, "I'm in!"

Charles lifts his hand, grinning back at me. But then something in his eyes flickers and his cheeks go a little pink. He quickly turns his high-five hand into a

188

half-hearted wriggly-fingered wave as his focus shifts to somewhere over my shoulder.

Jenny's worried voice comes from the doorway where Charles is still gazing fixedly.

"Who are you talking to, Charles?"

I can't help enjoying his obvious embarrassment a little bit, cruel ghost-girl that I am. He goes a little redder in the face, coughs and mutters, "Oh, I'm just blethering away to myself."

Flicking his eyes back to me, he musters something akin to a real smile.

"I've been known to talk a whole heap of shite sometimes, Jenny, don't mind me."

I smile back at him. Those are my words, a reference to a conversation Charles and I had a long time ago. I feel a flush of warmth creeping over me as we share the memory, silently, secretly.

"Right, so . . ." Jenny says, sounding unconvinced, "I'll just put the kettle on then, will I?"

CHAPTER
TWENTY-ONE

Around the time Jenny hooked up with Tom Devine, I found myself occasionally feeling pretty glum about the whole situation. When we were all hanging out together it was fine, but once I was alone, with only my own thoughts to listen to, it really stung that she had a boyfriend and I didn't. It wasn't that I didn't wholeheartedly celebrate the fact that they were such a good match and that they had found each other, it was just a little bit lonely to be the single one, the one who *hadn't* found anybody, a bit of a failure really. Not that I had actually failed with anyone in particular. Far from it, I had yet to meet a boy I didn't think was a complete waste of space. It was just ... I kind of wanted *somebody*. Even if they were a waste of space. Maybe I just wanted somebody to want me. Oh hell, I was a teenager, so there was a whole lot of angst around wanting, not wanting, wanting to be wanted and all the rest.

I suppose it's always pretty tough when your best friend gets into their first serious relationship. Especially for girls. Jenny and I had been so inseparable, so joined at the hip, that we might as well have paid rent at each other's houses. Suddenly, she was interested in other things (Tom) and busy with other things (Tom) and therefore not always at my beck and call. To be fair, they included me in most of the stuff they did, which was great fun, but sometimes it was just an unavoidable fact that three was a crowd.

On one such occasion, they'd headed off to some dodgy Chinese restaurant in town to celebrate their two-month anniversary or something equally gag-inducing, and I was bored and fed up with the whole me-being-single-and-lonely scenario. I'd already managed to entertain myself by rowing with Chris over him scratching my Backstreet Boys CD (he denied it vehemently, "Why would I be listening to that shite?" being his defence, "Because you're GAY!" being my counter-attack, etc.) and irritated Mum by mooching about the house complaining that *normal* people had televisions and why did I have to be born into a family of *freaks*. Regular teenage behaviour all round, I guess.

So, not feeling all that welcome in the house for obvious reasons (I was being a pain in the arse) I took myself off with a jar of Nutella and my diary to my "thinking place". My intention was to stay there just long enough for my mother to start worrying about my whereabouts, but not quite long enough to miss dinner, as we were having shepherd's pie.

My "thinking spot" was where I always went when I didn't want to be disturbed; when I needed some space to sulk, have a good cry, daydream, or write in my diary. It was inside a wonderfully camouflaged, dilapidated old tree-house, which wasn't actually on our property, but had clearly been long forgotten about

191

by whoever had built it next door. The only person living in the run-down old house beside ours was a chronically shy old bachelor farmer called Paddy anyway, and even if he had had a problem with me clambering over his wall and up into the thick branches of the huge old oak tree he wouldn't have been able to report it.

The tree-house itself was ancient, with treacherously rotting floorboards, barely any roof left and one wall completely missing. There was one little corner though that managed to stay relatively dry in all but the most vicious kind of West of Ireland weather, and this was my "thinking spot". Our two large ginger tom-cats, Puss and Boots, shared my love of this peaceful little haven and would generally follow me up whenever I was in residence, snuggling like a great, purring, orange blanket across my knees.

I had one big church-style candle up there, and a lighter in a sandwich bag, squeezed into a small hollow in the wood right in the corner. I'd be up there with my feline companions in the flickering candlelight until all hours sometimes, enjoying my own personal hideaway. I'd never even shown it to Jenny, from whom I had no other secrets. It just felt right to keep this place as my own.

Which was why, on this particular day, I was infuriated to see Charles's big dumb head appear through the entrance hole in the floor shortly after Puss and Boots had arrived and settled themselves on my lap. He was facing away from me, so I watched the back of his head as he looked this way and that, before shifting his position on the branch below and turning to face me.

"*Shite!*" he exclaimed, nearly falling out of the tree when he came face to face with me and my hostile expression. "Rosie, you nearly scared me into an early grave lurking there like that!"

"I'm not lurking, Charles," I responded, haughtily. "*You* are snooping."

"Sorry!" he responded, cheerfully. "Hang on a sec, I'll just . . ." His head disappeared for a moment, then reappeared alongside his two great big man-hands, followed swiftly by his shoulders, torso and swinging legs.

"Be careful!" I snapped, unwelcoming in the extreme. "The floorboards over there are about to give way as it is. You need to move slowly with your body weight kind of evenly distributed."

I had to laugh as Charles blanched and started shuffling over-cautiously on his backside across the filthy floor, like some type of large clumsy crab. Clearly the thought of crashing through the floor to the ground far below was one he didn't relish.

"It's not that bad," I relented, once he was a few feet away from the opening. "It's just that you're a bit heavier than me and I don't know how much weight it can take."

"You seem to be quite the expert on this place," he muttered through gritted teeth, as he finally reached me in the dry spot. He squeezed in beside me, ignoring my grumbling as his bulk squashed me against the wall. "It's a nice spot, isn't it?" he continued, peering out at the sun setting over the fields, the sheep dotted about the hillside, the cherry-blossom trees in full bloom in Paddy's back yard.

"Yes, it is, but it won't be for much longer now that you and Chris are going to take it over and wreck it!" I responded, bitterly.

"Why would we do that?" he asked, looking genuinely surprised.

"I dunno," I mumbled, still hanging on to my bad mood by my finger-tips in the face of his good humour. "Because Chris wrecks everything I love?"

"I don't know if that's necessarily true, Rosie," Charles said mildly.

"But I won't tell him about this place if that's what you would prefer? After all, you seem to have been the first to discover it. Your flag is, shall we say, planted."

"Really?" I squeaked, relieved that he was willing to keep my "thinking spot" a secret. "You really won't tell him?"

"Sure, no worries."

We sat for a few minutes without further conversation, as the sky turned various shades of peach and pink and red, and the candle flame's light grew stronger and brighter against the lengthening shadows.

"What are you doing up here anyway?" Charles asked, breaking the silence suddenly.

I bit back a sharp retort about him being a nosy fecker. After all, he was keeping my secret, I had to keep him on side, didn't I? So I told him. I intended to just say that I was a bit lonely, but before I knew it, the whole story had come gushing out of me and I had revealed all my deepest feelings of inadequacy and fear of never finding a boyfriend of my own, etc. Maybe it was something to do with the fact that he didn't say anything, just looked out across the darkening fields like a shepherd watching over his flock, nodding occasionally, glancing my way every now and then, making a small grunting noise of agreement when I got particularly vociferous about some point or another. Most importantly, he didn't do that awful, over-the-top-eye-contact thing people do when they're consciously trying to be *a good listener*.

By the time I stopped talking it was completely dark except for the flickering flame of the candle, which was just as well, because I could feel a hot blush creeping up my face with the realisation that I had just spilled my guts to none other than Charlie Walker. Nonetheless, I also felt a huge relief inside me, a weight off my shoulders, from talking to somebody about what had been playing on my mind for the last month. A little ray of sunshine spliced through the black cloud that had been following me around.

"So," I said, a little lamely, after the few slightly uncomfortable moments of silence that followed my storm of words. "That's why I'm sitting up here in a bit of a mood. I reckon I might just end up a lonely old spinster with only my big stupid cats for company. *Ow!*"

This last was directed at Puss, who had chosen this particular moment to open one eye and regard me disdainfully, while digging one razor-sharp claw just a little bit too deep into my knee.

"Well, I don't think that's at all likely, Rosie," said Charles, with all the wisdom of an eighteen-year-old male.

"You see, I think you are focusing a little too hard on the idea of 'The One', when really, 'The One' isn't what you're ready for at all. There are millions of fish in the sea, as they say. And they're all nice and tasty in their own way, you know?"

I didn't really. But I felt I ought to let him have his say. After all, I'd been blethering on for ages and ages. Charles continued without waiting for me to answer.

"So, you might try salmon and think, 'Wow, this is great,' and just stick with salmon for the rest of your life. Which would be a mistake, as you might then get sick of salmon if you have too much of it. But if you tried a few other kinds of fish, you could be like, 'Wow, sea bass is the *best*,' and yet still spend some time sampling trout, perch and plenty of others. You would enjoy them all, perhaps have some favourites for some stretches of time, but you wouldn't necessarily commit yourself to one fish just because that's what other people do, would you?"

"Er, no?" I hazarded.

"Exactly! You'd discover that you like lots of different fish for lots of different reasons. But then one day you would realise, after trying all sorts and experimenting with plenty of different ways to cook them all, that in the end salmon truly is your favourite, and that you'd never have known that for sure if you hadn't gone out there and made the effort to try lots of different types of fish, and . . . um . . . then maybe you would choose salmon as the fish that makes you happiest, the fish you want to be with, and . . . um . . . hmmm."

Charles seemed to be losing steam fast, so I piped up with the only thing I could think of to say at this strange juncture in the conversation, "There's something fishy going on here!"

He looked at me, a very confused expression etched on his young face. "Um . . ."

He seemed so funny sitting there with his brain tied up in knots by dubious fishy metaphors that I cackled long and loud, giving him a big bear-hug and a noisy smacker on the cheek.

"You do talk a whole heap of shite sometimes, Charlie!" I declared, as I shimmied across the floor and dropped out the hole. I threw a grin over my shoulder just before I ducked out of sight, leaving him with the parting shot: "Sure, I bloody hate fish anyway. Nasty, slimy, ugly things."

I could hear him chuckling as I hit the ground and took off at high speed across the lawn, hoping there was still some shepherd's pie left for me.

CHAPTER
TWENTY-TWO

Charles follows Jenny into the kitchen, breaking eye contact with me as the bitter-sweet memory of that conversation floods us both. I guess I'll never find my fish now. I grin despite the tragedy of that thought, wondering what kind of fish Charles most resembles as I traipse into the kitchen after the living folk. Probably a salmon, now that I come to think of it. Quite tasty, but bullheaded beyond belief. I mean, what's all that battling against the current about? Why not just spawn wherever's handy?

Jenny is subdued, but there's definitely more colour in her cheeks than there was last night. She busies herself making tea, slicing brown bread and setting the table. That's an awful lot of fussing for someone who usually stands in front of the open fridge with a spoon in her hand at breakfast time. She's finding it hard to look at Charles, probably feeling awkward after reliving her ordeal last night. After all, even though Jenny has always thought Charles is a big ride, she hasn't actually ever spent all that much time one on one with him. She always preferred to tag along with me and occasionally hurl flirtatious abuse his way instead of actually communicating with him. And that wasn't just when we were kids either — it pretty much sums up their adult interactions too.

"Would you consider going to the Gardaí with what you told me last night, Jenny?" Charles asks suddenly, as he spoons sugar into his milky tea. She freezes momentarily, then turns around and sits down heavily in the chair opposite him.

"I've been thinking about that all morning." She sighs, shaking her head. "I know I should, I know it might help with the whole Rosie investigation, I just . . ." She swallows hard before continuing. "I just don't think I'm ready yet. I don't think I could cope with all the attention, all the fuss, all the drama, what with everything that's happened lately, with us losing Rosie. Do you think I'm being awfully selfish?"

"No." Charles says simply.

"It really helped, talking to you last night." She breathes out heavily as her shoulders relax a little.

"It was weird, even though it was you I was speaking to — I really felt like I was finally telling Rosie too, you know?"

Charles's eyebrows only twitch a little at this, fair play to him, especially as I'm excitedly hissing in his ear, "Maybe you should tell her I'm here. You can be like Whoopi Goldberg in *Ghost*, giving her messages from me and stuff. Go on, tell her I said 'Hullooooooo' in a big spooky voice."

Charles clears his throat loudly, surreptitiously waving a hand around his left ear in an obvious attempt to get me to shut up.

Jenny immediately drops her head down and regards her lap intently, saying in a small voice, "Oh, I know I sound crazy. I miss her a lot, Charles."

"No, no!" Charles says in a rush, "I don't think you're crazy at all."

He pauses, weighing up his next words carefully, and I take the opportunity to butt in, "She's starting to think YOU are though, hahaha!"

He ignores me, which I must admit he's getting better at doing of late, the bugger. "I do believe that Rosie is definitely around us," he says eventually. "Her spirit, her energy. It's only human to believe that the ones we love leave something of themselves to comfort us in our grief — that's not crazy at all, it's healthy. And what harm is it doing anyone to feel the presence of someone who was very much an important part of our lives. There will never be any proof, but who needs proof to believe in what one feels?"

"Oh bravo, your spiritual highness, now tell her that I'm standing right here doing this." I yank hard on a small clump of Charles's sideburn, causing his eyes to water a little.

Jenny looks up and gazes at Charles compassionately. She clearly thinks he's welling up with emotion. "Is that who you've been talking to when you're on your own?" she asks, in something akin to the gentle, understanding tone mothers must use when they're first addressing the topic of masturbation with their sons. The whole "It's-nothing-to-be-ashamed-of-you-can-talk-to-me" thing. She must be trying to repay him for listening to her last night.

200

"Er . . . Well, yes," Charles says, rather uncomfortably. There follows a long silence, broken only by me sniggering in the background.

"Poor Charlie," I wheedle, "go on and tell her the truth, she won't have you committed."

But I know he won't confess that he sees me. And I know she probably *would* harbour serious doubts about his mental state if he did. Jenny would be the last person on earth to buy into the concept of actually communing with the dead. In fact, I'm mostly only trying to convince him to tell her so that I can laugh at the result if he does. Mean, I know, but I have to get my jollies somewhere. And it's all the more fun because he knows what I'm up to.

Jenny unfortunately chooses this moment to rain on my parade in spectacular style.

"You know, I always thought you and Rosie would end up together."

My jaw drops as Charles's eyebrows shoot up. A slow, sneaky smile spreads across his face as he regards my horrified expression, and says softly to Jenny, "Oh? Why's that?"

"*She did not!*" I bellow, incandescent with rage at this sudden turn in the conversation.

"You did not, Jennifer McLoughlin."

"I did," she says softly. I almost think she's responding to me for a mad moment, until she elaborates on her deluded theory: "You two just always seemed to be the perfect match. Not that she'd have admitted it. She'd rather have shaved her head and committed hara-kiri than admit it, but I reckon she always carried a torch for you."

"*Treacherous wench!*" I roar, flushing a deep red, even though I know what she's saying isn't, *couldn't be*, true.

I can't look at Charles right now, so I have no idea how he's taking this ludicrous accusation, but I do growl at him under my breath. "She's talking shite, Charles. I wouldn't have told you, but the gloves are off now: It's *her* who's always mooned after you, not bloody *me*. Tell her that! Tell her you know *she's* into you and let's see how she explains herself."

My rage kind of splutters and dies in its prime though as Jenny's eyes once more fill with tears. "I can't believe she's gone, Charles," she wails, sniffling into her sleeve. "It shouldn't have happened this way."

I huff and puff a little bit more, but she doesn't say anything else about her bizarre unrequited love theory, and by the time he's comforted her and brought her back to a reasonable frame of mind, the subject seems to have been thoroughly dropped.

Thank God. I mean, come on. This must be affecting her more deeply than I thought. She pulls herself together relatively quickly though and disappears off to the loo, leaving me alone with the supposed object of my affection.

"Not a word!" I demand, as soon as she's out of the room. "That's what you call complete hysteria, and I'm not in the mood for you to get any mileage out of it, you hear me?"

202

Charles merely gives me a smug little half-smile and replies mildly, "Why would I?"

He then explains that he has to go artificially inseminate a donkey or something equally gross and vetlike, but that he'll be back this evening. I agree to stay with Jenny just to ensure she's okay (even though I still kind of feel like strangling her myself), and that once Charles is back I'll head off to spend the evening haunting Jack. I can't wait. I've got a fair bit of pent-up, pissed-off steam to let out, that's for sure.

Carrying a torch for Charles Walker, my arse.

I spend the day with Jenny, who spends it watching all sorts of shite on the telly and, let me tell you, *Countdown* isn't half as much fun when you can't show off your superior intellect by yelling out seven-letter words here, there and everywhere. It doesn't stop me, of course, but Jenny stubbornly refuses to hear me, even when I solve the conundrum before the child-genius competitor.

This only adds fuel to my resentment of her declaration of love on my behalf earlier. I wear a cross scowl all day, which leaves my face only briefly when I exact my revenge in the only way I feel able — by hiding her Terry's Chocolate Orange. This entertains me for a good twenty minutes. One moment it's on the coffee table in front of her, the next, in the coal scuttle. Where, obviously, she doesn't look. She does retrace her steps, right back to the freezer (Jenny keeps all her chocolate treats in the freezer, the weirdo. I'm the opposite, I love it when I find a piece that's been in my handbag for a week and is all melty and smooshed up. It totally freaks her out). She checks her bedroom, even the loo. She crawls around the floor of the sitting room several times before finally giving up.

And I'm in no mood to relent. I feel no sympathy as I regard her puzzled face.

"Serves you right, you mad cow." I smirk to myself.

I'm so relieved when the doorbell rings in the early evening and it's Chris, popping round to check on Jenny. It's starting to get dark outside, but Charles isn't due back for several hours and I'm raring to get going on my mission. I can hear Jenny telling my brother all about the case of the disappearing chocolate as I tear out the door, leaving her in the safest of hands.

It's pelting with rain outside, but after my initial, instinctive hunching up, I realise that it doesn't feel like it used to when I was alive. In fact, it feels wonderful. Instead of landing on my skin in big, wet splodges gradually soaking me to the core and making my clothes slap against my flesh like cold seaweed, each raindrop passes straight through me — hundreds of them at once — sending delicious little individual shivers racing through me on their path. Finally, something that feels good when you're dead! I slow down and take my time getting to McMorrow's, relishing the tickly Irish rain shower. I'm actually giggling aloud from the sensation by the time I reach the door. If I didn't have some pressing work to do inside, I'd stay out here all night.

Jack's behind the bar covering my shift. They clearly haven't hired anyone to fill my size eights yet. This is good. He's stuck there and we have an audience. I wonder if he's got his gun on him. Wouldn't it be brilliant if I could get him to pull it in here in front of several witnesses. Although I'm not sure any of these witnesses would be all that admissible in a court of law. Good Auld Ross Moriarty is on his usual stool (very few other people ever try to sit there, due to the strange, lingering, miasmic odour hovering around that one spot) ranting animatedly to his good friend Liam Sullivan. Liam and Ross are such good mates not because of their similar age or background, but because Liam is deaf as a post and seems to have little or no sense of smell to boot.

Further along the bar sit Larry and Gerry McGarry, the red-headed bachelor twins who come in every Tuesday evening and sink an impressive amount of Guinness between them. Always the same amount, always at the same pace. They don't talk at all if they can help it, just sit side by side, sipping in unison and watching whatever sport happens to be on the telly.

A brief nod in the direction of the tap is their own unique way of letting me know they're ready for their next pint to be put on to settle. I've become pretty good at predicting the exact point they get to before The Nod. Four good sips before the end of the pints they have going is the usual, although if they have a particular thirst on them of a night it could be as early as halfway through. In fact, from the manner in which their heads are currently bobbing up and down in Jack's direction, I can see they're quite eager for their next pints right now. Jack is typically glued to the football on the TV, while Roger and Lydia are bowed over some paperwork at the end of the bar, completely disinterested in their customers as always.

I tut-tut loudly, purely for my own benefit. If I were behind that bar this kind of nonsense wouldn't be tolerated. Actually, that gives me an idea.

I hop over the counter with very little effort and sneakily grab two pint glasses. So far so good, nobody seems to notice the levitating glassware. I pull two pints of Guinness to the exact level they need to be left at to settle, and leave them neatly aligned under the tap. Nobody bats an eyelid at the tap apparently working of its own accord. If I'd known people were so unobservant I'd have got up to a lot more when I was alive.

The twins are getting a little frantic now, their heads wobbling like the bobble-head toys you see in the back of cars. Jack's muttering under his breath, something about "offside", so I decide to alert him to the fact that there are some customers in need of service. I kindly jab him in the ribs, very much like I did last night, and watch as his face registers first annoyance, then confusion, and finally, satisfyingly, panic.

Yes, Jack, it's happening again.

As he casts about to make sure there really is nobody behind the bar with him, he finally notices Larry and Gerry's empty pint glasses, and the veritable frenzy of head-bobbing that's going on.

"Two more, is it, lads?" he asks shakily, as he reaches for a couple of clean pint glasses. I cackle with delight as he freezes in his tracks. He's noticed the half-pulled pints! "What the..? Who the..?" His head spins this way and that, and his eyes start to look like they might pop out of his highlighted head. He peers suspiciously at Roger down the end of the bar, obviously wondering if he could have got past him and pulled those two pints unnoticed.

Roger looks up briefly, feeling the weight of Jack's gaze, and snaps, "Is something the matter, Harper?"

Lydia's head jolts up and she regards her secret lover with a shocked grimace. Oooh, she really doesn't want Roger's attention to be on Jack, does she?

"Oi, Rodge," I tinkle, as Jack splutters his denial, "this young fella has been riding your wife sideways and he's not a very good barman either. I say he should be fired on both counts, what do you reckon?"

Jack is topping up the twins' pints, holding them as if they're radioactive, and Roger isn't paying me any attention of course, so I casually poke a couple of wine glasses off the shelf beside me. They make a sufficient clatter to have everyone in the place looking at Jack, who goes a whiter shade of pale and stumbles about looking disconsolate. Roger's face turns a funny puce colour, but he doesn't get a chance to say anything as Lydia jumps in behind the bar, simpering over her shoulder,

"Don't worry, darling, I'll help Jack!"

She shoots a poisonous look in Jack's direction, bending to retrieve the dustpan and brush, and taking the opportunity to mouth silently up at him, "Calm down!"

He glares back at her, his mouth a tight line of stressed-out bafflement. It seems there may be trouble in paradise, I note, taking savage pleasure in the obvious tension between these two. Well, they deserve each other. And they deserve to make each other miserable too.

I find plenty of ways to wreak havoc for poor Jack throughout the evening. Careful not to let anyone else get a whiff of the paranormal activity that's taking place, I ensure he alone senses my presence. Aside from the obvious regular poking and tripping up that keeps him on his toes, I keep up a steady stream of smashing glasses, flicking on and off taps and stealing bar equipment. I develop a very entertaining method of turning up the music in the bar gradually until it's reached a pretty deafening level, which Jack keeps not noticing as he's so stressed out with all the other stuff that's happening. Several customers have complained already. He's turned it right back down on a number of occasions, but I just can't get enough George Michael tonight.

Roger ups and leaves at one point, declaring that he can't get any more work done in a madhouse like this, and that Jack better pull his finger out if he wants to keep his job. Jack retaliates hotly that this isn't officially part of his job description and he wouldn't be doing it if his girlfriend hadn't recently passed away. He actually manages to put a lot of emotion into that statement, the rat-fink, you'd think he hadn't had a hand in said girlfriend's untimely demise the way he sells it. Roger's chilly reply as he stalks out the door is short, sharp and to the point. "That's precisely why I haven't fired you yet."

Yikes! There's a lot of drama in McMorrow's tonight. And I'm right in the middle of it, where I belong. Thoroughly enjoying myself, I continue tormenting Jack. Lydia stays only another ten or fifteen minutes after Roger has left. She pulls Jack aside as she grabs her awful fox fur jacket.

"What the hell are you playing at, Jack? My husband is no fool, you know."

"This isn't about us, Lyd," Jack hisses back at her, his eyes wild with a combination of frustration and terror. "I'm telling you, something crazy is going on here!"

"Oh, Jack, it's not even a busy night, pull yourself together." Lydia turns on her heel to stalk out the door.

Jack casts about himself, realises that there's only Auld Ross left in the bar, and that even he's making ready to leave, and grabs her arm desperately. "Stay, Lyd," he wheedles, fear making his voice exaggeratedly high pitched. "Please, stay with me tonight?"

"Don't be ridiculous!" Her eyes are full of contempt and for just a millisecond I actually feel sorry for Jack. I make up for the moment of weakness by stamping on his foot as Lydia storms out the front door.

Jack's loud squawk of pain proves the last straw for Auld Ross, who looks him up and down with all the disdain a man in a pair of stained, second-hand women's riding jodhpurs can muster and says, "Jaysus, bud, you shud gessome sleep," before making to follow Mrs Smith out the door.

"Ross!" Jack yelps, as his last chance for company seems about to escape, "Would you have another pint on me?"

Now I know I've been doing my job right. He's genuinely scared. Nobody in their right mind would beg Ross Moriarty to have a drink with them. I can't help bursting into unrestrained laughter when the gnarled, hard-core alcoholic turns back and says piously, "I think you've had ennuff from the lookaya, son." But he stops and holds out a hand, "I'll take a can off ya since yer offerin'."

Jack reluctantly hands over a can of Bulmers and watches in despair as Auld Ross shuffles out the door. His hands are visibly shaking as he pulls the keys out of his pocket and makes his way over to lock the front door. I skip along in from of him, casually pulling chairs into his path, wooden legs screeching on stone floor, each one making him sweat a little more, fumble a little more, come a little closer to breakdown. There can be no doubt in his mind anymore that there's a malevolent presence here. I wonder if he has any clue yet that it's me. He *should*, unless I'm not the first poor innocent he's murdered.

Well, I'll be the last, that's for sure. I'm going to make life hell for Jack Harper. And then, all going well, he'll be cracking up enough to confess his sins to a priest, or preferably the Gardaí! He'll be punished, I'll be avenged and hey presto! I should be on the move to wherever I'm headed.

I wonder where I'm headed?

Jack finally has the key in the lock, after several attempts, when the door swings open and nearly brains him. My brother's head pops in.

"Howaya, Jack?" he asks, and I can tell instantly that he's got a few beers in him from the slight softness at the edge of his consonants. Chris is a squishy, cuddly, lovable drunk. I feel a sharp stab of loss as I look into his sad eyes. He's obviously having a tough time with my death. I keep forgetting about the hard fact of it and the effect it's having on the people I love. Mainly because I'm still hanging around them, even though they don't know it. Their pain just keeps on hitting me between the eyes like a nasty surprise and there's very little I can do about it.

"Any chance of a late one?" my brother enquires, with a hopeful nod at the bar.

"Chris!" Jack is almost crying with relief. "Of course, of course, come on in."

He blanches a little when Charles enters the bar after Chris, but covers it well. Charles gives him a curt nod, then shoots an apologetic moue my way. Clearly not his idea to come in here then. Well, it wasn't part of the plan, and my haunting is a little bit curtailed by the presence of my brother, who I certainly don't want to upset any more than he already is, but I'm not as cross as I feel I should be. I can't muster much enthusiasm in my voice when I sarcastically gripe, "Oh sure, come on in and have a party with my killer."

The fact is, I'm a little bit shaken by my own reaction when Charles came in. My tummy kind of flipped a little and I was really rather pleased to see him. A little bit . . . glowy even.

Damn Jenny and her stupid theory. I shake it off and plonk myself down on the bar as far away from him as possible. *I do not have feelings for Charles Walker.*

End of story.

CHAPTER
TWENTY-THREE

Jack busies himself taking Chris and Charlie's coats, pulling up bar stools for them and asking them what their pleasure is. He's bustling around like a happy housewife fussing over unexpected visitors. Well, I don't blame him. Anything would be better than being alone with me, the way I've been tormenting him.

Charles is still eyeballing Jack with obvious dislike, but he's acting oblivious. A different animal entirely to the angry, bullying young man Charles had pinned against the fridge in Honeysuckle Cottage last night, he's all smiles and chit-chat as he pulls the lads a couple of pints and pours himself a stiff gin and tonic. He never drinks beer or Guinness, says they go straight to his gut. For some reason, this suddenly seems like a major turn-off. I always thought Jack was so gorgeous, but from where I stand now, his orange-tinted, toned, fashionably clad body and his highlighted, carefully styled hair are just . . . Yuck. Not for the first time, I ask myself the obvious question:

What was I thinking?

I can't help myself comparing as my gaze strays to Charles, who sits moodily staring into space, half his pint down in one long draught. His shaggy, dark hair looks like he cuts it himself. With a pair of shears. Left handed. And possibly blindfolded. His great club-like hands are a million miles from Jack's manicured (*manicured!*) digits; short-clipped nails with a few traces of stubborn dirt around the edges, which quite clearly doesn't bother him in the least. He's built like a brick shithouse, but somehow his muscles look *useful*, rather than decorative. Yes, he has a slight gut straining against the belt of his worn old jeans, but it's more comforting-looking than unattractive. Charles looks like he'd give the best cuddles, like a friendly brown bear or something. My mouth goes very dry all of a sudden, as I realise my eyes have dropped below the waistline of his jeans. I'm staring at his crotch. And it's making my lower belly do some more of those strange little jumps.

"*Whoa!*" I involuntarily yell at myself, hopping a few steps backwards away from the danger zone. Charles immediately looks up at me, raising his eyebrows in a silent query: Am I okay? When his eyes lock onto mine, I feel my face flushing bright red.

WHAT is happening to me?

He regards me for a long moment through narrowed eyes, as if reading my mind. Then with a tiny little smile tugging at the corners of his mouth, he returns his attention to the bar, where a fresh pint is waiting for him.

Infuriated, I lash out at the nearest thing to me, which happens to be a low-hanging light-fitting over the bar. It swings wildly around in a half circle, connecting with a dull thud with the back of Jack's head. His eyes cross slightly with the impact, as Charles snorts Guinness down his shirt front and Chris looks up with a start. The light is still wobbling around in decreasing circles. I make eye contact again with Charles briefly, and the two of us dissolve into helpless giggles.

Even Chris cracks a smile. "Careful there, Jack," he says, softly. "You'll knock yourself out if you don't watch where you're going."

"But . . ." Jack stammers a little, then gives up, rubbing the back of his head and glaring at Charles with naked dislike, before catching himself and hastily rearranging his features into a more pleasant expression.

"Yeah!" he says, forcing a smile. "I've been pretty clumsy today, to be honest! Thought my P45 was in the post."

Chris's smile fades a little. "It's only to be expected, mate. How are you coping?"

Jack looks a little flustered, casting about for something appropriate to say, no doubt.

"Oh he's grand!" I pipe up, slinging one arm around him and squeezing hard. "Starting to think he's losing his mind a little, but other than that, just fine, thanks!"

Jack's arms are pinioned to his sides by my superstrong grip. Beads of sweat start to pop out of his pores and a pulsing vein appears in the centre of his forehead as he struggles to lift them. Charles is struggling to maintain a straight face and Chris is staring at my traumatised ex-boyfriend with obvious concern. He shakes his head sympathetically. "I know, I know. It's hard for all of us. One minute she was here, larger than life, full of energy and fun, the next, she's just gone." His voice breaks.

Instantly, all the satisfaction I've been deriving from tormenting Jack leaves me in a rush. I let go of him. Relieved, he rubs his biceps, as Chris continues, "Rosie's gone, and there's a chance someone out there took her from us." He turns to Charles, who clouts him on the back in support as he speaks, the words tumbling out now on a slightly slurred torrent of grief. "My little sister, who used to wreck our heads trying to get us to play with her. Who used to follow us round and thought we couldn't see her spying on us, who was the reason we invented BMX code."

(I knew it! I knew they couldn't have actually been that boring!)

"My little sister, who used to sneak into my room when she'd had a bad dream and sleep at the end of my bed like a little puppy." His eyes are welling up with unshed tears now, causing mine to burn in response. "My little sister is gone, just gone, 'poof' just like that. She's not in that body they've taken away from us. She's gone and I don't know where and that's what's so damn difficult. If I could just know for sure where she is, what remains of her, what's left of Rosie . . . Where is she? Where's she gone?" Chris trails off as the tears finally start to spill down his pale cheeks.

The two other men maintain the studied blank expressions that men always assume when one of their kind begins to weep. It's a far cry from the comforting chatter of reassurance that women give each other in the same circumstances, but there's compassion in both

216

scenarios. Charles keeps a heavy hand resting on Chris's shoulder and Jack casually lifts a pile of napkins onto the bar while still gazing intently in the direction of the TV. They aren't ignoring him. They're just *pretending not to notice that he's crying.*

"I'm here, Christopher," I whisper, my heart full of love and sorrow for my brother. "I'm right here."

"Ahem," Jack clears his throat, addressing Chris in a slightly strained voice, while still maintaining eye contact with the TV. "I don't know if this will be of much comfort to you," he says, taking a hefty slug of gin straight from the bottle before continuing, "but I think she might be here."

All eyes in the room, undead and alive, swing to regard the shaking barkeeper. He smiles nervously at the other two men. "I know it sounds crazy, but I . . . er . . . Well, I think Rosie might be haunting me?"

The end of his sentence tapers away into a squeaky question mark as Charles eyeballs him like a hunter would his prey. "And why," growls the hunter, biting off every word in a low, menacing tone, "would she be doing that?"

Jack gulps, not meeting Charles's unblinking gaze. He wipes his damp forehead with the sleeve of his Calvin Klein jumper.

Chris is blurrily looking from one to the other. "*Haunting* you?" he repeats, disbelievingly.

"I know it sounds mental," Jack shakes his head, his voice taking on a horrible, whiney tone, "but honestly, there's some stuff you don't know about me."

"Like his arse is abnormally hairy and he waxes it himself," I cackle excitedly, eliciting no response at all from Charles who still seems to be having a staring competition with the side of Jack's head.

"Why don't you tell us then?" he suggests, in the same threatening growl.

"Okay. Yeah, absolutely." Jack is nodding frantically, clearly aware that he's treading on thin ice in this situation.

"So, I was working in Dublin just before I moved here, mostly freelance stuff, loads of DJing and a bit of event management. I took on a job involving a wee boutique hotel in the city centre, the Laramie, which is where Jenny McLoughlin was working at the time." He shoots a nervous glance at Charles here, no doubt wondering just how much he knows after the compromising position we found him in last night with Jen. Charles's blank face gives nothing away. "She was a sweetheart, always going on about her hometown, a real country girl. She actually mentioned Rosie a few times, and this place too. It all sounded great, if a little rural for my tastes.

"So, one day, I'm at the front desk having a chat with Jenny, and this immaculate looking blonde bird walks in. I was surprised when Jenny introduced her as Lydia Smith from Ballycarragh. She seemed a bit of a glamour puss for such a small town, you know, very up-market. I could tell from the word go that this chick wanted me, she was totally giving me the eye and laying on the little giggles and the hair-flicking. You know what I'm talking about, eh, lads?"

218

When the only response from his two-man audience is stony-faced silence, Jack clears his throat and shamefacedly continues, "Anyway, she came on pretty strong, we had a few drinks that night in the residents' bar, and one thing led to another . . . She told me all about her husband, about how he was so wrapped up in his work he never paid her any attention, just gave her wads of cash to play with. And that she didn't really have any friends in Ballycarragh, that all the local women were jealous of her and that she really hated the quiet country life. It was just too boring for her, but hubby wanted her to get pregnant and be a chained-to-the-sink country mammy. She confided in me that she was still getting her contraceptive injections even though she'd told him she was happy to try for a family. She was obviously pretty unsatisfied in her life, and let's face it, she's a very attractive woman."

Once again, he's clearly looking for approval from Charles and Chris. The best he gets is a non-committal shrug from my brother. Charles remains tight lipped and non-responsive.

"Well, I was a free agent at the time anyway," Jack adds, a touch defensively.

What about the play you were making for Jenny, you slimeball? I wish I could push a button and make the truth come pouring out of his mouth, but Jack is lost in his own heavily edited version of events.

"And I wasn't going to turn down what was being offered to me on a plate, was I? So I started a bit of a thing with Lydia. We'd meet up whenever she was in the city, have a bit of fun, spend a bit of hubby's money, and I'd send her off home satisfied and recharged for another couple of boring weeks in the sticks. Soon she was coming up every weekend, and it was pretty clear she was falling for me. The feeling wasn't mutual and I tried to tell her that, but she just brushed me off, saying I didn't know what was good for me. It was shortly after that that she came up with the idea of me moving down to Ballycarragh on a permanent basis. I wasn't all that sure about the idea, but she came back to me with an offer of a ridiculously high salary to take over the entertainment side of this place, plus free room and board, and all I had to do was keep servicing her on a regular basis. Well, I wasn't going to turn it down, that's for sure. Most guys would find that a pretty ideal set-up, am I wrong?"

Jack's final attempt to get the two other men on side falls flat on its face. I can see the temper bubbling behind his eyes. Usually he doesn't have to work this hard to manipulate people into liking him. Then again, usually he's working on vulnerable females, not thick-skinned, strongly built men.

"And it was a sweet deal," he goes on, shaking his head and assuming a sad, faraway look, which gives me the creeps. "Until your sister walked into my life."

Chris's expression softens a little, even as I'm making hysterical vomiting noises behind the bar.

"No, no, no! Charles, don't let him fall for this bullshit." The frustration is almost too much for me to bear. I briefly consider stalking out and gathering myself outside in the fresh night air, but Jack is waxing

220

lyrical about me now, and despite my fury I can't help being a little interested in what he has to say.

"She just blew me away. I swear to God, I'm not a romantic type, but it was like love at first sight. She was so smart, so cute, so funny and sharp and harsh, and yet so soft and vulnerable under all that."

(Ah, yes, VULNERABLE, you like that in a girl, don't you?)

"And it didn't hurt that she was quite frankly the most stunning-looking woman I'd ever laid eyes on. Imagine that. I, who have travelled the world, lived and worked in some of the most fashionable cities on the planet, with some of the hottest, sexiest models and playgirls around —"

To my delight, I can see that the sympathy is rapidly draining from Chris's eyes as the sermon on "The Greatness of Jack" goes on. But then Jack notices too, and swiftly changes tack. "I knew that this was the woman I wanted to spend the rest of my life with. This was a woman who could make me a happy, settled man, who I could in turn strive to keep happy and content for the rest of her life." His voice cracks artfully here and a pretty, glassy effect comes into his eyes as if he's struggling to hold back unformed tears.

Dammit, he's good.

Chris is once more hanging on his every word, nodding in an understanding manner.

"Sorry, sorry," mutters Jack, making a big show of pulling himself together. "The only fly in the ointment was my arrangement with Lydia. I knew I couldn't continue the way I had been, but I was also worried about what would happen to my job and my prospects if I finished it with her. I mean, there was nothing else for me to do here, and I really didn't want to leave Ballycarragh now that I'd found Rosie. For a while we just kept our relationship quiet, while I tried to figure out what to do."

"Then Lydia found out herself, when she found a necklace of Rosie's in my bathroom. She was surprisingly okay about it. As far as she was concerned, Rosie was a great cover story for us and threw any suspicions Roger might have had about our affair right off course. But she wasn't willing to give up the physical side of it, she was hooked on that. I have to admit, I didn't have the balls for a long time to actually try to finish it until it came to a head one night in the middle of summer. I'd been avoiding Lydia for most of that time, only sleeping with her when I absolutely couldn't get out of it, and she was getting a bit fed up with the whole situation.

"She followed me to a party out at the lake and we had a huge row about it. She told me that it was her who brought me here and she could just as easily get me run out of town too. She threatened to tell Rosie all about us if I tried to stop our affair and she said I'd be out on my arse if I dared to tell anyone myself. So all in all I was in a pretty dodgy situation. I knew what I was doing was wrong, but I also knew that it was all driven by love for Rosie. I agreed to keep seeing Lydia, but it was Rosie I loved. As far as I could see, Lydia wasn't ever going to leave Roger. I knew that someday she'd get sick of me and move onto her next bit on the side.

And then I'd be free to be completely faithful to Rosie for the rest of our lives together. I even planned on telling Rosie all about it some day in the future, when we were all settled down and it was nothing but a memory from our youth."

Jack pauses, looking intently at Chris and filling his voice with sickeningly false, pleading regret. "After all, I didn't love Lydia. I didn't even like her, especially after it all became about deceit and blackmail."

I can't help it; at this stage I am so incensed I'm fit to burst. "*Bullcrap!*" I roar, making Charles flinch with the sudden loud noise. "Seriously, this is ridiculous. Why the hell was he snogging the face off this blackmailing, deceitful, black-hearted nymphomaniac he didn't even like, minutes — *MINUTES!* — after he found out I was dead? Ask him that, Charles, go on, *ask him that!*"

Charles doesn't ask him that. He asks instead, his words steeped in the warning of impending danger, "So you think Rosie knows now what you did?"

Jack nods slowly.

"And she's haunting you for it?"

Jack nods again, looking pleadingly at Chris, who appears to have been won over by this pathetic sob story. Every now and then his eyes nervously dart back to Charles, who's clearly unconvinced. "Yeah, pretty much," he says, his voice wobbly as he awaits their verdict.

Charles stays silent.

Chris shakes his head sadly before speaking. "I hope you can get over your guilt, man, because that's the only thing that's haunting you. I'm glad you told us though. It's good to get these things off your chest. What you did really wasn't right, but it wasn't the worst thing a person can do."

At this, Charles fixes Jack with another one of his full-force death stares. "Absolutely not. Not the worst thing by a long shot."

He's pretty intimidating, I must admit. The tone of his voice and the level of hostility pulsing through it are enough to make my hair stand on end, and he's not even directing it at me. Jack must be shitting himself, wondering what Charles knows.

"Everything, buddy!" I smirk, pushing my face right up close to Jack's. "He knows *everything*!"

Even as I say it I realise that this isn't such a good thing for him to be aware of. After all, he has a gun. What if he comes after Charles in order to silence him? Does he have that in him? I stare at Jack in horror, taking in the sweat beading his brow and the slightly panicked, trapped look that's been in his eyes for the last twenty-four hours. My guess is yes, absolutely, this is a man at the end of his tether. He's capable of anything at this point. Here we are trying to drive him to confess but what we're probably doing in reality is spurring him on to further acts of madness.

"Right then!" I declare, all of a sudden desperate to get these two precious men of mine out of here and away from the nutcase I've been baiting all night. I force a note of cheer into my voice. "I think it's time we all head off to bed now!"

224

Charles shoots a slightly confused look in my direction, but doesn't show any signs of moving. Nobody stops Jack when he pulls another round of pints either.

Thankfully, though, there's not much chat left in the three men. They sit in relative silence, drinking their beverages, lost in their own individual thoughts.

After half an hour of this, Chris finally says, "Better get home."

Charles and Chris start to pull on their jackets as Jack frantically grabs a bottle of whiskey from the shelf behind him. "Are you sure, lads?" he asks, waving it around like bait. "You won't stay for one more?"

"Don't bother, you sad tosser." I hiss in his direction as the other two shake their heads firmly. "I'm done with you for tonight."

Besides, I reason, as the three of us begin the long trudge home, someone has to look after Charles tonight. Who knows what Jack might try next?

CHAPTER
TWENTY-FOUR

"What do you make of that?" Chris asks Charles, after several minutes of silent trudging, during which I have been fruitlessly trying to make my breath plume out into the chilly air like the two living folk beside me.

"I think he's full of shit," Charles says shortly, making me snort.

"Understatement of the year," I mutter, exchanging a brief, knowing glance with him.

"You're a bit biased though, aren't you?" This strange comment from Chris hangs in the air for a moment.

I'm certainly flummoxed as to what he's on about, and Charles seems to be likewise from the expression on his face. Probably the beer talking.

"What do you reckon?" Charles asks gruffly, ending the awkward pause. "You've known him longer than I have, haven't you?"

"Never really liked the guy to be honest," Chris shrugs, non-committally. "I mean, he's harmless enough, but he's rather full of himself. I seriously don't know what women see in pretty boys like that. I never thought it would last with him and Rosie. You two would have eventually —"

Charles breaks into a sudden, loud bout of coughing, drowning out whatever Chris was about to say. I pound him on the back, possibly a little too hard, as he stumbles forward a few steps from the impact and has to brace himself against a tree to regain his balance.

"Sorry," I grin at him, not sorry at all. "Don't know my own strength!"

"Do you think he could have been involved in Rosie's death?" Charles blurts out, causing Chris to stop in his tracks and peer at him intently.

"Do *you*?" my brother asks, still regarding Charles as if he's holding a live grenade.

It's Charles's turn to shrug. "I just have a bad feeling about the guy."

Chris starts walking again. "Yeah, I know what you mean, he is a complete sleazeball. But I don't know about accusing the poor bugger of murder. I mean, look at the state he's in, thinking Rosie's haunting him because he cheated on her!"

"And violated my best friend and shot me in the head, if we're being clear." I butt in, indignantly.

"He hardly strikes me as a hardened criminal. He doesn't even have the balls to stand up to Lydia Smith, let alone kill anybody. Especially my little sister. Why would he hurt Rosie?"

His voice cracks again and his shoulders start to shake. He adds quietly, "Why would anyone? Why, Charlie?"

Charles slings an arm around my snuffling brother's shoulders and walks him the rest of the way home in companionable silence. By the time we get to the gate of my parents' house, Chris is dry-eyed and serious.

"Do you really think Jack did it? Do you have any solid reason to believe that?"

Charles doesn't answer for a whole minute. I can practically see the cogs turning in his head. What can he say?

Well, Rosie seems to think so?

I see dead people?

Your dead sister isn't haunting Jack, she's haunting ME, and to be honest, it's getting to be a bit of a pain in the arse?

"No," he replies, eventually. "I don't have any proof. But I don't trust him, and I wouldn't rule him out entirely."

Chris nods, slowly taking a few steps up the lane. Then he stops and turns back. "Thank you for being such a rock for me, man. I know you must be hurting a lot too underneath it all. I know how you felt about her. It shouldn't have happened like this."

It looks like he might continue, but then he turns on his heel and with a final lift of his hand, disappears into the darkness.

Charles and I set off in the direction of his rambling farmhouse over the other side of Walker's woods. I hold off for as long as I can before I just have to ask. "How you felt about me?" I finally blurt.

228

"Drop it, Rosie," Charles grunts, his chin tucked inside his scarf and his hat pulled low on his brow so all I can see of his face is a pair of deeply shadowed eyes and a cold red nose.

"Your brother is shit-faced."

"But . . ."

"And so am I, come to think of it," he interrupts, as he trips slightly over his own feet.

"Why are you following me anyway?" he grumbles, crossly. "Shouldn't you be staying with your family, or with Jenny or something?"

I stop dead (not that I could stop any other way, really) and assume an affronted expression, fully expecting Charles to stop walking too and look back at me. But he doesn't. He just keeps on trudging into the murky darkness ahead, the grumpy arse.

"*Oi!*" I yelp, finally finding my voice and employing my super-speed to overtake him and stand directly in his path, poking him in the chest with one extended digit. "Why are you being so nasty all of a sudden?"

"Get out of my way, Rosie, or I swear to God, I'll walk straight through you."

I open and close my mouth a few times, like some kind of dumb silent-movie character, before sheepishly standing aside. After all, he does look like he's about to set off again and I really don't want him to walk through me. I'd feel like a cannibal.

He starts walking again. Well, I'll be damned if I'm going to toddle off home like a good little girl just because he says so. I continue to follow him. "For your information, I'm coming with you because I think you're more at risk from that psycho than anyone else. Especially after acting the tough guy last night and being all suspicious with him this evening," I say prissily, as if I had absolutely no part in the behaviour described. "So can you please stop being so mean and let me protect you without biting my head off every few seconds."

"I'm not biting your head off, but I don't need your protection either. I mean, what are you going to do, poke him into submission?" Charles snorts derisively. "Knock a few ornaments off their shelves and hope one lands on his toe?"

"Hey!" I can't believe he's being like this.

"What the hell have I done, Charles? Have I offended you in some way? Am I not good enough at being a ghost for your standards? Because it's a lot harder than it bloody well looks. And it's not exactly a barrel of laughs that my boyfriend hated me enough to kill me either, so can you please stop giving me such a hard time?"

We've reached the sprawling, run-down farmhouse that Charles has been living in and renovating since he was nineteen, when he inherited it off his crazy Grand-Uncle Geoffrey. He pushes open the very heavy, ten-foot-high, antique front door (which he never bothers to lock because of Lady and Tramp, his two huge, terrifying Irish wolfhounds) and looks back at me wearily.

"Do what you want, Rosie," Charles says, his eyes flat and bloodshot. "Just let me get some damned sleep, I'm worn out from all this."

And with that he's gone, leaving me standing in the doorway, two hulking canine shapes edging slowly towards me out of the shadows, growling menacingly.

"Um . . . Good dogs..?"

Despite being undead, invisible and fairly superstrong myself, the two slobbering mutts still put the frighteners on me. I guess that's their job, but I've always felt that Charles could have trained them to be a bit more friendly to people he actually *likes* (not that he's acting as if he likes me at all at present, the big wally).

I spent a long, uncomfortable afternoon stranded up a tree when I was seventeen, with these two horrible hounds pacing below, bloodlust in their nostrils and the threat of considerable violence in their eyes. I had only come round to retrieve a board game of mine that Chris had illegally leant to Charles. To be fair, they were puppies at the time (so merely the size of a couple of fanged donkeys). And they had infuriatingly transformed into tail-wagging, wriggling, hand-licking sweethearts the moment he returned from work. It still makes my blood boil to think of the bollocking he gave me for letting them out.

"They're only puppies, Rosie."

"!"

"Look at the poor things, they're completely freaked out."

"!!"

"What if they were hit by a car?"

"Somebody would have a hell of a panel-beating job on their hands!" (Finally, I'd found my tongue after several minutes of being struck dumb by shock and terror.)

"That was totally irresponsible of you."

"Fuck off, Charles."

"And what on earth were you doing climbing bloody trees at your age?"

"I'm going home. Where's my flipping Game of Life? I want it back."

Things are different now though. I manage to get a grip on my irrational fear. I'm a grown woman, for goodness' sake. Also, they can't exactly get those great big teeth into me, can they, seeing as I don't have a corporeal form anymore?

"Goooood doggies."

"GrrrrrrRRRRArrarrrrRRR."

Bugger it, I'm not taking any chances. I vault clean over their dumb-looking heads and dart quick as a flash into the kitchen, kicking the door closed behind me as I go.

"Ha!" I taunt, peering through the small glass panel in the wooden door. "Some guard dogs you are!"

Tramp launches himself against the door, causing it to shudder considerably, and causing me to quickly cease all taunting of psycho dogs.

It dawns on me slowly that I'm alone in the ultimate farm-boy bachelor pad, free to explore (snoop) to my heart's content. However, after rifling through the barren cupboards for a while somewhat disinterestedly, I realise my heart isn't really in it. I mean, what am I actually looking for? I know Charles pretty well already. The most exciting thing I'm likely to come across is a giant pair of tongs used for something indescribably gross like birthing deformed calves who've grown too big because of their mammy cows ingesting the chemicals used to make the grass grow quicker or something like that.

Dejected, and now unable to get the disturbing images of mini-cows with oversized heads out of my twisted mind, I wander through several freezing-cold, unfurnished, spooky rooms. Charles has been working on the house for twelve years now and, like any man left to his own devices, he's pretty slap-dash about it, doing up a room here and there on a whim whenever he has the spare cash and/or time. Thus, there are two inhabitable bedrooms, the kitchen and a study completed, a half-finished bathroom (basic isn't the word) and many, many dark, neglected spaces in between. It takes me a while to locate the study, which is my favourite room, tucked away right at the back of the house.

It's a gorgeous room. It was, bizarrely, the first he renovated (who needs a bed, or a functioning toilet for that matter, when one can put up lots of heavy mahogany bookshelves and sleep in a gigantic leather armchair?). The heating miraculously works in here, making it cosy and inviting, with lighting that's all discreet and soft, coming out from interesting angles under shelves and behind understated shades. I'm pretty sure Charles spends most of his time in his study when he's at home. The air carries the same distinct smell of maleness that wafts about him all the time, kind of like hay and bonfires and freshly turned earth, and a little bit of something spicy and warm. Very pleasant, actually, if you like that kind of thing.

I breathe in deeply, plonking myself down in the luxuriously grand leather chair behind the desk. *Ahhhh*, yes. I've only ever been in here when Charles himself has been occupying this chair and I've always wanted to have a go in it. I spin around a couple of times. (Of course it spins! I always suspected it would. And it kind of bounces from side to side too, and rises and falls with a hiss of air at the touch of a button.) My legs are a blur as they pass through various items of furniture. But then I stop suddenly, as something on the desk catches my eye. Something goes wrong in my distracted state, and my body stops way before the chair does, leaving me with several mouthfuls of spinning leather as I reach out to pick up the photograph that sits atop a pile of documents on Charles's desk.

It was taken not long after Charles moved in here. I remember how excited I was at the potential of a whole house uninhabited by *any adults at all* and how tirelessly I campaigned for it to be a party house, a free house, a place where Jenny and I could skip school without fear of retribution. Imagine my dismay when I realised Charles wasn't going to behave like a normal nineteen-year-old male and do what I wanted, rather acting like a stuffy adult himself and declaring his house out of bounds for such uses. I held a grudge for

234

the rest of my school life, nick-naming him "Old Man Walker" and ridiculing his sedate lifestyle any chance I could. In fact, I never stopped doing that, now I come to think of it.

This picture was taken only about a week after he had received the keys to the property, before any of my delirious teenage dreams of freedom had been dashed. It was the first time Chris and I had explored the property inside and out, and I remember Chris taking tons of photos of everything from the stable yard to the crumbling staircase in the entrance hall to the mouldy old portraits on the wall. I was waxing lyrical about what a great ballroom you could put in the huge dining room at the front when Charles grabbed me around the waist and started spinning me wildly around the room, lifting me off my feet and making me shriek with slightly hysterical laughter.

"What?" he had demanded, as I begged him to put me down, "I thought you wanted to party?"

Chris snapped a picture as we twirled past.

I never saw it. I forgot all about it, to be honest. Charles put me down eventually and I clambered up the precarious staircase and explored the rest of the house, giddy with plans and dreams.

It's a great picture. Our smiles are wide, our eyes full of laughter, our expressions completely unposed and free of self-consciousness as only the best, most unexpected photographs can capture. My stomach twists into a painful knot as I look at the young girl in the image.

She was so alive.
She was so happy.
She was so obviously in love with Charles Walker.

CHAPTER
TWENTY-FIVE

Uh-oh.

There it is, dammit. I think I've known since I first laid eyes on him at my parents' house that this realisation was hurtling towards me. My spidey-senses were on high alert but I was trying so hard to avoid it, and I was doing a pretty good job too. I must have known it was going to hurt way too much. Worse than discovering that I was dead. Worse than finding out about Jack's cheating, or his likely involvement in my death. This is a knife in my non-beating heart. The sense of loss is overwhelming.

I quickly make my way up to Charles's bedroom, the enlightening photograph clutched tightly between ghostly fingers. The dogs watch me as I move through the entrance hall, but they don't move a muscle or make a sound. They must sense that I mean business.

I only pause for a second outside his door, considering knocking. Then I just walk on through. There's no point in standing on ceremony anymore. I need to be with him, and I need to be with him now.

His eyes are closed, an old-fashioned feather quilt hanging off one corner of the high-set bed, only a small portion of it (thankfully) managing to preserve his modesty. His skin is pale and scattered with plenty of thick, dark hair in all the places it should be. I feel a bubble of regret burst deep inside me and have to swallow hard not to burst into tears. What was I doing wasting all that time with a vain idiot like Jack Harper when this beautiful beast of a man was clearly mine all along?

Because it's not just *my* eyes in that photograph that tell a story. And all the pieces have finally slotted together in my mind. Jenny knew it. Chris knew it.

And this man right here knew it all along too.

I sit down as lightly as I can beside him, reaching out a hand and holding it just millimetres from his warm skin. I watch his chest rise and fall with each breath. Life flows through him.

Not through me though. Something is flowing through me but it's not life.

"Oh God, Charlie," I whisper, trying to push away the rising tide of rage that threatens to engulf me. "Why didn't you just *tell* me?"

"I did," he murmurs, through barely moving lips, his eyes still closed.

I drop down to my knees beside the bed to get a closer look at his face. "No, you did not!" I hiss, scowling at eyelids that refuse to lift. "You most certainly did not tell me that you've been madly in love with me since we were rugrats!"

A niggling voice in the back of my head is trying to make itself heard over my righteous indignation.

238

Well, he did, actually. In the raspberry patch. All that talk about salmon. And countless other times. How else would you be so sure he does love you?

But I'm very good at ignoring those sort of voices. So I push on regardless. "It's all your fault! I would have realised much sooner if you'd just *said something*."

"I did," he insists. "An' I cleared out the shed too."

"What?"

"It's only a surface job really. N'thing to worry about."

"WHAT?"

A loud, stuttering breath escapes between Charlie's (suddenly immensely kissable) lips, and it dawns on me that he's fast asleep. I grunt, frustrated, but don't have the heart to wake him up. It's been a hard run of it for him, I can really see that now.

Imagine what it's been like, trying to be strong for everyone else — even me.

I sit back up on the bed and resume my non-contact stroking of his shoulder. He is so very beautiful. I could sit here like this all night. But underneath the peaceful scene I'm painting, there's still trouble brewing deep within me, coursing through my veins in place of a life force.

This is the man I should have been with. The man I could have made a life with, the man I always knew deep down inside I wanted more than anything in the world. I wasted so much time, because I didn't know that my time was so severely limited. And now my hands are completely tied. There's no possible way I can ever have that life now; the sweet, sweet life that suddenly seems so clear, so obvious, so tantalisingly close. I could almost reach out and touch it. I don't have any life anymore, I'm just clinging on by my fingertips to the remnants of my old, snuffed out version.

I don't want to be here any longer — it's too hard. I want to go wherever it is I'm supposed to be going.

Why am I still here anyway?

The answer starts to dawn on me with icy, hard certainty. I'm not here to haunt anyone. I'm not here to torture myself over what might have been. I'm not here to comfort my family or Charles, or prove that Jack is the one who killed me, or protect anyone from him.

How often do they actually solve cases like this anyway? How often do they bring rapists to justice? How can he just get away with what he did to Jenny? How dare he take away my future; my happy, joyous, perfect future with Charlie? The way it could have been, should have been, was meant to be?

I'm here to see that justice is done. I'm here to stop him once and for all. I'm not here to haunt Jack Harper, I'm here to kill him.

It's starting to get bright outside. I'll go soon.

CHAPTER
TWENTY-SIX

I wait until the first glimmer of golden sunshine spills across the courtyard before setting off. The grandfather clock in the corner of the room says it's twelve minutes past eight. I'll be at McMorrow's before it hits eight fifteen. Charles's phone starts ringing just as I leave. Well, he'll wake up now, no doubt, but he's not going to stop me doing what needs to be done. Nobody is. I don't have a plan as such, but I don't need one. I just know what has to happen. The how and the where will sort themselves out.

It's a fresh, bright winter morning outside. The sky is blue and the sun is out, but there's no warmth in it. There was a heavy frost last night and an icy coldness lingers in the air. The prettiness of my surroundings and the cheerful chirruping of the waking wildlife around me only serve to fan the flames of my fury. Why should I have to see all the beauty of this world where I don't belong anymore? I'm an alien here now. I can no longer enjoy this place. I round a corner at high speed and the pub looms into view. Even as I near the door, it bursts open and the object of all my wrath bursts out. Jack is pulling on his jacket, looking rumpled and unwashed, his mobile phone pressed to his ear.

"Well, how would it look if I *didn't* go?" he's demanding in a harried, exasperated voice. "You're just going to have to come in yourself to take the delivery, Lydia. I don't know how long I'll be . . . Ah, look, I'm late enough as it is."

He snaps the phone shut on a high-pitched retort. Typical Jack. I'm filled with a sense of loathing so strong it almost buckles my knees. I don't particularly like Lydia myself, but this man has no respect for anybody. He's a self-serving pig and he deserves all he's going to get. It's time for payback.

I slide through shiny red metal as he slams the driver's door of his fancy, sporty-looking Hyundai. He doesn't put on his seatbelt. I always used to remind him, and he'd make a big show of doing it just to please me.

"I'm a fantastic driver, Rosie," he used to say, cocky as anything. "I'll never crash."

He takes off with a squealing of tyres and a spray of gravel, the flash fucker. I used to love sitting right here in the front seat, window down, wind in my hair. I didn't even particularly mind the thumping, annoying dance music he insisted on blasting out. I do now though. As soon as he flicks on the radio, I reach over and change the channel to a rock station that's much more to my taste. The tinny, bleeping, repetitive tones of pointless techno are instantly replaced with the much more pleasing screech of guitar riffs. I laugh mirthlessly as Jack absently changes back, and I retaliate like an annoying sibling. This pattern is repeated several times before he clearly catches on that

242

his radio isn't on the blink and that something else is going on. He gulps visibly and leaves Metallica blasting through the speakers.

That's not going to help you, mister.

I'm really enjoying watching the fear take hold of him; I can almost smell it. And for the first time I feel absolutely no pity, no uncertainty, no empathy. I want him to be scared. I want him to be *petrified*. I want him to suffer horribly. Look at all he has taken from me and from others, like Jenny and Charlie and Roger Smith and God only knows who else. I don't feel anything except cold, hard certainty. We're coming to a sharp corner and inspiration strikes me. This should be fun.

As Jack eases into the bend, I reach across him and grab the steering wheel. I let him notice my grip for a split second, just so I can see the realisation begin to show in his horrified eyes, then I yank hard. The super-sensitive steering responds beautifully, sending the low-slung car into a terrifying spin, before we smash through the fence at the side of the road and flip high into the air. The speed of our rotations is keeping Jack pinned to his seat, but not for long. As the nose of the car makes contact with the ground outside, he is thrown forward with considerable force against the windscreen, which cracks and buckles, but doesn't actually break. From there, we begin to roll, still at high speed, down a steep incline. Jack is thrown about the interior of the car like a rag doll, as the crunch of metal and the shattering of glass provide a cacophonic soundtrack.

I am, of course, completely unharmed, though when we finally do come to a stop, I'm sitting pretty much inside the engine. The car is upside down and has come to rest against a tree at the bottom of a sloping field. Through the gap in the fence that we burst through, I can glimpse an occasional car passing above, but nobody's stopping as yet to see what's happened. Which is good news for me, as I'm only just getting started.

He's crumpled against the driver's side door, one of his arms bent at an impossible-looking angle and a considerable amount of blood staining his face, but still breathing. I step out of the mangled wreckage of the car and walk around to his side. In one smooth, powerful movement, I pull the impact-warped door wide open, making the twisted metal scream in a satisfyingly creepy way. Jack slithers out of the car into a pathetic heap on the damp grass. He moans, trying to sit up. Realising too late that his injured right arm won't bear his weight, he collapses with a girlish squeal of pain.

"Ouch! That looks pretty painful," I say, my voice heavily laden with sarcasm. I really wish he could hear me; there's a lot I'd like to say to him. As if reading my mind, Jack starts to whimper my name.

"Rosie, Rosie, please." He rolls onto his back and pulls himself slowly up against a tree-stump, panting like an injured animal. "Don't do this to me. I'm sorry . . . I loved you so much."

This pathetic appeal serves only to infuriate me further. I pick up a wing mirror and pitch it at him.

"You don't know the first thing about love, you selfish prick, and you stole my chance at it too!"

My aim has never been very impressive, but the sharp edge of metal where the mirror was torn from the car does catch him on the cheek, causing a fresh line of crimson blood to materialise and begin dripping down onto his collar. He starts to cry, his lower lip trembling in a manner that seems completely fake, even though I can see the real fear and panic in his eyes. Even when he's being genuine the creep looks like he's putting it on.

"Rosie, I never meant to hurt you. You know I wouldn't intentionally hurt anyone, don't you?"

The filthy, lying monster! How I wish I could . . .

Inspiration strikes me, and I grab a sharp-looking piece of machinery from the grass near my feet. Using the nearest undamaged surface of the car as my blank canvas, I carefully scratch the paintwork, watching Jack's expression change as he reads my message.

WhAT AboUT jEnnY?

"What? Oh come on, Rosie, is that it? Are you jealous about *Jenny?*"

I don't know what I had expected, but it certainly wasn't the defiant, petulant attitude he's exhibiting now.

He continues, clearly not knowing what's good for him, "She was begging for it, Rosie. And she meant nothing to me, you must know that?"

"*Arghhh!*" I scream, feeling the last vestiges of control leave my mind and hurling my writing device at him as hard as I can. This time, my aim is true; it wedges deep in his thigh, causing him to scream along with me in harmony.

Now there's a change in him. Now he's finally starting to get it. I'm not just a jilted girlfriend looking to hear that he truly loved me after all. I'm not just the lingering ghost of a girl whose feelings got hurt. Oh, no. I am a vengeful spirit. A force to be reckoned with.

It's judgement day, shithead.

I kick another scrap of Jack's car at him where he cowers, trembling with uncontrollable fear. I have no merciful feelings, none at all. Even the tiny part of me that thinks this is all a little bit over the top and dramatic wants to see him pay for all that he's done. Did he feel pity when he cold-heartedly took away *my* young life? Would he even have given me a second thought had I not returned from the dead to wreak havoc?

Not a chance.

As I cast about for something else to fling at my whimpering target, I spot a small, heavy, shiny object poking out of the smashed glove box inside the car. Oooh, perfect.

Almost poetic, in fact.

I pick up the gun and step closer to where Jack is slumped prone against the tree-stump. He watches the deadly weapon float towards him, his mouth gaping in a rictus of terror. I could swear he's looking directly into my eyes as I sight along the barrel, aiming for the

246

centre of his blood-smeared forehead. Looking into his pretty, reddened, tearful eyes, I finally feel my resolve cracking. I can't really do this, can I?

He probably carries this very gun around in case he feels like killing another innocent woman. Of course you can do this. You have to do this. This is why you're still here, disembodied and heartbroken.

I take a deep breath and tighten my grip on the weapon. I had never even seen a real gun before the other night when Jack pulled it on me. I always hated the bloody things, saw them as the root of all evil in this world, a glaring symbol of the uniquely human disregard for life that sets us apart from all the other creatures on this planet. Now that I'm standing here, though, with the solid weight of the weapon in my not-really-there-at-all hand, I can feel its power, the raw seduction of its potential. I snap off the safety catch, and Jack squeezes his eyes shut, jabbering nonsensically under his breath. As I wrestle with my conscience, I notice a dark stain spreading quickly down the left leg of his designer jeans.

Nice!

I can't help it, I feel a giggle welling up inside me. He's such a pathetic sight. The warmth of laughter pushes up through the anger and the hurt and the vengeance, and obliterates it all with a giddy relief.

A screech of brakes sounds on the road above, and I look up to see a familiar green Land Rover reversing at high speed back to the gap in the fence where we broke through, what seems like an age ago. Lady and Tramp leap off the trailer like a pair of trusty side-kicks as

Charles tumbles out the door and comes racing down the steep incline at an insanely high speed.

"Rosie, STOP!" he yells at me, as I stand there with the remnants of a chuckle still plastered all over my face.

What's his problem? I wonder dumbly, forgetting that I'm still holding a loaded weapon two feet from a battered, bruised and thoroughly frightened man's head.

Look at him, all hero-like and cute, running full tilt towards me like he's going to save the day. Hmmm . . . he'd want to slow down a bit now, or he's going to —

Charles tackles me in true rugby-player style. The impact is like being hit by a small lorry as we both hurtle through the air and land winded in the damp grass.

Which I can feel soaking through the fabric of my pyjamas.

And the crushingly heavy weight of the large man lying on top of me feels pretty real too. His dark eyes look into mine and mirror the shock and surprise he finds there. Tentatively, I reach up with my free hand and brush an unruly lock of black hair behind his ear. Yup. This is happening, all right. We're touching. I can feel his heart beating hard, as if it's somehow in my own chest.

Charles seizes the moment, fair play to him. Conditions may not be perfect, what with a semi-conscious ex-boyfriend just a few yards away, and a firearm still clutched in my hand, but credit where credit is due, he doesn't let any of that stand in his way.

248

He kisses me. He presses hot, firm lips against my own, and I sink into the kiss that I never knew I'd waited my whole life for.

It's perfect. Passionate, tender and imbued with infinite meaning. It's the best kiss of my life. It's the *only* kiss of my afterlife. And goddamn it, I enjoy every moment of it.

Several minutes later, we finally, reluctantly, separate. Charles cradles me in his arms, and I start to cry; great big, hot, salty, real tears that roll down my cheeks and splash onto the backs of his hairy arms where they rest around my waist. Neither of us asks how or why we can suddenly hold each other. I think we both know the answer is beyond our understanding. But we also both know somewhere deep inside that it won't last long either, which is part of the reason I'm crying (the other part being that I'm also feeling a ridiculous level of happiness, and being a woman this makes water squirt from my eyes).

It's indescribably lovely to feel the solid warmth of Charles's embrace. The silent communication of love, trust, energy and understanding that's passing between us in this magical, fleeting moment. We watch the two giant wolfhounds snuffling around Jack, where he lies curled into a tight little ball, his eyes squeezed shut against whatever horrors lie beyond the safety of his eyelids, rocking back and forth like a man on the edge of reason.

"I didn't mean it . . . Tell her, Charles, please tell her . . . I'm sorry, I didn't mean it . . . Jenny wasn't asking for it, what I did was wrong, *wrong!* I shouldn't have done it, tell her I'm sorry . . . I'm sorry Jenny . . . Rosie . . . *I'm sorry!*"

I can tell Charles is impressed at my handiwork. He doesn't say anything to that effect, but he does grunt at Jack, "Shut up, Harper. I'll tell Jenny you confessed all right, but you're ruining my moment here."

We sit for a long time, fixing these precious minutes in memory as best we can, before I finally break the peaceful silence.

"He wee'd himself, you know."

Charles snorts with mirth. "You do have a pretty scary temper, Miss Potter."

He grins down at me, and I grin back up at him, admiring his sexy Charlie Walker lop-sided smile. We spend quite an inappropriate amount of time just grinning inanely back and forth at one another, before he drops his bombshell.

"He didn't kill you, by the way."

CHAPTER
TWENTY-SEVEN

It takes quite a while for me to actually formulate a response to this new piece of information. After all, there's a lot going on in my head, most of it completely fuzzy and blurred by the overriding feelings of love and lust buzzing around my body. Eventually, I settle on the most appropriate.

"What?"

Charles looks at me tenderly, concern written all over his face. *Mmm*, lovely Charles-face. All ruggedy and crinkly, with a lovely big nose and stubble all over his slightly squishy jaw-line . . .

I shake my head vigorously to clear the pesky loved-up fog in there, almost headbutting Charles in his lovely face as I do so. "What the *what*, now?"

"Jack didn't kill you," Charles repeats, jerking a thumb in the direction of where Tramp is sitting on Jack's head, to illustrate his point. "The Gardaí say —"

"Stop! Now hold on there just a minute, big guy," I interrupt, waving a finger under his nose. "Were the Gardaí in your bedroom this morning?"

"Er . . ."

"Exactly!" I bark, triumphantly. "Why don't you start from the beginning then? And don't leave anything out while you're at it."

Charles squints at me, all twinkling wolfy eyes, before grabbing my chin and kissing me deliciously.

"Right you are, Miss Potter," he declares, when he finally releases me, somewhat dizzy and limp in his arms.

"At a ridiculously early hour this morning, your brother telephoned me and told me the Gardaí were on their way round to the house with the final conclusions of the investigation. They said that they'd had some very unusual results and that it would probably be for the best if Jack and Jenny were present as well so they could clear up all possible avenues of enquiry. I left as quickly as I could. I did try to find you, but when you didn't appear I thought you must be off sulking somewhere over our words last night."

"Hey!" I glare up at him.

He smiles, cupping my cheek in one hand. "I'm sorry about that by the way. I was feeling incredibly hard done by, having to listen to that slimy prick go on about you like you were *his*. Having lost you before I even had a chance to tell you how I felt, and your brother nearly letting the cat out of the bag, I was just behaving like a fool really. Pretty much the effect you've always had on me, come to think of it."

"Well, yes. You were actually," I mutter smugly, nuzzling closer into his arms. "Now, continue. You were off to my parents' house this morning."

252

"Yes. I figured you'd be around somewhere, and if you weren't you'd find me with your weird superpowers if you wanted to. So I hotfooted it over to the house. The Gardaí were there already and so was Jenny and everyone except Jack. But we didn't really give a second thought to him; Chris said that he'd spoken to him already and that he was on his way, so we just started without him."

That explains where Jack was off to in such a hurry this morning then.

"They told us that while accusations had been levelled at Jack, there was absolutely no way he was responsible for your death, not least because he had a rock-solid alibi for that night — he was exactly where he said he was — DJing in front of a couple of hundred punters in McMorrow's. The only time he left the DJ stand was on his break, when he was with Mrs Lydia Smith having a 'meeting'."

Charles smirks knowingly at me, but I can't share his private-joke moment. Something has just snapped into place in my memory and I can sense an extremely unwelcome tsunami of information mounting on the edges of my mind.

I think I remember something...

"So there we all are, taking in what the Gardaí are telling us, and I suddenly put two and two together, and realise you've probably gone after Jack to torment him some more. All of a sudden I had this overwhelming urge to come find you, I just felt that something wasn't right. It was weird, like you were in my head or something." Charles blushes a little bit, obviously embarrassed to be spouting what sounds remarkably like the New Age claptrap he always teases my mother for believing in. I decide against letting him in on the fact that I spent the night sitting by his bedside, plotting (quite possibly aloud) things I might do to Jack Harper.

"Frankly, I didn't think it would have got to this point," he gestures vaguely at the carnage around us: the smashed-up car, the discarded gun, the battered and bruised ex-boyfriend.

"I was heading back to McMorrow's. I thought that's where I'd find you, hiding his car keys or something. I noticed the skid marks on the road and the broken-down fence, and I just happened to glance into the field to make sure nobody was hurt. Lo and behold, there you were about to shoot Jack in the head!"

"I wasn't really going to shoot him," I protest weakly, as Charles looks probingly into my eyes.

"What happened, Rosie? What made you lose it all of a sudden?"

"I just . . . got mad." I say blandly, reluctant to explain the sudden and overwhelming sense of loss, grief and rage I felt when I finally admitted to myself that I was madly in love with him.

Charlie widens his eyes and exaggeratedly looks around the field of debris. "You can say that again."

After a long pause, I ask the question that's been tripping around the edges of my mind since he arrived: "So who the hell did it then?"

Charles shifts a little uncomfortably, suddenly refusing to meet my eyes.

254

A little *ping* goes off again in my brain.

Ah, I'm not sure I'm quite ready to remember this.

Still, I stubbornly persist, "Charles! Who killed me?"

"Well, um, that's where it all gets a little bit . . . unusual."

With a whirring of cogs, a kaleidoscope of images, and a stomach-churning sense of discomfort, it all comes back to me in a rush.

I remember that night. I remember exactly what happened. I know who killed me.

Oh, bugger.

CHAPTER
TWENTY-EIGHT

Halloween night was the most miserable of nights, with a cold wind howling down the chimney, whistling through cracks in the windows and under the doors, causing the cottage to develop its own chilly little internal-weather systems.

I was sitting at the kitchen table, right beside the pot-bellied stove in the corner, wearing my favourite old blue-flannel PJs and painstakingly stitching together my sexy belly-dancer costume for the Halloween Monsters' Ball that night at McMorrow's. Sure, a belly-dancer didn't exactly fit the bill for the "Monster" theme, but I'd built my entire concept around a pair of to-die-for shoes I'd found on the internet (on a drag-queen costumier's website catering for "the well-endowed shoe lover". I kid you not).

I glanced lovingly at them where they occupied pride of place on the kitchen table. Pretty, pretty shoes. Gold all over — apart from the spindliest, silver stiletto heel I'd ever laid eyes on — they consisted of not much more than a thin leather band across the toes and a delicate gold chain around the ankle, from which there dangled lots of dinky gold coins. Absolute bloody torture to walk in, of course, but so, so worth it for someone who had had to spend most of her life in men's trainers, or the rare, ugly, rejected items found in the bargain bin at the back of shoe-shops. And the best bit was, there were loads and loads more where these came from on www.hishotheels.com, signalling the end of all my giant-feet dilemmas forever.

The back door crashed open on a gust of wind, causing me to stab myself in the thumb with my needle and bark a few well-chosen profanities at the weather gods. A flurry of hailstones and several curling brown leaves accompanied Jenny as she struggled against the ferocious weather, hauling the door closed behind her with Herculean effort and then collapsing against it.

"Well, good evening to you too," she grimaced, drily.

Her hair was sodden, plastered against her flushed face like it was painted on. Her cheeks and nose were red. Not the cute pink flush you see in the ads on telly, but a real, freezing-cold, blotchy redness that's typical to Irish skin. Water was actually dripping down her face, stained here and there with muddy mascara.

I felt a little churning in my stomach, much as I felt most days when I saw Jenny. Things had never really gone back to normal with us since I'd started going out with Jack. Not in a nasty, bitchy way, of course. Just in a kind of uneasy, unspoken kind of way. There were a lot of topics off-limits, especially because pretty much everything I did involved my boyfriend, and she didn't want to hear anything about him. I also had a lot of guilt holed up inside me because, shameful as it was to admit it, I'd actually been avoiding her a lot of late.

Precisely because of the guilt and the unease, and all the rest.

I missed her a lot.

She muttered something about the weather being distinctly unfriendly out there and declared that she was getting into her pyjamas and not budging from beside the fire until the morning. I almost asked her if she wanted to come to the ball, but caught myself at the last minute. She never came to McMorrow's anymore. Not unless she knew for a fact that Jack wouldn't be there, and on those occasions I was invariably absent too. Tonight was a night when he would definitely be there, DJing, mingling with all the revellers and having a blast. I'd been looking forward to this party for weeks and had even wangled the night off so I could really let my hair down and enjoy myself.

It came as some surprise to us both then when I suddenly blurted out that I'd like nothing more than to join Jenny on the couch for a girls' night in. I couldn't quite believe what I was saying as the words left my mouth, and for an instant I wished I could gobble them back up. But when Jenny turned and hugged me with such a look of genuine delight on her face I knew why instinct had made me suggest it.

I could go out another time. I could hang out with my boyfriend another time. I could wear those delectable shoes another time. Some instinct in me was telling me that I shouldn't go out tonight, that I couldn't neglect this loving, sweet, loyal friend for one minute longer, that if I was ever going to repair our friendship it would have to be tonight.

While she showered, I uncorked a delicious bottle of Prosecco I'd been saving for a special occasion, lit the fire in the sitting room, put on some lovely Nina Simone and organised a plate of nibbles. By the time I was sitting on the couch, watching the flame of a candle dance in the draughty air, I had almost convinced myself I was missing nothing at McMorrow's anyway. Almost.

Jenny came in, wearing her matching pink version of my flannel PJs, and flopped down into an armchair with an exaggerated sigh of relief. She took my proffered glass of bubbles and toasted me.

"To friendship," she said.

"To us," I countered.

I was glad to be there. We drank and laughed and drank some more (opening another bottle of wine and a bottle of port that was lurking in the back of a cupboard, of dubious quality, but reasonable effect). We talked and reminisced and looked at old photos, and not once did either of us broach anything to do with Jack. It was really lovely, just like old times, and as the fire burned and the night got wilder outside I really felt that we were getting things back on track.

So when Jenny suddenly turned serious, fixing me with her big, cat-like eyes and announcing that there was something she really needed to tell me, I dodged her gaze and slipped off to the loo. When I came back, I had my own suggestion. "Let's go to McMorrow's, Jenny?" I pleaded, slurring my words only slightly.

"We've had such a fun night — why not finish it the way we always used to? Down the pub! I promise Jack is DJing, we won't go near him at all. I'll stick with you and we'll just have heaps of craic. Please! I don't want tonight to be over yet, and I really wanted to go to this ball, and I have these killer heels to wear, and I don't want to sit here and argue about my stupid boyfriend again."

"I wasn't going to argue with you," Jenny said, quietly.

A long moment passed, in which I thought all hope was lost, and she was just going to head off to bed. A small part of me didn't care either way. I'm ashamed to admit it, but I'd already made up my mind that I was going to go to the ball after all, Cinderella style.

But then she smiled up at me and I knew I'd won her over.

"On one condition," she said.

"Name it."

"We go like this, in our PJs."

I squeaked in protest, but she held up a finger and continued. "And you come home with me after, no disappearing off and staying at Jack's tonight."

I scowled and nodded sulkily. I could tell there was more to come. *One condition, eh?*

"And we sit down and finish this chat later. There really is something I need to tell you. I should've told you ages ago. It's important."

"Okay, no problem, but I'm bloody well wearing my new shoes!"

Half an hour later, considerably worse for wear and dressed in the bizarre combination of flannel pyjamas and spike heels, I found myself crushed against the bar in McMorrow's with a zombie to my left and what appeared to be an extra from *Fame* to my right. Jenny was directly behind me as I ordered us a couple of glasses of red. I hadn't spotted Jack yet, but then again, he'd made a big fuss of keeping his costume secret, so he could have been anywhere in the throng really. Probably outside having a cigarette in between sets.

I fully intended to keep my promise to Jenny and stay by her side all night long. But she had to go to the loo at some stage and I was hoping to use the opportunity to seek my boyfriend out, explain the situation and maybe sneak a little kiss when the time came.

Almost as if she was reading my mind, Jenny tugged on my sleeve and roared over the music, "*I need a wee!*", jigging her thumb in the direction of the Ladies. I nodded and grinned, and mouthed, "Okay", and the minute her back was turned, headed for the door.

The chilly night air took my breath away as I stepped outside, and the whipping rain stung my eyes. Nobody stood out the front to smoke their ciggies in this weather. But there was a little side door just round the corner where anything up to six or seven people could be found squeezed in, sheltering from the rain and puffing away. I made my way round, spilling wine from both the glasses clutched in my hands as I went (gravel and spike heels are not conducive to steady walking). I got close enough to the doorway to make out a couple of figures and then stopped in my tracks, slightly embarrassed. There were only two bodies in there and

261

they were, from the looks of it, having quite the make-out session. I certainly didn't want to intrude.

Jack was probably in the loo, I reasoned, disappointed. I was about to turn away when something clicked in my head. That werewolf looked very familiar.

So did the Barbie doll.

Oh my God, NO!

I staggered away from the horrifying scene playing out in front of me, stumbling and landing heavily on my knees as I fled. I tore my shoes off and set off for home, not thinking about what Jenny would do now, not thinking about the cold, wet ground under my toes, not thinking about anything except the fact that my boyfriend was lip-locked (and gropingly entangled) with none other than Lydia Smith. I actually threw up on the way home, I was so freaked out.

When I got in, I collapsed against the front door for a few minutes, gasping for air after the exertion of running all the way home. I felt numb. Then I started crying. Then I started to feel really, really mad. I stumbled into my room, and the first thing I saw was the framed picture of Jack and me on my bedside locker. With an almighty shriek of rage, I flung my shoes at it, sending my lamp and several other items flying.

That felt good.

I spun around and grabbed a painting off the wall, bringing it down hard on my dressing table.

Better.

I became a spinning force of destruction, channelling my pain and disappointment into anger, thoroughly trashing my bedroom, even though a reasonable voice in the back of my head was keeping up a steady commentary of: *Oh dear, you really loved that cushion . . . Uh-oh, you might need that mirror some time . . . Um, do you really think you should throw that . . . Oops! Never mind, you can go to Egypt again someday and replace that...*

As I began to wind down, I flung myself bodily at my bed with the intention of having a good old weep. Unfortunately, wine and over-exertion played their part and I ended up missing the bed entirely and landing on the floor beside it with an almighty thud. Two things crossed my mind simultaneously:

There's my La Senza bra that's been lost for months, dangling behind the headboard.

And:

OUCH! That really, really hurt.

I cautiously sat up, my head spinning rather nauseatingly. Oh boy, was I going to have a headache when I woke up. I dragged myself up onto the bed and lifted a hand to rub my throbbing head where I had basically landed on it.

Only, my hand didn't make contact with my head. It touched something that went *jinga-linga-ling*, jutting out from where my head should be.

I pulled on it and it came loose, with a funny wet, sucking noise.

I gazed dumbly at my gorgeous gold shoe for several seconds. There was a horrible, sticky, red substance all over the heel, dammit.

Come to think of it, there was some on my pyjamas too. Lots of it, in fact.

Oh.

I gently collapsed backwards against the pillows behind me. As the room started to spin faster, and my eyes started to feel distinctly heavy, I had the vaguest notion that I should call someone for help.

But I was so tired . . .

With a dull thud, the blood-soaked shoe fell from my lifeless hand, and I sank softly into unconsciousness.

CHAPTER
TWENTY-NINE

Charles stares at me in silence for several long seconds after I finish telling the story of my untimely demise. I'm finding it hard to meet his eyes, especially after making such a fuss of my so-called "murder". But when he suddenly guffaws loudly, I fix him with an indignant gaze.

"Charles!" I declare, outraged by his insensitivity.

"Sorry, sorry!" He holds up one hand as if to buy himself some time to regain his composure.

"It's just . . . *Bahahahaha!*"

I glare, rethinking my love for this heartless fiend all of a sudden.

"It's just . . . Killer heels?"

And with that, I'm laughing too. He's right. It's all just a little too ridiculous to take seriously. I decide to join in.

"There's been a 'shoeing' in Ballycarragh!"

"You made a right heel of yourself this time!"

"I told you they were 'to die for' . . ."

We continue to giggle away like a pair of irreverent teenagers for several minutes until I playfully attempt to swat Charles, squealing, "Oh, stop, please stop. I think I might do a Jack and pee my pants."

We both stop laughing abruptly. My hand only made semi-contact with him this time, his body offering some resistance, but still giving way in the end and letting my hand glide through him like a knife through butter. I meet his eyes and see my own concern mirrored there.

"Come on," Charles demands, jumping to his feet as if something's bitten him on the ass. "We can't just sit around here all day."

"Where are we going?" I ask, clambering to my feet and casting a glance in the direction of the still-gibbering Jack. "More to the point, we can't just leave him there, can we?"

Charles ignores me, his mobile phone already pressed to his ear as he starts striding up the steep incline. I catch a few words as they drift back over his shoulder.

"Been a road accident . . . severe shock . . . suspected broken arm and head injury . . . ambulance . . ."

I cast one last look at my ex-boyfriend. Even though I now know he had nothing to do with my death, I still reckon he deserves all he got. He'll probably never be prosecuted for what he did to Jenny, and to who knows how many other girls. At least now he's learned his lesson. I don't reckon Jack Harper will be messing with any other innocent young things in the future. Indeed, from the blank, zombie-like look in his eyes, I'd say it'll be quite some time before he regains any semblance of his former cocky self.

"Serves you right!" I bark at him, as I swivel on my heel and follow Charlie back to the Land Rover.

I could swear I hear him muttering as I retreat what sounds like: "Serves me right, serves me right, serves me right."

Charles's piercing whistle brings the two dogs thundering past me as I pant and wheeze my way up the hillside. Where have my superpowers gone to when I need them? My body feels much more solid and human than it has since I woke up that morning several days ago and stepped out of it. Maybe I'm not really dead after all? I have a wild flash of hope as I clamber into the passenger seat and regard my beloved Charlie. What if this has all been some kind of inspirational dream and I'm going to wake up any minute, and I can run round to his house and tell him all about it, and then we really can live happily ever after?

Charles looks at me. I reach out and pinch him.

"*Ow!*"

"This isn't a dream, is it?"

He closes his eyes tightly and I can see the strain written all over his face. When he opens them, though, his gaze is strong and clear.

"This is real, Rosie."

His voice sputters in my ear, like someone's fiddling with the reception dial on an old wireless radio. There are tingling, fizzing sensations creeping up my arms and legs. Something is definitely going on here.

Charles starts the engine and throws the car into gear. "Hold on a little longer, Rosie," he says through gritted teeth, taking off with a squeal of rubber. I put my hand over his where it rests on the gearstick. Thankfully I can still feel the warmth of his flesh even though I can actually see through my own hand at this stage.

I'm not ready to go yet. There's so much I haven't said.

"Charles, I'm sorry!" I blurt out. And before I know it, the words that have been welling up inside me start coming thick and fast.

"I was such an idiot, I can't believe I denied how I felt about you for so long and wasted so much time, so much precious, precious time that we can't get back. My most meaningful relationship was with an absolute horror of a man, and I could have been with you all that time. I could have been with you *all my life*. I should have been with you! Oh God, if I'd only worn slippers like Jenny did, or if I'd not drunk so much wine, or if I'd just stayed home with her like a good friend, none of this would have happened and our hearts wouldn't be breaking, and I wouldn't be sitting here feeling like E.T. about to take off, and you wouldn't have to be listening to me talking nonsense and fading away before your eyes."

With that, I run out of breath and start crying; great big, heaving sobs that seem to come from the very core of me, the hot tears actually crackling as they run down my rapidly deteriorating facial planes. Charles says nothing, he has pulled up outside his house and leapt out of the car. He stalks around to my side and wrenches open the door, scooping me into his arms and tucking my face into his broad shoulder. I can sense how unbearably light my body is at this stage; he's barely touching me as I hover in his embrace.

268

With several long strides, Charles kicks open the front door, and then another, before stopping and gently tipping my chin so that I have to look up from where my face is buried in the warm, sweet-smelling folds of his waxy coat.

We're in the old dining room where that photograph was taken years ago. It appears that this is one of the rooms that's received Charlie's full attention, as it's almost unrecognisable. It has been lovingly and ornately transformed into the ballroom of my dreams. It's breathtakingly beautiful. Gilded mirrors, sparkling chandeliers, luxuriously heavy curtains . . . I can almost picture extravagantly dressed guests waltzing elegantly around the room as I gaze around, my jaw hanging open in surprise and awe.

"Wow," I sigh. "Charlie, it's so lovely."

"This is your room, Rosie," he speaks softly into my ear. "This is where I hoped to ask you to be my bride one day, and if you said yes, to make it happen right here too."

I start to cry again, and whisper, "I'm sorry —" but he cuts me off.

"No," he says firmly. "No more apologies. You have nothing to apologise for. I've never been much of a believer in fate and all that stuff that you and your mother bang on about, but over the past few days I've had to rethink my opinions. There's no doubt in my mind that all of this has happened for a reason. I am completely at peace with it. Imagine if you had just been gone, just like that, and I hadn't had this amazing time with you. *Then* I would struggle to understand, *then* I would fight against it. But you came back to me. You gave me these precious days of your undivided attention. You gave me the chance to experience your love, and no matter how short the time we've had together has been, it's enough for me. It will sustain me for a long, long time. I'm ready to let you go, Rosie, because you deserve to go wherever you're going. If you could see yourself right now, you would understand. You're glowing, you're shining, you are so very, very beautiful. And I will always hold you in my heart. Just as you are in this moment. Just like this."

As Charles has been speaking, all my pain has dropped away, all the sadness is gone, and in its place I feel only warmth, joy and love. My entire body is tingling. When I look down, I can see why; there's only the faintest outline of my physical form left and it's shimmering and sparkling like the reflection of moonlight on water. I look into Charlie's eyes and smile up at him. It's a relaxed, peaceful smile. He drops his lips to mine, and as sparks (actual sparks, I kid you not) fly, kisses me the way every girl dreams of being kissed. His face is suffused with golden light for several seconds. It's beautiful and I know it's coming from me.

And then I'm soaring high, past the tinkling chandeliers, looking down on the love of my life where he stands, arms outstretched, bathed in a zillion twinkling little points of light, a soft smile on his lips.

He whispers, "I love you, Rosie Potter."

I love you too, Charles Walker.

Epilogue

Jack Harper will be found suffering only minor injuries, but in a complete state of shock, after losing control of his car on a sharp bend on Ballycarragh Road. He will not recover from the stress of this traumatic crash for some time. Indeed, he will be admitted to St Gertrude's care home for the mentally unstable for a year or so, after trying desperately to convince the doctors tending him that he has been visited by a vengeful spirit and needs protection. He will find that institutional life suits him quite well, and when he does finally make a full recovery from his psychotic episode, he'll stay on at St Gertrude's as a voluntary carer, expressing no desire to venture into the outside world ever again. He will always have a deep-rooted fear of red-headed women.

Jenny McLoughlin will start going to McMorrow's again, and on one particular night will find herself sitting in the snug alone with Chris Potter. Chris will confide that he has always had a considerable crush on Jenny, and she will declare that she has always secretly fancied him too. The pair will cause a scandal by running off three months later and getting hitched in Las Vegas. The happy newlyweds will buy Honeysuckle Cottage, where they will live in peaceful harmony for almost a year before the first Potter grandchild appears. After that, noise and chaos and laughter preside, as Jenny births five more beautiful, red-headed babies in quick succession. The sixth will finally be a girl and will be named Rosie.

Lucy Potter will have a very interesting conversation with Charles Walker, and as a result will give him a small urn containing some of the ashes from her daughter's cremation. She will become insufferably smug and more bullheaded than ever in her views about life and death, declaring only that she *knows for certain* that she's right, but never actually explaining why. She will confide in her husband what Charles told her, but John Potter will merely smile and say, "Well, that's nice, dear."

Lydia Smith will always deny the accusations levelled at her about a so-called affair with Jack Harper, her only comment on the matter being, "Ah sure, that young lad is mental, isn't he? You couldn't seriously believe a word that comes out of his mouth." Several years down the line, after Roger walks in on her in a clinch with her personal trainer, André, she will find herself living in a one-bedroom apartment on the outskirts of Dublin, with André and his three Doberman Pinschers, unable to afford even one measly shot of Botox.

272

Roger will keep working away, quite content to be a single man again, until he finally retires at age seventy-two and moves to Italy, where he will fall madly in love with a chubby, passionate, older woman called Sofia and finally learn what life is all about.

Auld Ross Moriarty will wake up one day and decide to stop drinking. He will get broadband fitted in his mother's house and complete an internet course in business, after which he will start a very successful online-networking site for recovering alcoholics and drug addicts. He'll be asked to appear on a television chat show to tell his remarkable story and the host will be so taken with him that she'll give him his own permanent spot. He will undergo a considerable makeover, becoming one of the most beloved men on Irish TV. He will never marry, preferring to stay at home with his mammy, but rumours will abound about Rosso's devilish success with the ladies.

Charles Walker will keep working on his rambling old house in Ballycarragh. He will continue to tend to all the animals in the locality and maintain a strong bond with the Potter family. He will eventually meet a kind, intelligent woman called Sinead, who he'll have a long courtship with and finally marry when they are both well into their forties. They won't have children. They will share a deep love and respect for one another and many years into their marriage, Charles will tell Sinead all about Rosie Potter. Then she'll understand at last why he never allows the spectacular ballroom at the front of the house to be used. Occasionally he'll go in there, when Sinead isn't at home, to sit beneath the twinkling chandeliers with a little silver urn clasped in his hands.

When, after a long and happy life together, Sinead is at his bedside as he takes his last breaths, she will place this urn in his hands, kiss him gently on his fevered brow and whisper, "Go to her, my love."

And he will smile up at his loving wife.

And come to me, where I've been waiting impatiently . . .

To start where we left off.

THE MAKE-UP GIRL

Andrea Semple

Faith works in a fabulous PR company, has loads of gorgeous, glamorous friends and, best of all, a handsome boyfriend. He never wants to watch the football, and thinks Faith is the most beautiful girl in the whole world. The only problem is, he doesn't exist. Faith has made him up, just like she's made up her perfect life. It's what she does. She's a single, lonely, low-paid make-up girl, and it's far too late to tell her family the depressing truth. Except that her sister has just got engaged, which means she's finally run out of reasons why her family can't meet her perfect, imaginary man. It's time to turn fantasy into reality . . .

RIVER ROAD

Jayne Ann Krentz

It's been thirteen years since Lucy Sheridan was in Summer River. The last time she visited her aunt Sara there, she'd been dragged away from a wild party by the guy she had a crush on. Obviously Mason Fletcher was the over-protective type who thought he had to come to her rescue. Now, Lucy learns there was more to the story . . . Mason had saved her from a very nasty crime that night. Soon afterward, Tristan, the cold-blooded rich kid who'd targeted her, disappeared mysteriously, his body never found. Mason is still a protector at heart, a serious (and seriously attractive) man. And when he and Lucy make a shocking discovery inside Sara's house, Mason's quietly fierce instincts kick into gear. He saved Lucy once, and he'll save her again . . .

TEMPTING FATE

Jane Green

In 20 years of marriage Gabby has never doubted her love for Elliott — even when he refused to give her the one thing she still wants most of all. But now their two daughters are growing up, Gabby feels restless. And then she meets Matt . . . Intoxicated by this young, handsome and successful man, Gabby is momentarily blind to what she stands to lose. And in one reckless moment she destroys all that she holds dear. Consumed by regret, Gabby does everything she can to repair her mistake. But are some betrayals too great to forgive?

TAKE A LOOK AT ME NOW

Miranda Dickinson

Nell Sullivan has always been known as "Miss Five-Year Plan". But when she finds herself jobless and newly single on the same day, she decides it is time to start taking chances. Blowing her redundancy cheque on a trip of a lifetime to San Francisco, she meets a host of colourful characters, including the intriguing and gorgeous Max Rossi. Very soon the city begins to feel like her second home. But when it's time to return to London, will she leave the "new Nell" behind? And can the magic of San Francisco continue to sparkle thousands of miles away?

THE HOLIDAY HOME

Fern Britton

Two sisters. One House. The holiday of a lifetime . . .

Each year, the Carew sisters holiday at Atlantic House, the family's Cornish retreat, but they are complete opposites. Prudence, hard-nosed businesswoman married to the meek and mild Francis, and Constance, loving wife to philandering husband Greg, who has always been outwitted by her manipulative sibling. Suspecting that Pru wants to get her hands on Atlantic House, Connie won't take things lying down. When an old face reappears, years of simmering resentment reach boiling point. Little do they know that a long-buried secret is about to be exposed. Is this one holiday that will push them all over the edge?

A CROWN OF DESPAIR

Jenny Mandeville

Having sent his last wife to the block, the tyrannical Henry VIII sets his lustful sights upon an innocent and unworldly gentlewoman, the recently widowed, Katherine Parr. In mourning for her late husband, and yet desperately in love with another, Katherine is forced to choose between the man she loves and a crown of despair. In the years that follow, as Henry's terrified sixth wife and queen, she battles to contain her fear and revulsion of her bloated and monstrous new husband. The real threat of execution and the humiliation that she endures only strengthens Katherine's resolve that somehow she will escape the gruesome fate of her predecessors and ultimately be with the man she loves.